INFINITY DRAKE:
GIANT KILLER

Books by John McNally

The Infinity Drake series in reading order

THE SONS OF SCARLATTI

THE FORBIDDEN CITY

GIANT KILLER

To [signature]

INFINITY DRAKE

GIANT KILLER

John McNally

[signature]

HarperCollins *Children's Books*

First published in Great Britain by
HarperCollins *Children's Books* in 2017
HarperCollins *Children's Books* is a division of HarperCollins*Publishers* Ltd,
HarperCollins Publishers
1 London Bridge Street
London SE1 9GF

The HarperCollins website address is:
www.harpercollins.co.uk
1

ISBN 978-0-00-752169-2

John McNally asserts the moral right to be identified as the author of the work.

Typeset in Berylium by Palimpsest Book Production Ltd, Falkirk, Stirlingshire
Printed and bound in Great Britain by Clays Ltd, St Ives plc

MIX
Paper from
responsible sources
FSC C007454

FSC™ is a non-profit international organisation established to promote
the responsible management of the world's forests. Products carrying the
FSC label are independently certified to assure consumers that they come
from forests that are managed to meet the social, economic and
ecological needs of present and future generations,
and other controlled sources.

Find out more about HarperCollins and the environment at
www.harpercollins.co.uk/green

For my wife, Louise.

Thanks for winning me in that raffle

FILE NO: GNTRC 9457549-OP/DRAKE-∞ TOP SECRET

TOP SECRET - MOST CLASSIFIED - RESTRICTION ULT9

FILE ABSTRACT: NARRATIVE ACCOUNT OF OPERATION GIANT KILLER.

(.1) BASED ON DEBRIEF INTERVIEWS CONDUCTED BY ████████ , TECHNICAL AND
SURVEILLANCE METRICS/TIMELINE COMPILED ████████ BIOMED SUPPLEMENT MDI
ZURICH GMBH, UPDATED ████████████ (.2) TO REFLECT TESTIMONY AND
INTERROGATION OF ████████ . FULL OPERATIONAL DETAILS. DECISION-MAKING
PATHWAYS. FULL PSYCHOLOGICAL/EMOTIONAL CONTEXT.

ACCESS: PRIME MINISTER/CABINET SECRETARY/SECRETARY OF STATE DEFENCE/
SECRETARY OF STATE FOREIGN/CHAIRMAN JOINT CHIEFS OF STAFF/CHAIRMAN GNTRC.

LIFETIME ACCESS: A. ALLENBY/ ∞DRAKE.

STUDY ACCESS: LEADERSHIP AND TACTICAL COMMAND LEVEL 009.

FILE MOST SECURE - NOT TO LEAVE REGISTRY

Then the LORD said to Moses and Aaron, "Take handfuls of soot from a furnace and have Moses toss it into the air in the presence of Pharaoh. It will become fine dust over the whole land of Egypt, and festering boils will break out on people and animals throughout the land."

Exodus 9:8–9

It's far more important to know what person the disease has, than what disease the person has.

Hippocrates

PROLOGUE

FEBRUARY 19 10:54 (GMT+1). La première
table de roulette, Casino de Monte-Carlo,
French Riviera

"Place your bets! *Mesdames et messieurs – faites vos jeux!*" The croupier's voice rang out.

The roulette wheel spun, numbers flashed past, and for a few moments all possibilities existed at once.

An agent of the Global Non-governmental Threat Response Committee (commonly known as the G&T) prepared to place a five-hundred-euro bet on number 35 black.

The agent, beneath a heavy disguise, was Dr Al Allenby, six foot two inches of angular, eccentric cool; a scientist trapped in the soul of an artist.

His nephew, Infinity Drake – aka Finn – thought him the best uncle in the world. Al thought himself the worst. It was all his fault Finn had been shrunk, all his fault he'd subsequently been captured, all his fault for creating the Boldklub reduction process in the first place, something the world's greatest terrorist, David Anthony Pytor Kaparis, wanted so badly.

Twice Kaparis had tried to blackmail the world into handing over the Boldklub secret; once by releasing the apocalyptic Scarlatti Wasp, more recently by creating a swarm of deadly nano-bots in Shanghai. Twice he had been thwarted, by a 9mm high Infinity Drake.

Infinity Drake: missing, presumed dead.

Until now.

"Place your bets! *Mesdames et messieurs…*"

The silver ball began to lose momentum as it orbited the spinning wheel.

After months of silence – of endless searching, with no result – the G&T had at last received some grainy video footage of what appeared to be Finn, together with a message from Kaparis proposing a deal: a handover of the boy in exchange for the key Boldklub fractal equations[1]. To consent to the deal, a five-hundred-euro bet would be placed on 35 black at the casino in Monte Carlo at a specified time. An exchange would then take place in the smoking area on the street outside. The equations would be on a memory stick. The 9mm

---

[1] A mathematical set with a pattern that repeats as it expands or, as in the case of the Boldklub equations, contracts.

hostage, Infinity Drake, would be inside the aluminium tube of a Cohiba Espléndido fine cigar.

It was a fool's gambit, but Al was desperate.

"Last chance, *faites vos jeux!* Place your bets, *mesdames et messieurs...*" called the croupier.

The rich, mainly elderly players placed safe bets.

Al placed a blue five-hundred-euro chip on number 35 black. The deal was on.

The ball cracked against the spinning wheel then bounced like Al's heart around his chest.

"No more bets! *Mesdames et messieurs – rien ne va plus!*"

This was it. The culmination of five months of heartache and uncertainty. Al could not wait to see Finn, to bring him back to size at Hook Hall. He could not wait to hold him, to hang out with him, to eat junk food and play Xbox for nine hours straight. He could not wait to see his late sister, Finn's mother, in his eyes, or for Al's own mother – Finn's epic grandma – to find peace again.

Al could not wait.

He was already on his way out, heading for the smokers of fat cigars on the street outside. As he burst through the swing doors to join them, precisely as planned, a motorbike drew up. A rider with a passenger on the back – both Tyros[2].

---

[2] Aged between twelve and seventeen, Tyros are the foot soldiers of Kaparis, secretly selected from care institutions across the world and indoctrinated to serve him.

The passenger, a girl of fifteen or so, withdrew a Cohiba Espléndido cigar cylinder from a bag round her waist.

Al took out a small blue memory stick. The equations it contained were fake. Booby traps. If you ran them through any Boldklub machine it would blow up.

The Tyro thrust out the cigar tube. Al handed over the stick.

Then everything happened in a blur.

RRRRRRRRRRRRRRRRRRRRRRRRRRRR!

The motorbike roared straight off across the Place du Casino.

Al tried to twist the top off the cigar tube, hands shaking. It was stuck. One of the other smokers, another agent, ran to help. As they struggled, Al's microphone picked up his desperate incantation, "Finn... Finn... Finn..."

Then the top finally twisted off and – *POP!* – the tube emitted a spray of confetti.

FEBRUARY 19 10:59 (GMT+1). Hull of the *Shieldmaiden*, Mediterranean Sea

"Haaarrrurglurgl!" Kaparis gurgled in delight.

Heywood, his ever-faithful butler, leant over to suction excess saliva from the back of his mouth.

Kaparis had loved the casino since he was a spoilt boy holidaying on Cap Ferrat. It was where he first acquired a taste for cheating. Now, all

these years later, he lay paralysed in a steel sarcophagus, a great iron lung ensconced within the steel skin of a 30,000-tonne oil tanker. Around his head was a whizzing optical array that allowed him 360-degree vision, and above that, a domed screen array feeding him news, images and data from a vast criminal network, as well as real-time video of events 160 miles away in Monte Carlo.

He knew Allenby and the G&T would never willingly hand over the real Boldklub equations, so he had decided that he would taunt them instead, play games and bully them, wear them down until they got so mad that they did something stupid, or – better – got fired and replaced by someone who would cut a deal.

Over the course of the unfortunate Scarlatti episode, and the more recent disaster in China, Kaparis had managed to capture a great deal of video footage of Infinity Drake, and with it his engineers and animators had managed to construct a perfect hologram of the boy. And the G&T had fallen for it!

"FOOLS!" he roared.

Letting Allenby take on the mission himself showed how desperate they already were.

He had them in the palm of his hand.

RRRRRRRRRRRRR!

A second motorbike shot across the square in pursuit of the first. The rider was an athletic young woman, Delta Salazar. She was the finest pilot in the USAF and she jived her Ducati Multistrada through the traffic as the Tyro bike ahead of her took a sharp left up a side street.

Like Finn, Delta had been shrunk for Operation Scarlatti; but unlike Finn, she had not been captured in the Forbidden City. Her little sister had though. Carla. She was still missing and Delta was going to find her or die trying.

She rounded the corner. The Tyro bike was forty metres ahead, roaring up a narrow street of boutiques.

BANG! The passenger fired back. Delta felt a bullet rip past. In a whip's beat she drew her own SIG Sauer P226 service pistol and returned fire – *BANG!*

The bullet punched through one Tyro's shoulder and into the other's neck. *SMASH* went the bike through a boutique window.

Delta powered up, but by the time she reached them, both Tyros had detonated suicide capsules.

Back at the casino, as the last of the confetti settled, a great stone of despair sank through Al's chest and he fell to his knees.

His fellow agent kicked over a table in frustration.

"HAAAAAHAHA!" Kaparis laughed to see such fun – and then choked as he saw something that spoiled... everything—

"Huuu... hgaah!"

For as Al and his fellow agent tore off their false beards and prosthetic faces, Kaparis instantly recognised the second agent.

Captain Kelly of the SAS.

Missing, presumed dead... Or if not, presumed to be just 11mm tall.

It could mean only one thing.

"NNNMMMMARRRRRRRRRRRRRRRGH!"

It was to be a day of highs -- and lows.

PART
ONE

PART
ONE

ONE

FEBRUARY 19 15:11 (GMT+2). Carpathian
Mountains, Romania-Ukraine border. Alt.
1,995m/6,545ft

He drank her blood.

They were, after all, in vampire country. Thick forest, thicker snow, a picture-book landscape of peaks and abandoned castles.

Finn was no vampire, of course, nor even a flea, but he had to eat to stay alive, and Carla's scalp was pockmarked with tiny wounds where he had broken the skin to feed[3], using a spike of metal he'd

---

[3] The digestive systems of nano-humans can absorb only 10 per cent of normal food and water. Blood, however, being more refined, can be absorbed at nearer 25 per cent.

picked up in Shanghai as a sword. Carla's once-luxuriant hair had been his sanctuary on the never-ending death march, a jungle thatch that had given him cover, warmth and sustenance.

For five months, mostly at night, Baptiste – their captor, and one of Kaparis's worst Tyros – had dragged them across the ancient spine of the world: up through the Taklamakan Desert, through icebound mountain kingdoms, then across an endless frozen plain, until mountains rose once more, thick forests full of bears and wolves. The only clue to how far they'd come in the faces of the few peasants they saw; even at a distance and wrapped up against the cold, they had grown pale and round-eyed.

Baptiste, bearded and unholy, had no other function but to go on in dumb, endless flight, driven by an urge he could make no sense of. His brain had been so damaged as he escaped Shanghai with the girl that he could barely remember who or what he was. All he had left was a brute sense of purpose, a homing instinct, and a capacity for violence. He knew the girl was his prisoner, but little else. And he had no idea, nor could he conceive, that she carried a thirteen-year-old boy in her hair called Infinity Drake, who was just 9mm tall...

Finn finished his drop of blood and wiped his mouth. "It's less sugary. You're getting weaker."

"Between you and the fleas, I'm surprised I haven't run dry," Carla complained, resisting the urge to scratch.

The thuggish form ahead of her grunted and yanked the cable that shackled them together and bound her wrists. She staggered on.

They were traversing the tree line below a steep ridge, Baptiste and Carla high-stepping through deep snow. Finn climbed through her hair to take him in.

How do you kill a giant?

How do you kill someone two hundred times your size? Finn had been trying to figure it out for three thousand miles. Even in this zombie state, Baptiste was still many times faster and stronger than them, many times the murderer.

Finn's plan was always to attack, but Carla knew better – if they could just hold on long enough, they would eventually get close enough to civilisation to summon help.

Right from the start (when Carla had thought Finn was just a kid on an army base in England who hung out with her older sister), they had enjoyed seeing the world in entirely different ways – America versus Europe, art versus science, girl versus boy. Sometimes she thought it was only the pointless circular arguments that kept them alive, as she slogged on through the real world and Finn ran around her head, full of crazy ideas—

"Hit him with a rock!"

"Build a signal fire!"

"Steal his knife!"

It was a strategy that had lost ground since Yo-yo had gone missing – Finn's faithful idiot of a dog, who'd trailed them every step of the way from Shanghai. If Carla attacked, Finn had assured her, Yo-yo would join in. Trouble was, since wolves had closed in a few nights before, Yo-yo had kept his distance.

Was he even still alive? The further they'd gone, the weaker they'd all become.

One thing was certain – the brutal trek might never end, but one of them surely would, unless something happened soon.

How do you kill a giant?

Finn, lulled by Baptiste's pace through the snow, suddenly got a flash of inspiration.

"Hey! We could *hypnotise* him!"

"Why didn't I think of that?" said Carla sarcastically.

"No, listen. We went to this show once," said Finn, trying to remember the night in a theatre with Uncle Al and Grandma. "Next time we stop, stare at him, tell him he's feeling sleepy, then – click your fingers!"

"Click. Right," said Carla.

"Then loop the cable around his neck and pull like hel—"

"You know what I'm going to do if I ever get out of this?" Carla interrupted.

"What?" said Finn.

"Shave my head. I'm going for the totally bald look. That way no one will ever climb into my hair agai—"

"*AAAAAAA!!!*"

Baptiste stopped dead and his sudden cry echoed around the valley like a rifle shot.

"What is it?" said Finn.

Carla followed the thug's gaze. There, peeping just over the top of the ridgeline ahead... was a cross of stone.

Saliva dripped from Baptiste's open jaw and he fell to his knees, gasping, overcome. Whatever he was looking for, he'd found.

"*UUUUH!!*"

Carla couldn't believe it. Finn couldn't believe it. There he was, a metre away, his neck exposed. Helpless in shock. For the first time. Helpless...

How do you kill a giant?

"NOW CARLA!!!" Finn screamed, but her instinct beat him to it.

Adrenalin surged and with her best softball hitter's cry, Carla jabbed her bound wrists forward to loop her shackle round Baptiste's exposed throat, then she yanked back – hard – with every ounce of her weight and being.

Baptiste gasped, reeled and rose.

"YES!" screamed Finn, nearly pulling a clump of Carla's hair out in excitement as she rode the back of the raging, exploding form, clinging on like a rodeo champ as they fell back – *SPLASH!* – like a great whale in the snow, turning and careering down the slope in a snowball fury, Carla hanging on for dear life, Finn confused, crushed, the mad frozen world tumbling and... *THUMP!*

They hit something, stopped dead. A boulder?

"GAHH!" – with his free hand, Baptiste forced the shackle from his throat to take desperate rasping breaths – "GAHH! GAHH! GAHH!"

Carla pulled harder, every cell of muscle stretched to breaking point, every sinew hard as nails. "GAHH! GAHH!" cried Baptiste, as they lay locked in the snow, moments stretching to eternity... He was dying... he was dying...

Until the wolves came.

OWWOWWWOOWWW!

Finn saw them first, charging down the slope, leaving powder trails like missiles.

"INCOMING! CARLA!"

OWWOWWWOOWWW!

Carla looked up and in that split second – "*GHAUH!*" – Baptiste flipped like a salmon, slipped the noose and grabbed the back of her scrawny neck, and before she knew it she was thrown onto her back in the snow – *SLAM* – and Baptiste was above her, drawing back his fist—

RRRRAAW! The first wolf hit him all claws and teeth.

Baptiste, furious, beat it away as if it was a fly, then roared caveman-like at the rest of the incoming pack.

"*AARRRRRRRRRGHGHGH!*"

Fear ran through the wolves and they scrambled to avoid him, sudden cowards. From the snow, Carla saw high above the mayhem an eagle break its glide, disturbed, and at the same time... she felt the earth explode.

BRBRBRRBRRBRRRRRRRRRRRRRRRRRRRRRRRRRRRRRRRR...

Thunder rose from the mountain. She saw Baptiste's momentary confusion, then – *WHAM!* – the mountain hit him as a wall of white, a wall of energy, of cascading snow.

"Avalanche!" Finn yelled in her hair. "Hang on!"

But nothing could be heard, nothing could be sensed in the all-encompassing chaos, the liquid totality of it…

BRBRBRRBRRBRRRRRRRRRRRBRBRRBRRBRRRRRRRRRR…

FEBRUARY 19 15:22 (GMT+2). OBS post South, Carpathian Mountains, Romania

The Tyro lookout sharpened the focus on the Zeiss T-star image-stabilising binoculars. Her pulse quickened.

She zeroed in on the white scree slope on the Kalamatov Ridge. The avalanche was obscuring her view, but she could see at least one figure in the snow. Immediately she hit the hard comms link back to the monastery.

"Trespass alarm! Seven kilometres south-east on Kalamatov!"

BRBRBRRBRRBRRRRRRRRRRRBRBRRBRRBRRRRRRRRRR…

Carla felt only pain – the shackles biting into her wrists as her unseen captor twisted and turned, then a *SNAP* of sudden release as the avalanche ran itself out, fading from a roar to a sigh…

She came to a halt, daylight leaking through the snow crystals.

She must be near the surface. For a few moments she lay in the profound silence and whiteness. She was still alive, but…

"You still there?" Carla whispered. Her greatest fear was to lose

17

him. He was annoying, but he was in every sense her blood brother.

Finn opened his eyes in the curled sanctuary of her hair.

"Are you kidding? This stuff is like a bulletproof duvet."

She let out a "Ha!" in relief.

"Is *he* still there?" said Finn in turn, hardly daring to hope.

Carla tried to move and got a shock. She still felt the pain of the shackles, but her wrists moved freely through the powder... Nothing at all binding them. She opened her arms... Smooth, delicious nothing. She felt like a princess waking in a fairy tale.

"HA!" Finn yelled when she brought her hands to her face in disbelief. "GET AWAY!"

Powered by euphoria and panic, Carla began to swim up to the surface.

"Careful!" Finn called out as the sun hit her face and she took a deep lungful of free, freezing air.

"Careful..." Finn warned again.

"OK..." Carla whispered. Slowly she wriggled and worked her head above the surface.

Baptiste...

Three feet away.

Head and shoulders out of the snow, stock-still like an Easter Island statue. Except this statue was bleeding and wisps of cloudy breath leaked from its mouth...

Carla held her own.

"Slow, slow, slow..." Finn urged.

Staring intently at the statue, Carla began to inch her way out. First her shoulders, then her arms, her knees... until she was able to take a first high step, a second...

She turned to wade down the slope, heart thumping. Three steps, four, five... She'd not been this far from him in months. The invisible chains that bound her to her captor seemed to be breaking one by one, until—

His eyes snapped open.

"AAAAARRRRRGGGGHHHH!" screamed Carla.

"RUN!" Finn yelled.

Carla ran, kneeing through the deep powder, stumbling as Baptiste exploded from the bank – "*WAAAAARRRRRGGGGHHHH!*" – avalanching after her, reborn in rage.

Finn shot to the top of her hair and grabbed his favourite long curl, flying free at its end like a mad bungie jumper able to bounce around and see all ways at once.

"RUN RUN RUN!"

Baptiste had pulled a knife from his belt and was closing fast.

Finn had to do something. Finn had to kill the giant. How?

"Arrrggghhhhh!" – Carla cried out suddenly as she ran onto nothingness and dropped a dozen feet before a rocky outcrop, coming to land – *WHUMP* – in a snowdrift at its base.

Baptiste followed – *WHUMP* – thumping further down the slope.

Carla instinctively rose to run again, but as she did so she heard Finn warn – "DON'T MOVE!"

She had fallen at the mouth of a cave, smashing aside the snow that concealed it. Now its contents were exposed. She sensed stink and stored heat. She saw fur. A pair of black eyes zooming in. A mother roused from a hibernating huddle.

"BEAR!" yelled Finn unnecessarily. "BROWN BEAR!" Always the naturalist.

Its massive salivating jaws opened – "*ROOOOOOOOOAAAAAAAA-RRRRRRRRRRR!*"

Carla screamed. The huge female swung round to check its pile of young, then swung back.

Finn, from the flying curl, saw Baptiste rising up the slope with the knife.

"KICK THE BEAR!"

"What?!" said Carla.

"KICK IT AND RUN!" screamed Finn.

Carla kicked at the dirt and ice before her, sending a spray of filth and grit into the bear's face, enraging her and flipping her from defence mode into attack.

"*ROOOOOOOOOAAAAAAAAARRRRRRRRRRR!*"

"GO!" screamed Finn.

As claws and jaws flashed towards Carla, she rose like a rocket and threw herself as far down the slope as she could, straight past the rising Baptiste...

"ARRRRRGGGGGGHHHHHHHH!" Man met mammal.

Carla sensed the force of the blow and heard a gasp of air as the claws of the bear ripped Baptiste clean open. She felt hot blood spray against her, felt life end – and thanked God she couldn't see it – as the bear's jaws snapped home round Baptiste's neck, breaking his spine like a dry stick.

Finn caught a glimpse of it. Saw the crimson arc whiplash across the snow and sky. A final obscenity. But not final for long...

"*ROOOOOOOOOAAAAAAAARRRRRRRRRR!*"

"RUN!" This was one mad bear.

Carla fell and tumbled and ran and staggered down through the forest as the bear pounded after her.

Carla had seconds.

Moments.

She would be obliterated.

Finn braced himself for the incoming final hit and yelled, uselessly, finally, "NOOOOOOO!"

YAP!

Hope.

Yo-yo galloped through the undergrowth and gave it everything, put every ounce of jelly energy into his spring and sank his teeth into the bear's hind leg.

ROOOOOAAAAAARARARARARARR!

Yo-yo let go and – using the momentum of the bear's reeling body – flew like a stone from a slingshot down the steep slope.

ROOOOOAAAAAARARARARARARR!

The bear roared again as it barrelled after the pelting, yelping mongrel, splintering the forest and exploding the snow.

"Run..." Finn managed to say through his astonishment.

TWO

Kaparis reviewed the tapes of the Monte Carlo sting.

He saw Captain Kelly. He saw Delta Salazar. Both were full-sized.

The last time he'd seen them, they were just 11mm tall.

He ground this new information round in his massive mind.

Like Allenby, Kaparis had been able to create a subatomic vortex within which all matter could be reduced, but his was crude, only capable of shrinking machines. Allenby could not only reduce living humans to nano-scale, he had now worked out how to reverse the process and restore them to normal size without killing them... Allenby was not just ahead in the race, he had made a great leap forward. It was like being in an old propeller biplane and watching a jet fighter shoot past.

Given an infinite amount of time, Kaparis could and would deduce the four elusive fractal equations at the heart of the Boldklub process. But he did not have for ever. Yet.

Now everything had changed. There was no contest. The game was up.

FEBRUARY 19 17:48 (GMT+3). Carpathian Mountains, Romania-Ukraine border

As she crested the Kalamatov Ridge, Carla fell to her knees. Just like Baptiste had done, just like many a pilgrim in times past, at first sight of the Monastery of Mount St Demetrius of Thessaloniki.

Against the brilliant orange of the setting sun, perched on top of a thousand feet of sheer white cliff, was a ruined cluster of ancient buildings, a nest of towers and tiles and a once-golden dome, tipped with the Orthodox cross. It was, in its way, magnificent, a crown of thorns on a snaggletooth of limestone, and only madmen could have built such a place.

"What is *that*?" asked Finn from the crow's nest of Carla's hair. There was not a whiff of smoke or any other sign of life.

"A Holiday Inn?" breathed Carla. "I don't know, but if we want to get through the night alive, we better check in..."

"You're not serious! How would you even get up there?" asked Finn.

23

"We've got to get out of this wind. Baptiste may have been a psychopath, but he was heat, body heat, and when we crawled into a snow hole, that's what kept us alive."

Yap! Yap!

"What was that?" Finn said, and held his breath to better listen through the wind.

Yap!

Carla looked back to the ridge.

"I *knew* he'd make it!" said Finn.

"YO-YO! HERE! HERE, BOY!" cried Carla.

Yap!

Over the ridge shot a spray of finest pink-sunset snow, a skittering cloud – and at its centre, an effervescent black scribble: a bounding, dishevelled, filthy, injured, exhausted, idiot of a dog.

"YO-YO!" cried Carla.

"YOYOYOYOYO!" yodelled Finn.

Yo-yo danced and circled, fearful of any trace of Baptiste, but Carla laughed and called his name and finally he came to her, yapping and wagging and loving the Finn-ness of her. Where his master had disappeared to nearly a year before was a mystery beyond Yo-yo's tiny brain, but not beyond his quite brilliant sense of smell.

Carla collapsed in the snow and submitted herself to an assault of licks and kisses. "Good dog. Smelly dog."

"Warm dog," Finn said. "You can snuggle up in a snow hole with him. We can make it down the valley in the morning. There must be some kind of settlement serving that place. We're almost ho—"

He bit back the word "home". It was too much. The thought of speaking, actually saying something, to Al and Grandma... There was an emotional avalanche banked tight in his chest and this was no time to let it sweep him away.

"...Almost there," was all he could manage.

But Carla wasn't listening to Finn. She had noticed something on Yo-yo's collar.

"Wait a minute – there's something here."

Yo-yo's collar was as filthy as the rest of him, but on one side of it was a lump.

"What is that?" said Finn. He crawled out of the thick of her hair to dangle from the curl at her forehead again as she rubbed away some of the muck. It was some kind of plastic cylinder attached to the collar, the size of a large battery.

"They sent him into the Forbidden City to try and find us! It's a tracker! It must be!" said Finn.

"Why haven't they been tracking us then?" said Carla.

She found the catch and took the whole collar off. "Maybe it ran out of power?" she said, examining it more carefully. "Or maybe it's not a tracker. Maybe it's some kind of comms device, or—"

But before she got any further...

YAP!

Yo-yo was off his haunches, nose high in the frozen air, stump of a tail curled like a tongue in concentration.

"Bear...?" asked Carla, fear returning.

"No," said Finn, hearing a distant buzz. "Machines...? PEOPLE!"

Carla shoved the dog collar into her top and scrambled down the steep snowfield, Yo-yo bounding ahead of her, crossing the tree line and disappearing into the forest.

"BE CAREFUL!" yelled Finn.

"Yo-yo, come back here!" ordered Carla and the dog yapped back, already lost.

She ran into the forest after him, the last rays of the setting sun needling through the pines to light the dog's progress through the snow. The further Carla ran, the darker it got, but the more they could hear the noise – engines, definitely the sound of engines, somewhere ahead.

Yap!

"Yo-yo!" said Carla, changing direction, heading for the bark, till…

"ARRRGGHHHH!" – the ground fell away. Nothingness. She shot out a hand and grabbed a sapling, then clung on hard and closed her eyes and felt the tiny tree take her weight, its roots clinging to the earth.

She gasped. Her eyes adjusted and she saw she'd just saved herself from running straight off a steep drop.

Yo-yo appeared and yapped at her, as if she was an idiot.

"No more short cuts," said Finn at her ear, then before she'd had time to catch her breath, he shouted: "Look!"

There beneath them, headlamps slicing through the darkness, three snowmobiles slaloming through the trees, tacking their way up the slope.

"HERE! OVER HERE!" Carla cried.

"They're climbing this way," said Finn. "They must have seen us on the pass."

Finn looked across at the silhouette of the ruined monastery through the trees. Surely it was the only spot they could have been seen from? As Carla pulled herself back up, he looked down at the snowmobiles again. It was hard to tell in the fading light, but all three carried a driver and a passenger, and slung across the back of each passenger... an automatic rifle with a distinctive curved magazine.

"AKs..." said Finn.

"UP HERE!" yelled Carla.

"*OWOWOWW!*" howled Yo-yo, to help her out.

"SHUT UP!" said Finn. "They're carrying AK47s!"

"What?"

"The only place anybody could have seen us from is the monastery. Who would live there? Who would hide there? Who would send out men with guns?"

"Hunters?"

"You don't shoot bunnies with AKs," said Finn.

Carla looked back down at the whizzing skidoos. "That would be cruel..."

"Baptiste fell to his knees when he saw it," said Finn. "Kaparis has headquarters all over the world..."

"You think it's where he's been headed all this time?"

"Want to find out?"

Carla answered by turning to run in the opposite direction down through the forest.

Finn could hear the skidoos climbing towards them, beams of light starting to flick through the trees.

"They're coming!" said Finn, lashing himself into place in the hair just above her forehead, poking out like a tiny tank commander.

Carla slogged on, but the skidoos were cutting through the forest like a wind, engines raging, lights strobing. In a flash of white light, they were spotted—

"*DA! ESTE!*" went up a foreign cry. Carla dived out of the beam.

"*ACOLO, ESTE!*"

Again she ran, but all three were closing in. Before she could be spotted again, Finn's yell matched her instinct: "HIDE!"

She dived forward and buried herself in the snow, clutching Yo-yo to her.

VROOM! VROOM! VROOM!

The three skidoos overshot.

"Stay down!" said Finn.

Carla hugged the panting dog closer and he licked her face.

The skidoos stopped. Finn and Carla could hear voices.

"Don't come back... Don't come back..." begged Finn.

Then – *DRDRDRDRDDRDRTT!* – muzzle flash lit the iced canopy as shots tore high through the trees in an attempt to flush them out – *DRTRRTRTRT!*

Yo-yo took violent fright, bursting out of Carla's arms to bite back. *YAP YAP YAP YAP!*

"*ACOLO!*" went up the cry. Yo-yo barked and, as headlights

wheeled once more, Carla launched herself into the darkness, running without hope or direction, running into...

Nothing.

Suddenly she found herself falling like Alice – but not like Alice, as she *hit* (and hard) a slide of ice and flew down it, a toboggan run of hellish thumps and spins and whacks that sent her winded and flying – *WHAM!* – into a blue-black final darkness...

THREE

Is she dead?

Finn woke upside down, still lashed into her hair.

Is she dead?

He struggled and turned himself round. Saw stars in a slice of night sky above, saw fast-moving clouds, heard the wind. Where the hell were they?

Is she dead?

She couldn't die. She had carried him through hell, they had come too far... He untied himself and dropped to her scalp. At once he could feel her pulse beneath his feet, feel her warmth. Alive...

What a girl, Finn thought, and not for the first time.

How long had he been out of it? Hours? Minutes? He pushed through to examine her scalp. There seemed to be no blood, no great crush of her skull.

Had they fallen down the cliff? He looked up. The slice of night sky was sandwiched between slabs of blackness. Were they inside the mountain? Inside some kind of split in the rock?

The skidoos had gone. So had Yo-yo...

"CARLA!" Finn yelled, as much to force back his tears as to rouse her.

"WAKE UP!"

Then from above – movement – a scratch – a thump.

Chunks of dislodged snow and ice fell towards them.

Wolves? A bear?

"CARLA!"

WHAP! – with a slap, the end of a heavy wet rope nearly knocked Finn clean off his perch. He clung on and looked up as a huge leg appeared over the edge of the crevasse, then another, then a squat muscular figure slid straight down the rope.

Every hair on Finn's tiny body stood on end as the figure blotted out the last slice of sky. He braced himself.

The figure stopped dead. Grunted. Struck a match.

Light stung the darkness and a figure from a nightmare squinted at Carla. A boy, medieval in dress and form, with a huntsman's bow across his back, dark face scarred and twisted, a misshapen thing. His bulging eyes looked at Carla and absorbed her.

Carla, as if in response, briefly opened her own, beautiful eyes.

They widened in momentary shock then lapsed back into unconsciousness.

"*Esti...?*" the boy started to say, and tried to shake her a little.

When he got no response, he fed the rope around Carla's back and secured it. "Yes!" said Finn. "Get us out of here..."

The boy braced himself against the walls and hauled on the rope.

Back out on the rock face, Finn saw no sign of skidoos. The starlit sky was clouding over and sharp flecks of snow were whipping in on the wind.

He felt himself flip upside down as Carla was picked up and slung over the shoulder of the extraordinary boy, who did not pause as he picked a treacherous mountain-goat's path down the slope without slipping or stopping. By the time they'd reached the valley floor, a blizzard was blowing. The boy dropped them on to a toboggan and jumped on behind them, steering them through the forest. After a few minutes, the ground began to rise again. The boy hopped off and pulled the sledge along until eventually they stopped before another rock face.

The snow was wild around them.

Finn saw the boy work away at something, pulling a rope that disappeared into the darkness above. It could only lead to one place – they must be beneath the ruins, beneath the castle in the air. As the rope began to run free in his hands, the boy jumped back and – *WHUMP* – a great basket dropped out of the darkness.

The boy tipped Carla unceremoniously over its side and leapt in after her. Again he hauled on ropes, and Finn felt the basket rock and sway as they began to rise. In a short time, the boy's hauling became easier; a great falling counterweight passed them, then the rope was running through his hands as they rose relentlessly. Finn saw they were rushing up towards a perfect square of light, a trapdoor in the floor of heaven. Finn gasped as the basket thumped home into a blindingly torchlit timber wheelhouse.

As Finn's eyes adjusted, he could see their saviour more clearly – a hunchback half-man clothed in rags. Again Carla was thrown over his shoulder and he set off on a mad rocking run, almost too fast for Finn to make sense of where they were. There was a long, narrow stone passage, lit by dim oil lamps, with many passages and doorways leading off. After a minute's run, the boy veered off into a much broader passage, then shouldered through a large oak door, and they arrived in the peace and sanctuary of…

Books.

Candle-light.

Words.

Thousands of pages, rotting and reused, torn and shredded, lining the floors and jamming the gaps to keep out the cold. Fuelling tiny fires.

A library. Finn knew it was from the smell, the musty, trusty smell of books. But he had never seen a library as tragic or as strange as this. A huge high ceiling topped ranks of splintered shelves lining damp walls that seemed to run from earth to heaven, an illusion reinforced by the religious decoration on the smoke-blackened pillars and frescos, saints' faces, red and gold and ruined. An ornate, crumbling wedding cake of a library transformed into a slum, its desks and furniture upturned and adapted, knocked and nailed into an encampment of shanty shacks, out of which devilish and dead-eyed children stared and shivered, dressed in grey sackcloth and buried like hamsters under the piles of yellowing pages. A dormitory of the damned. And at the far end, on a raised dais with a commanding view over the whole cavernous room, was a large desk on pillared legs, where sat, surrounded by bells and dangling tubes, a striking young man.

Their deformed saviour headed straight for him, letting Carla down off his back to offer her like a cabbage to a king.

"*Draga... Primo?*" said the boy.

Primo? thought Finn. He could see his face in shadow – handsome, sherry-skinned, dark eyes with a thousand-yard stare. He had seen the dangling tubes around him before, in old war films, speaking tubes used to communicate on ships and submarines.

"*Ce facut?*" asked the Primo, suspicious.

"Santiago find," the boy explained in English.

He lifted Carla higher and the Primo reached out a hand. His fingers sought and gently traced the detail of Carla's face as Finn looked again at the Primo's black eyes... and at the same moment, Carla came round, shocked at the touch of the sculpted youth staring straight through her. She drew breath to scream—

"No! He's blind, Carla!" shouted Finn, running to her ear.

Carla caught the scream, and flinched from the hand, turning away, only to see the mashed-up face of Santiago for the first time.

"ARRRRRRRRGGGH!"

"It's OK, Carla! The freaky kid rescued us!" Finn insisted in her hair.

"Stop!" demanded the Primo, quelling her at once.

"I don't know what's going on, but we're in the castle, I think they're OK!" said Finn. He could feel her pulse thumping through her scalp.

"Romana? English? Deutsche? Française?" demanded the Primo.

"What's happening?" Carla managed.

"Santiago found you. You should not be here," said the Primo. The deformed boy, Santiago, shuffled.

"What do you mean?" said Carla.

A bell rang on his desk. Then two bells. Distant orders began barking out of the speaking tubes.

"Hide her!"

FOUR

Carla felt no fear – she felt warm for the first time in months.

They'd been hurried out of the library as the main doors opened to three brutal-looking adults in black, AK47s slung across their backs, "*Siguri*" the ragged children called them, as they were smuggled down to a cell-like storeroom, where Carla had been urged to hide in a wooden chest.

They'd heard a fair amount of crashing and yelling, then nothing for a long time.

"Finn," Carla whispered.

"Shh!" Finn said, listening hard in her hair – then "AHH!" as he found his legs being tasted by a pair of snout-headed lice the size of fat cats, their organs visible beneath their maggoty skin. "GETAAWAYAYYYY!" Finn grabbed the spike that never left his side, but before he could swing, the lice were off through Carla's hair, roadrunner legs whirring like outboards.

"Are you OK?" said Carla.

"Bookworms," said Finn.

"Worms in my head?!" she hissed.

"No, not 'worms' – that's just what they're called. They're bugs that feed off mould – and me—"

Finn stopped. He could hear something.

Footsteps.

"Someone's coming!"

The lid of the chest lifted and candle-light revealed a scrap of a girl with a thick Slav accent. "Come! Be quick!"

Moments later, Carla was running behind the girl back along the stone passage to the library.

Some of the shacks had been kicked down, and bedding and pathetic belongings lay around in a tangled mess, but the Siguri had gone. Some of the younger children were gathered around the Primo's dais, anxious. Carla was rushed straight up.

"Santiago has been taken by the Siguri guards. You must save him," said the Primo, urgent. "They know he has been out now. They are searching for s stranger."

"For me?" said Carla.

"Santiago found an injured climber last year – they killed him. So now they think, if he finds another, he'll hide them."

"What have we walked into?" Finn asked above Carla's left ear.

"Why would they kill an injured climber?" asked Carla.

"Because it is the Will of the Master," said the Primo.

"Oh great. Oh, just perfect," said Finn, his heart sinking. "Ask him if they're *Tyros*."

"Are you Tyros?" said Carla.

"We are the Carriers. We serve," said the Primo. "The Tyros are in their dormitories."

"Dormitories?" said Finn.

The scrap of a girl threw a sackcloth robe over Carla's head, and Finn had to duck in case he got dragged out.

"The Abbot has called for more fire," said the Primo. "Go with Olga. Santiago must live. He is one of us. You are a stranger."

"But a Tyro dragged me here from China! A monster! I only just escaped. I—"

"If Santiago is dying, you must give yourself up and save him," ordered the Primo.

"Sacrifice myself?"

"If you do, you will become one of us," explained the Primo solemnly. "We will try and save you too."

"And if I refuse?" asked Carla.

"Then they will find your body at the foot of the cliff," the Primo stated matter-of-factly.

Carla's temper flared.

"You're threatening to kill me?"

"I'm making you an offer – honour or death. I must protect the Carriers. If Santiago talks, he puts them all in danger," the Primo stated.

The Carrier kids watched and waited. A curious bunch – all sizes, shapes, colours and ages, dressed in the same sackcloth as Carla.

"Keep him talking. Buy some time," said Finn at her ear. "We need to weasel a way out of this."

"I choose honour," Carla answered.

"I said stall!" complained Finn.

"Santiago must live," repeated the Primo. "Go!"

"Go!" answered Olga, and she pulled Carla in a skinny grip towards the exit.

Finn climbed through Carla's hair, still complaining as they left the library and hurried up a main passageway that curved up through the building, its flagstone floor polished smooth by centuries of footsteps.

"We need to get out of here," said Finn.

"And leave him to die?" said Carla.

Olga scurried through some doors ahead of them and suddenly they were in cavernous kitchens, dead at this hour, but with a great black iron furnace at its heart. Olga opened the furnace door to reveal a nest of large stones, white hot, like dragon's eggs. She lined up a pair of iron buckets and with some huge tongs grabbed and dumped a glowing stone into each one – *donk, donk*. Then she handed Carla a thick glove and indicated towards a bucket.

"Go!" Olga urged and picked up her own shimmering load.

Carla followed suit and Olga led them out of the kitchen and into the black heart of the complex—

The Forum.

Carla stopped dead at the sight. For Finn with his gamer head on, it was like a new map revealing itself.

Lit by flaming torches, it was a courtyard hollowed out of a hotchpotch of buildings, a core three storeys deep. A single round opening in the centre of the roof let in curls of snow and huge filthy banners proclaimed the words *Honour*, *Obedience* and *Master*. Doors and entranceways, some ancient, some more recent concrete, peppered the four sides of the courtyard, and a rising irregular spiral of stairways and open walkways connected them all together. It was like something out of a painting by Escher.

"Freaky…" said Finn.

"Go!" Olga scolded and led the way, little legs rushing up the mad spiral. Carla set off after her and tried to keep up. The hot bucket swung and she could feel her gloved hand starting to burn.

Halfway up the spiral was the entrance to a great concrete space hidden beneath the ancient monastery roofs, hundreds of bunks in serried ranks, full of sleeping teenagers.

"Tyros…" said Finn at Carla's ear. "This is some kind of hive. We need to make a phone call, *now*."

"Olga! Where is there a phone?" Carla called and mimed a handset. "A telephone?"

Olga just looked perplexed. "Go!" she said, and they were off again, climbing past another dozen entranceways.

"Tell her!" yelled Finn. "We have to find a phone or a computer, or... the collar! That thing on Yo-yo, whatever it was. Have you still got it?"

Carla grabbed her pocket. Nothing. Had she taken it off Yo-yo? She could barely remember.

"I must have lost it somewhere on the mountain."

"*ARRRGGHHHH!*" – the sound of screams was coming from the top floor. Olga hurried them through an arch guarded by Siguri, then on through a huge door into a church of crumbling beauty... and the screams of Santiago.

"*AARRRRGGHHHHHH...*"

He lay stretched out on a rack in the centre, the heart of the High Chapel, face down, his arms being pulled up behind his humped back by the Siguri chief, a thickset Turk. The screams echoed off the painted saints and gilded icons. Looking down on him was the Abbot, the leader of the monastery and the Siguri, a man in Roman robes, with a face so badly burnt it resembled the surface of a planet.

Half a dozen Siguri and a severe female secretary looked on.

The secretary flicked her head at Olga and Carla, indicating an iron stove.

"WHERE is the STRANGER?" raged the Siguri chief.

Carla wobbled the last few steps to the stove, but almost dropped her bucket as she became aware of a strange sound.

It was a sound Finn knew only too well.

Schlup-schlup-schlup – dinner time.

"Yo-yo!" said Finn, hardly believing it. "I think Yo-yo's here."

He could feel Carla's heartbeat spike through the scalp beneath his feet.

"Oh no, if he gets a sniff of me…" said Finn, becoming suddenly worried.

"It is all quite simple," the Abbot said, wearily looking down at Santiago. "You like it out in the woods. It's where we found you. It's where you belong."

"Yes, Padre…"

"We know there was a trespasser, a stranger. We spotted him. We found his dog."

He gestured to the far corner of the chapel. There, unmistakably, was Yo-yo's rear end, his head buried in a pan of stew which he was transferring to his stomach in great wild gulps.

"It was very clever of you to find them."

"No, Padre…"

"Yes. You left your toboggan out. Did you bring the stranger in? Did you hide him?"

"Santiago no bring dog!" he answered.

"No. We found the dog," the Abbot reassured him. "In the woods. But you were in the woods too."

"Pine cones. For the fire…"

"You were gathering aromatic fuel? In a snowstorm?"

Santiago wriggled an approximate nod, ashamed to be lying.

At the stove, Olga used some tongs to drop off their hot stones, taking her time as Carla watched Santiago on the rack. Finn could almost feel the morality rising through Carla's scalp, but counselled – "Don't do anything. We have to figure something out."

"Who was it, do you think, that the lookout and the searchers saw then?" the Abbot asked Santiago, letting the question hang. Santiago could not help but fill the silence.

"An... angel, Padre?"

"An *angel*?" said the Abbot. "With a *dog*?"

Santiago shook in disagreement. "NO DOG, Padre – dog run away! Crazy dog!"

"Could it be a stray?" the Abbot asked the Siguri chief.

"No, sir. A stray would have starved by the time it got up here. This dog has been regularly beaten; its master must be the stanger."

Olga started to lead Carla back out.

The Abbot waved, the rack wheel turned, and Santiago cried out again in excruciating pain.

"*Arrrrrrrrrrgggghhh!*"

The cry stopped Carla in her tracks – at the very moment Finn's scent finally rang a big bell in Yo-yo's tiny brain – *YAP!*

Yo-yo whipped round. There! There was the good girl! There was the Finn smell!

YAP YAP YAP! YAP!

The Siguri chief, the Abbot, even Santiago, turned to look.

"It has the scent of its master!" said the chief.

Yo-yo was straining at the rope that held him, pointing only one

43

way: at Carla, halted before the great door, ready to turn and declare herself.

"Let the dog go!" ordered the Abbot.

"No, Yo-yo! PLAY DEAD!" Finn yelled uselessly from Carla's hair.

The Siguri holding Yo-yo released him and he sprang towards Carla like an accusing finger, all skew-whiff as the stew sloshed about the wire rack of his body, until... *BANG!*

The doors behind Carla burst open and in came the severed head of Baptiste, ravaged by bears and dangling from a Siguri gauntlet.

HOWWWLLL! – Yo-yo cowered back in fear.

CLANG! – Carla dropped her empty bucket in shock.

"*Stupido!*" cried the secretary, and slapped her so hard Finn had to cling on as she fell.

The Abbot was shaken. "Bring it closer!"

Baptiste's head was marched up and dangled before him.

There was one lidless eye, the other was missing, as was the top quarter of his skull. A wafer edge of white bone stood proud of the blood and brain on what was left of his brow. His skin was ghostly, ghastly pale, and his black mouth gaped open. A section of collarbone dangled from ligaments at his neck. Here was the master. Here was the stranger.

The Abbot recognised him at once. "Oh, my dear boy..."

FIVE

Santiago was released and led back through the labyrinth, held between Carla and Olga like a broken bird, eyes tight shut, muttering some mad, grateful, polyglot incantation (*"Fo me ca Maria – fo me ca Primo – fo me ca Jesu – fo me ca Master – fo me ca Dei"*) while Yo-yo strained at the end of a rope just ahead, anxious to put as much distance as possible between himself and the severed head.

They arrived back in the library to exclamations in a dozen tongues. Carriers crowded round. Excited, Yo-yo began to yap, then – just like it would in the playground – a handbell broke up the scene – *Ding-a-ling!*

"Quiet! Do you want the Siguri back?" demanded the Primo.

Santiago limped over to him.

"What did you tell them?" the Primo asked.

Santiago recounted what had happened in a breathless, dramatic babble.

At the end of it, the Primo asked, astonished, "*Baptiste?*"

"His head – just his head," Carla confirmed. "He dragged me here from Shanghai. When I got away from him, the bears got him."

Santiago grunted confirmation. There was murmuring among the Carriers.

"They know him... They're impressed," Finn said at her ear. "Make the most of it!"

"I did what you asked," Carla told the Primo. "I brought Santiago back. Now I must make contact with the outside. I must call for help."

"There is no means. We are not meant to exist," the Primo said. "There are no phones, no electric. Even fires do not burn by day. We are made to live as of old."

Finn looked at the bells and the speaking tubes hanging around the dais and started to understand. This place was undetectable.

"There are NRP machines in the infirmary, but nothing else," said the Primo.

"What are NRP machines?" asked Carla.

"Neuroretinal programming," explained the Primo. "A probe is put through the eye into the brain, to program Tyros with expertise, strength, character."

"That's what made you blind..." Carla realised, appalled.

"The Master searches care institutions across the world for children of exceptional intelligence. I am from a local orphanage, but others are from the farthest corners of the earth. If we are suitable for NRP, we become Tyros and begin our training. If NRP fails, but we are still of use, we are put to work with the Carriers – local unwanted children," the Primo said. "If we are not of use, we die."

Finn felt Carla give a shiver.

"Your Master is a monster," she said.

"We are here. Nowhere else," said the Primo, dead simple.

At Carla's ear Finn said, "These NRP machines must use computers of some kind, they must be connected to something?"

"Primo, these machines, are they computers? Do they have electricity?"

"They are connected by wire to the Caverns, but no Carrier can go there."

Finn's ears pricked up.

"What caverns?" asked Carla.

"Beneath us. Great halls within the mountain."

"What is in them?"

"We cannot know. But flying machines go there at night sometimes."

"Flying machines?" said Carla.

"We have to get out and tell someone about this," insisted Finn. "We have to get off this rock!"

"In the morning, I have to leave, I have to get help," Carla told the Primo.

"You will never make it. First you have to escape the Siguri, then the peasants – who all depend on the Protectorate – then the elements themselves."

"Santiago gets out," said Carla. "How else did he find me?"

"They know Santiago will never leave. He was the unwanted runt

47

of some peasant girl. As a babe he was left to die in the snow, but an old crone heard his cries, rescued him from wolves and nursed him back to health. Later, when she was dying, she brought him here. He knows nothing else."

"I got dragged across half the world by a mad Tyro – I'll make it," said Carla.

The Primo, not used to being challenged, tilted his perfect chin and turned his blind eyes on her. She felt as if they were staring through her.

"For every runaway the Siguri catch, they let the Tyros kill another five Carriers for sport. To set an example."

Finn sank back against Carla's scalp, challenge fading in the face of such cruelty. A lump rose in Carla's throat.

"Baptiste was the worst," the Primo added, more conciliatory. "We are grateful he is dead. He would have killed me, but the tutors stopped him."

"Why?"

"They need me. For the Carriers to be effective slaves, they must be led," he said simply.

Carla looked around at the ragged Carrier kids. They were all shapes and sizes, all colours, all abilities and disabilities. They certainly needed someone.

"This place is like an evil fairy tale," Finn said in Carla's hair.

"We've got to help them," Carla insisted. "Primo, if I can get one message to the authorities, important people – and soldiers – will come, will stop this."

The Primo silently considered the matter and Carla stared at his face and wondered what it must be like to be without sight in such a place, a darkness within darkness, and yet be so strong.

"Nothing can be done before the spring melt."

"Before *spring*?!"

"Follow Olga. Tomorrow we will make you a Carrier. Live as she lives, do as she does. As long as you work hard, you will be safe."

FEBRUARY 20 03:17 (GMT+2). Hull of the *Shieldmaiden*, Mediterranean Sea

Kaparis did not by nature sleep.

He seethed.

Usually Heywood would knock him out with a powerful sedative, but Kaparis had refused, wishing instead to pickle himself in fury and self-pity. He considered that he had got everything he had in life through application, imagination and sheer hard work. But never once had he had any luck – despite having inherited his vast wealth, good looks, charm and a brain the size of a small planet.

It wasn't fair. Other people got lucky all the time, while he had to slog his guts out. Or at least other people's guts, which was frankly messy.

Nothing was fair...

Then Heywood interrupted his musings and said, "Sir? The Abbot is on the line."

"At this hour?"

Moments later, coloured bars of data danced on his life-support monitor, like nymphs in spring, and Kaparis ordered: "Bring me the head of Baptiste!"

On the screen above him, the Abbot presented the gory remains of the Tyro's head on a cushion, like some precious jewelled thing.

"We retrieved it from a bear den on the Kalamatov Ridge!"

"HAAAHH!" Kaparis laughed, baring his teeth like a hyped primate.

"And where is she? Are you keeping her back as a surprise? Oh, I can barely stand it!"

"Who, Master?"

"THE SALAZAR GIRL!" Kaparis roared.

The Abbot was clueless.

"Three of them disappeared in China," he explained to the Abbot, as if to a fool. "Baptiste, Carla Salazar, and, very likely, Infinity Drake. If Baptiste walked all that way, do you think for one moment he would have left them behind?"

"We carried out an extensive search, Master..."

"RUBBISH!"

Fools. Morons. Scum. Could they not FOR ONCE match the scale of his intellect? He gurgled with rage, unable to speak a moment, as the Abbot whimpered...

"We scoured the mountain! We can assure you he was quite alone. All we found was a dog..."

Kaparis almost suffered a seizure.

A dog?

A dog?

A dog with a supernatural sense of smell that had successfully traced its

9mm master before? A dog idiot enough and faithful enough to follow that scent for three thousand miles?

"Get me a picture of Infinity Drake's dog!" snapped Kaparis.

An image flashed up on the screen array. Yo-yo. A vision of joyous furry idiocy.

"Was it, by any chance... this dog?" asked Kaparis.

The Abbot gulped. It was a thousand times cleaner than the one they'd found, but it was the same dog.

"We thought he must have picked it up along the way..." the Abbot tried to explain.

"WHERE IS IT?"

The Abbot's mind was blank. He dimly remembered someone kick it aside. He scrabbled around for some consolation. "Perhaps the Carrier children have it? They have value as rat catchers. We will have the whole complex searched! If there is a dog – if there is a girl – we shall slay them!"

The Siguri chief beside the Abbot was nodding vigorously, but Kaparis slammed on the brakes—

"NO! Don't you see what this means?"

His mind was a spinning Catherine wheel. If the dog was there, then Drake was there. If so, where? If Baptiste had brought the girl with him then was Drake somewhere on the girl? But where was the girl? On the mountain? In a bear?

"Find the bears, slice them open. The Salazar girl has to be somewhere—"

"Or Santiago found her!" exclaimed the Abbot.

"Santiago?"

"The idiot boy. The trapper."

51

"The hunchback?" said Kaparis, vaguely remembering the wretch.

"Sometimes he finds lost souls. He was out late on the mountain – we questioned him. But not about a girl…"

"Brilliant!" gasped Kaparis.

"Really?" said the Abbot.

Kaparis's voice fell to a rasping conspiratorial whisper. "If Drake is hidden somewhere in the monastery, we've caught him, with or without the girl."

No one was dumb enough to ask the obvious question: how? How do you catch someone 9mm tall in a complex the size of a cathedral? Nobody asked, because they knew the Master always came up with an answer more fiendish than they could ever conceive.

Nano-radar[4], thought Kaparis. They could scour the buildings, scour the mountain. But Drake could hide from it behind steel, behind rock. But why would he? If he didn't know they were looking for him, he would have no reason to hide. We must do it by stealth, thought Kaparis, we must lure him out into the open.

"We must set a trap, we must bait it…" Kaparis thought aloud.

What did Infinity Drake want more than anything in the world?

His father…

With a blink, Kaparis wiped the image of Yo-yo from his screens and directed his optically controlled cursor to retrieve a file marked ARCHIV23874378KAP-ENCRYPT. The title read: "Intel. report 498090bb – Drake, E."

It was the report Kaparis had commissioned thirteen years before into

---

[4] Nano-radar sets, shrunk to detect super-dense nano-material. Limited in range.

the mysterious disappearance of Ethan Drake, father of Infinity, during an experiment at a lab in Cambridge. He opened it across the screen array. Kaparis knew it almost by heart, though it had always posed more questions than answers, always deepened the mystery.

Ethan had built a machine – the forerunner of the Boldklub machines – a machine that proved his genius. It was not just a masterpiece of science and engineering, it was a work of art. It was more than the sum of its parts, more than all it was designed to be. It reached out beyond the boundaries of physical laws into the unknown. Kaparis had been furious. How could he compete? First he had lost the love of his young life to Ethan, now he had lost the future. Why? It made no sense. Kaparis considered himself the supreme applied human intelligence. Perhaps you could be too perfect?

Or did Ethan Drake simply have all the luck? If he did, it ran out the day he attempted an unwise experiment in quantum teleportation. He had thrown himself into the subatomic magnetic vortex at the heart of his machine... and disappeared without a trace. Not an atom of him remained. No one understood why.

Kaparis had taunted Infinity Drake with the existence of this report when their paths had crossed in Shanghai, taunted him too that Ethan had chosen suicide over life with his wife and newborn child. The boy had been enraged; he was clearly obsessed with his father's disappearance.

Here was the bait.

Now for the trap. If the boy was in the monastery, then...

Then out of nowhere it finally happened.

Luck.

As Kaparis turned his rational mind from nano-radar to all the practical-

53

ities and complexities of designing a trap, and a miniature jail, his eyes and his subconscious mind drifted across Ethan Drake's original notes. The notes were rough -- fast, shorthand equations, sketches like cartoons, thoughts caught and set down as they happened. Numbers and letters and symbols that danced down the page, all the way down to the final mysterious biro scribble: L = Place? Mysterious because, in conventional physics, L represented locomotion. And "Locomotion = Place?" was an impossible and perplexing statement. But because on this occasion he wasn't concentrating, Kaparis suddenly saw with his subconscious what the scribble really was: Ethan Drake had written the L lopsided. Because the L was actually not an L at all. The two lines of the L were in fact the crudely drawn hands of a clock—

Time! In Ethan Drake's hand, the cockeyed L was Time.

L = Place? became Time = Place?

Kaparis convulsed. His mind overloaded. Suddenly Ethan's notes began to come to life, growing and taking shape in three dimensions and glorious Technicolor. The whole system sprang to life in his head, the genius of Ethan Drake, dancing for him, only him...

Time = Place? The fabulous conclusion changed everything.

It had been there all along. Yet only he, Kaparis, had finally seen it.

The Boldklub fractal equations that he had so long sought, for which he had spent years terrorising and blackmailing Al Allenby and the G&T, were now blindingly obvious.

And there was more, so much more... The implications...

It was as if he had climbed out of a propeller plane and strapped himself onto a rocket.

He was about to seize control of the future.

SIX

FEBRUARY 20 08:53 (GMT). Hook Hall,
Surrey, UK

SPLASH!

Six foot six and sixteen stone of pure military meat hit the muddy water at the foot of the five-metre wall, sending it in all directions at once.

Unstoppable, Captain Kelly of the SAS (seconded to the G&T's informal military detachment) hammered every muscle in his body towards the next obstacle on the course that ran through the woodland surrounding Hook Hall, the stately home and laboratory complex in Surrey that served as the HQ of the Global Non-governmental Threat Response Committee.

55

Thirty metres of monkey walk lay ahead. Kelly grabbed the first bar and began to swing beneath the frame, enjoying the pain, loving it, the complications of the abortive Monte Carlo mission forgotten for a few blissful moments.

And they had to forget. All who had experienced life at nano-scale had found it difficult to adjust to life back at normal size, but more than anything, life without Finn...

THUD!

A four-inch, six-ounce throwing knife, travelling at 130mph, split the surface of the target post, transmitting the concentrated intent of the young woman who threw it from the far end of the Zen-white martial arts studio in the Old Manor.

Flight Lieutenant Delta Salazar bent her body over and took up her second position. When she wasn't on fire, chasing down Tyros on motorbikes, she was ice. Lukewarm tears were just not her thing. Except when it came to her little sister. About Carla – still missing, possibly captured, possibly dead... she was a complete mess.

Hence the yogic knife-throwing routine she indulged in every morning to try and clear her mind.

THUD!

Crinkle.

Engineer Stubbs unwrapped a boiled sweet, popped it into his mouth and began to suck. It was a twenty-two-calorie Werther's Original, containing soya lecithin and flavouring, and it was the first solid to pass his lips in forty-eight hours.

He was in his chaotic workshop in the old stables at the back of Hook Hall. He had not taken an active role in the Monte Carlo mission as he didn't "travel well" and just the thought of going to France caused him an upset tummy.

Also, he knew it would all go wrong. It was his default position.

He was a man not of action but of make do and mend. In his time at nano-scale he had improvised a jet-powered jeep and a hydrogen balloon on the hoof, as well as having designed the Ugly Bug experimental nano-vehicle.

Fat lot of good it had done poor Infinity though, he thought…

VVRVRRVRRRRRRROOOOOM!

The De Tomaso Mangusta had been designed to take the breath away, a beautiful piece of jet-age engineering built for speed and named Mangusta, or mongoose, to imply it would eat its 1960s rival, the AC Cobra, for breakfast. With Dr Al Allenby's customisations, it was capable of lunch and dinner too. Al didn't just drive it round the runway at Hook Hall – he tried to plough it into the earth, so brutal was his cornering, so crude his acceleration. The thrill ride used to take his mind off things.

Used to.

He passed the Start/Finish line for the ninth time at 145mph – *VVRVRRVRRRRRRROOOOOM!* – and saw the chequered flag.

The signal that the Monte Carlo post-mortem meeting was about to begin.

With a sigh, Al slowed, left the track, and drove down through the complex to the hangar-like building known as the CFAC (Central Field Analysis Chamber). The huge doors parted as he approached and he drove straight into the vast concrete space that was dominated by a ring of particle accelerators capable of whipping up an electromagnetic vortex that could shrink all matter.

His Boldklub machine. It had been used first during Operation Scarlatti, when Finn had first got caught up in the nano-world and where, somewhere, he remained. Now it stood idle, waiting for his return.

Al crushed the lump that rose in his throat and spun the Mangusta to a handbrake halt at the centre of the array.

Commander James Clayton King, the Hook Hall supremo, on his way up the steel gantry steps to the control gallery, didn't look down, break step or in any way acknowledge him. The impeccable figure who had coordinated saving the world any number of times hated showing off of any sort.

In moments, the G&T Committee were assembled: engineers, scientists, thinkers, soldiers. There were no formalities. Commander King reviewed the Monte Carlo débâcle using video to illustrate the handover, the roar of the motorbike, the pop of the empty cigar tube, the chase and kill. When the recording finished, he concluded: "We're not the first to leave the casino having incurred a loss. We knew this could happen, which is why we took precautions. Kaparis duped us. We duped him."

Pictures flashed up of the dead rider and the girl who'd made the exchange.

"Tyros, of course. Note that they've taken to wearing coloured contact lenses to disguise the scarring left by the brain programming."

The last known picture of Kaparis flashed up, able-bodied and evil, standing with a group of super-rich investors in Zurich, Switzerland, sometime in the late 1990s.

Al had to look away.

"As ever, he is playing games, displaying his power."

"What goes on in that pretty little head of yours…?" Delta wondered aloud as she imagined three separate ways she'd like to snap that pretty little head off.

"We go again," said Kelly. "We have no choice. He knows we have no choice. We wait for him to make contact again and we start again."

"And we look ridiculous, again," said Stubbs gloomily.

"Shut up, Stubbs," said Kelly automatically.

"We are prepared for every eventuality," said King. "Except one."

"What?" said Al.

"He may be stringing us along because he doesn't have Infinity or Carla."

"They are NOT dead!" cried Delta, who never welcomed this suggestion. "We have no evidence that they're dead. I was the last to see her and at that time she was alive!"

It was true that Delta had lost consciousness shortly after, but (attached to Yo-yo's collar and still at nano-scale) she had been the

59

last person to see her sister alive. Infinity Drake was presumed to be secreted somewhere about her person.

King waited a moment.

"We have no evidence, apart from a few doubtful videos, that Kaparis is holding either Infinity or your sister."

Delta took comfort in this and bit her lip not to show it.

Al looked at the Zurich picture again and felt his stomach twist. Whenever he thought of Kaparis, his body tensed to take a punch. *Exactly what Kaparis would have wanted*, Al thought. Maybe that was the problem. Al looked round at the experts at the table or on screen, perhaps the finest minds ever assembled. He had led them to disaster. All his life he had been the smartest guy in the room, the brain. He had surfed his intellect and got as far as Boldklub and nearly bust open the laws of physics, but now it seemed he was all washed up.

"Stubbs is right…" said Al (but Stubbs took no pleasure in it). "We should never have fallen for Monte Carlo. That was ridiculous. We've become too predictable. Too logical. We're scientists. We want the world to be rational, but we know that most of the time it isn't. Life is *random*, absurd. That scares and confuses us. That's why most of us are so bad at personal relationships!"

Al looked around. He was right. The room was full of blinking, uncomfortable nerds.

"If we can't logically figure a way through this, then we've got to embrace the irrational, the unconscious. Look for answers there. We – no, *I* – I've got to stop digging the hole we're in, I've got to step back and *feel* it, you know?"

"May I be excused?" requested Stubbs at this point.

"It's time to get Zen, get patient," Al continued. "It's time to look beneath. This is a game of chess, not noughts and crosses." He got up and paced. "We've got to think forwards, think backwards, think laterally; find the gap, the clue." He slapped the table – "Come on! Let's think outside the box! Let's *burn* the damn box! You're the brightest and the best. The only thing that trumps facts, that trumps time, that trumps the inevitable – that breaks $E=MC^2$ – is the HUMAN IMAGINATION!"

Al climbed on to the desk and threw himself into a headstand. His legs flailed and split, but he held it, just.

He regarded them all, upside down. They looked ridiculous.

"It seems," sighed Stubbs, "we're back to square one."

FEBRUARY 20 10:12 (GMT). Blue Valley
Mall, Woking, Surrey, UK

There were too many variables, thought Li Jun.

There were six small children and approximately six thousand polyurethane spheres in the ball pool, featuring nine different colours with a predominance of red, blue, green and yellow. Four per cent of the spheres were misshapen or dented. Every movement caused a chaotic chain reaction through the surrounding balls that was predictable only to a low standard deviation. Too many differential calculations were required.

But what was causing Li Jun's real distress was that the activity of the six small children in the ball pool had no point or goal. She looked out of the ball pool to where Grandmother Allenby stood with the other adults.

In an exaggerated mime, Grandma clutched her diaphragm and said, "*Breathe*, dear."

Li Jun took a deep breath. She should be able to cope. She had a formidable mind. She had been Kaparis's chief technician, after all—

"INCOMING!" Hudson cried, sprinting towards the edge of the pool while holding on to his glasses.

Grandma watched the speeding dork bellyflop in, causing an explosion of colour.

"Hudson! Really!"

"Come on, Li Jun! Get your shoulders under!" said Hudson, and he began to splash her with balls, an activity enthusiastically taken up by the little ones, so that Li Jun soon stood, uncomprehending, in the centre of a mad fountain.

"Is she... quite normal?" asked one of the other parents, looking at the slim teenage girl who seemed to be part Asian, part alien.

"She's from another culture," explained Grandma, biting back the urge to call Hudson and the toddlers off.

Li Jun was, in fact – thanks to Grandma – the world's only liberated Tyro. After they had been rescued in the South China Sea, she had managed to provide vital information about Kaparis and his Tyro programme, but more lay buried in her mind and scans proved her brain had been deliberately manipulated. How could they unlock the memories within it? Grandma had a simple strategy: Li Jun had to be normalised. So Grandma had taken her home to clean sheets, fresh flowers, and fun. Finn's best friend, Hudson, was brought in to act as a surrogate sibling and she had begun "play therapy".

Li Jun bloomed, even if she hadn't opened up completely yet. But most of all, it was good for Grandma, who liked Li Jun. She kept her busy and she kept her from thinking about Finn.

"INTO THE CASTLE!" cried Hudson, leading a Pied Piper charge on the coloured rope ramparts of the Maze Adventure. Li Jun stared after him like a frightened cat.

She is a jigsaw, thought Grandma with a sigh. *Like any teenager*. Except that with most young teenagers the edge pieces and corners were mostly in place, even some of the sky. In Li Jun's case, the bits that were in place were few and far between and the pieces looked as if they all came from different sets...

"HELP!"

Hudson, far too big for the soft play apparatus, had managed to get himself stuck.

"Oh, for goodness' sake..." said Grandma, and she started to wade through the coloured ball pool to rescue him.

It was while Hudson was being released – by Grandma, a four-year-old boy called Donald and a member of the security detail that followed them everywhere – that the first breakthrough occurred.

Li Jun had stepped out of the ball pool to wave goodbye to the other children. As their parents led them back through the shopping mall, the children played a game, which Li Jun instantly saw the logic of. The floor was made up of a series of tiles; the object of the game was never to step on the lines between them.

Li Jun looked down and centred her feet in the tile squares... and a thread tugged in her mind... She saw mountains... felt cold...

She moved forward, step by step, avoiding the lines. And with every step, stone slabs started to appear in her mind's eye and fit together to form... another floor, in another place...

"Li Jun? What is it, dear?" asked Grandma as she reappeared with Hudson.

"I don't know, Grandmother," she whispered. Then she asked in a trance, "Hudson? Do you have your tablet?"

Hudson took his iPad out of his pack and gave it to her.

Li Jun opened the Minecraft app. She took a step. Remembered a stone. Laid it in a blank landscape. Then another. Then another...

Grandma and Hudson watched.

"'Unless you change and become like children, you will never enter the kingdom of heaven'," said Grandma.

"What?" said Hudson.

"Call Al."

SEVEN

FEBRUARY 20 12:09 (GMT+3). Monastery of
Mount St Demetrius of Thessaloniki

Hoooowowwwoowoowowl!

Yo-yo wept as he was led through the back of the kitchens by a
Carrier. He noticed nothing, cared for nothing. He was miserable.
Why hadn't Finn and the good girl tried to stop this madness? He
had suffered greatly in the Carrier bathhouse as the water poured
down on him and he was washed by a dozen hands. Indignity had
been piled upon indignity as the Carriers then used shears to give
his fur a skintight cut, then stained him dark brown with some dye
– he was light brown, British tea-coloured to his bones! It was a
betrayal of his roots! He was inconsolable. Not that anyone cared...

Then he smelt something, something strong and getting stronger. Instinct took hold, his ears pricked up. He heard a *Yip!-Yip!-Rff!-Ackck!-Ouugh!-Puh!-Frrt!*

His tail began to wag at three hundred beats per second.

They approached a door, a door into a tiny courtyard, a forsaken pit down which light seldom shone. The Carrier kicked the door open – *YAP!*

Dogs, dogs, dogs! Leaping and spinning – *Yip!-Yip!-Rff!-Ackck!-Ouugh!-Puh!-Frrt!*

The ratters. The finest line-up of unloved mongrels ever assembled to hunt down rodents. Fantastically unattractive, they bore the names the cooks had blessed them with – Needy, Weedy, Livid, Fluey, Bulky, Sulky, and – lopsided on her three good legs – Barrel-Shaped-Fart-Wagon.

With unknowable joy, Yo-yo threw himself into the fray.

Finn woke from a deep sleep and tried to remember who, where and why he was.

Carla was awake beneath him. Rising groggily, urged on by Olga—

"Come!"

"I'm coming..."

Carla staggered out of their cell and down a stone passage after Olga as it all came back to Finn.

Oh yeah: mad castle, middle of nowhere, get the hell out.

They arrived at a bathhouse where Olga tugged at Carla's filthy clothes. "Come! *Lava!*" She went to open a sluice in the next room.

"You better wait here," said Carla. "I think they're going to clean me up." She stuck a hand into her hair so Finn could jump on to one of her massive fingers. He clung on and she deposited him on a windowsill. Then she left and Finn found himself alone.

He listened to the stillness, felt strange. He'd lived in Carla's hair for so long now that they'd become like Siamese twins. Through cracked and clouded glass, there was a stunning view down a snow-clad valley and a sheer drop to the valley floor. *What a strange, ancient and beautiful place to be*, Finn thought, *a million miles from schoolwork and screens*. After all they'd been through, what would ever feel real again?

Carla returned with a cup of soapy water scooped from her bath and set it on the windowsill.

"You're not going to believe how good this feels," she said, and dashed back out.

Finn climbed onto the window latch so he was above the steaming pool. He hauled his filthy clothes off and threw them down, then took a deep breath – *SPLASH!*

His body cut through the hot water. It was glorious, a well of warmth and loveliness, sunlight gilding the bubbles. He swam and splashed and the enamelled grime of the previous months seemed to lift in layers from his skin until he felt purely himself again.

He barely had time to wring out his clothes when Carla returned, transformed. The malnourished, filthy "thing" was now a glowing teenage girl. Finn was alarmed to see her great mat of mad hair now clean and cut back almost as short as Olga's.

"Do I look like the others?" Carla asked.

Finn took her in. With her big eyes and starved frame, she looked like some French film star. He should tell her, but he was a boy and luckily – "*Come!*" – Olga reappeared.

Carla picked him up and transferred him to... clean hair! What had been a dense jungle was now a bouncy castle, flea-less and fine.

One new world followed another as they arrived back in the library. It was a hive of activity by day, the Primo and two half-blind assistants responding to bells and speaking tubes, and snapping out orders to Carrier kids who came and went.

Olga and Carla were ordered straight to the laundry and from there hit the monastery in full swing, pushing a cart around and filling it with discarded linen as they went.

First they passed through the kitchens, picking up filthy aprons and caps, the place a buzz of noise, steam, running Carriers and swearing cooks.

The Forum came next, teeming with Tyros and tutors as they changed lessons, traversing the skewed walkways that connected every part of the building.

They collected table linen from a dining hall, then made their way up the walkways, collecting uniforms from Siguri stations and white robes from the tutors' quarters.

The whole place was a contradiction, thought Finn, a mix of medieval and modern, ancient stone and steel, oil lamps and AK47s.

They passed classrooms and a vast gymnasium, on their way up to the dormitories—

"Tyros!" shouted Finn, as a crowd of vile teenagers, steaming and dripping wet snow from some exercise on the slopes, burst into the Forum and began to pound their way up towards them. They were all ages and sizes and they piled past them into the dorms, shoving and snarling at each other, beating the warmth back into their flesh, many with swollen and bloodshot eyes. Olga and Carla pushed round their cart and picked up discarded fatigues as the Tyros stripped down, shameless, and struggled into red uniforms that made them look like inmates of some asylum.

"We've got to get out of here," Finn said as Carla worked the room.

"We can't just run, if we get caught we kill Carriers," she muttered back.

"Maybe the Primo's bluffing? Maybe he's on some kind of power kick?" said Finn.

"He's proud, that's all," said Carla. "We have to find another way. We need help."

"Santiago!" suggested Finn. "Maybe he can find Yo-yo's collar!"

"Out on the mountain? That would be like looking for a needle in a haystack. And he'd never go without the Primo's say-so," said Carla, dodging Tyros as they strode back out of the dorms.

Finn took in the reds of their eyes.

"Then we have to find the infirmary, check out these NRP machines," said Finn.

69

When they did finally arrive at the infirmary, they wished they hadn't.

A dozen Tyros were laid out on gurneys, fanned out in a circle like the petals of a flower around a large console in the centre. Wires led from the console to the heads of each Tyro. And out of each swollen eye, of each Tyro, stuck a probe that had been driven straight through the eye and deep into the brain.

The sight made Carla want to retch.

"NRP..." said Finn.

Two medics attended the stricken Tyros and made adjustments at the console (Finn could see the screen as plain as day – this place had technology, this place had electricity!) and a snake of cables led down from the console directly through an opening in the floor.

As they rolled the empty laundry cart back out, Carla said, "It will never be spring in this place."

"There were computers back there," said Finn. "Electricity fed from the Caverns, like the Primo said. We have to get down there. There must be something we can use to sound the alarm."

"But I'm a Carrier, and Carriers are banned," said Carla.

"Who said anything about Carriers?"

EIGHT

The two young teenagers convulsed, dancing, as the digital beat drove home the vocal loop for the umpteenth time.

"*Love dance. Love dance. Love dance dance dance dance – robot...*"

Li Jun's sharp black hair flicked and flew, her body throwing the weirdest shapes, while Hudson headbanged off the beat, holding onto his glasses.

Grandma sat and knitted and resisted the urge to yell, "Turn the bloody thing down!"

Via CCTV, Al and the Scarlatti crew and his technical team watched them dance.

"That girl can kick it," observed Delta.

"Truly," said Al.

The dance-offs with Hudson seemed to free Li Jun's mind and send her back to the model-making refreshed. To help, Al had put together a playlist of dad-dance classics, though tragically she preferred what Al called "Hudson crap".

Love dance robot climaxed and Hudson and Li Jun collapsed, giggling, onto the sofas.

"Time for a cup of tea, I think," said Grandma through the kitchen hatch.

"Mum, don't move! Let it happen naturally," insisted Al over the comms.

"But it's teatime?"

"Hey! No structure, no timetable." He was convinced his new, non-rational "intuitive" theory explained Li Jun's breakthrough. "Instinct over intellect, remember? Let's just set the parameters and let her play."

"They shouldn't be stuck in front of screens all day – it's unhealthy," Grandma complained, ignoring him to go and put the kettle on and look for Welsh cakes.

In the living room, Li Jun turned back to her task. One wall was now full of screens linked to Hook Hall. For the last four hours, she had worked away at the Minecraft model, just as she used to sit working away for Kaparis. Hudson's role was to lie on the sofa pretending to be in an iron lung.

The results, being pored over by Al and the technicians, were fractured 3D chunks of some extraordinary building – staircases, passages, a hall, fireplaces, a battlement – populated by hundreds of stick figures. But what did it all add up to? A prison? A castle? Architectural databases had thrown up thousands of possible matches, occupied and derelict, across the world. Way down on the list at number 2,453 was the Monastery of Mount St Demetrius of Thessaloniki.

"Let's ask her to work on the surrounding landscape again," said Commander King, convinced that the floating structures would make more sense in context.

"She just does clouds," said Stubbs.

"Let her follow her own path," said Al firmly.

Li Jun began to work again on what they thought of as the "courtyard" structure, adding detail to the walls and the beginning of a door.

"Maybe she's just playing Minecraft…" grumbled Kelly.

"Come on, Li Jun!" said Delta, as if she could snap her out of it by force of will.

Commander King looked again at the structures and began to wonder.

"What troubles me is it's too big... Look at how many figures she's drawn. Imagine having to support all those people. Every one of them is a security risk. Haven't they got homes to go to, bars to drink in, phone calls to make...?"

Al stared at the figures too, at the stone walls, at the fireplaces and candlesticks... Then he looked around the control gallery, at its lighting and stacks of computers and glittering screens.

"She hasn't drawn a single screen, a single phone, a single piece of hardware. There are no lights even..." said Al, thinking hard.

"So?" said Kelly.

"So they're off-grid!" said Al.

"Off-grid?" said Delta.

"I mean, living slow – no communications, no Internet, no conventional power. Goodbye modernity – hello total isolation."

"Total security," added Commander King.

"Rank all the possible locations by geographical isolation," said Al to one of the technicians.

Moments later, on the new list, the Monastery of Mount St Demetrius of Thessaloniki had shot up – to number seventeen.

"What else have we got?" said Al, still manically pacing. "Come on, Li Jun!"

Grandma handed Li Jun a cup of tea and a Welsh cake, looking over the girl's shoulder at the cloudscapes. "Looks heavenly, dear."

Heaven...

Something fired in Li Jun's brain. She thought of stained glass. She thought of a face.

She dived forward and immediately started to draw. Grandma, Al and everyone at Hook Hall watched intently as a face began to appear... A male face, a beard. It wasn't a very good face, but then Li Jun added another detail that gave it away—

A halo...

Al turned to the technicians and shouted, "Cross-reference with religious buildings! Or a building with some kind of church or chapel in it!"

The technicians entered the filter and a new ranking list was drawn up, by age, materials, isolation and religious use. At number nine on the list was the Monastery of Mount St Demetrius of Thessaloniki.

Then Li Jun added colour to the halo – *gold*... and a great fissure opened up in her mind. She said the word "Abbot" aloud and immediately started to draw an Orthodox Christian cross...

Now only one name remained on the list.

NINE

Hearing his name called and smelling Finn, Yo-yo ducked out of the rough-and-tumble in the ratters' yard and ran up to the kitchens. He found the good girl among a forest of legs – *Yap!*

"Good boy! Come!" said Carla.

She took Yo-yo into the service passage, ran her fingers through her hair and deposited Finn onto Yo-yo's head.

Finn disappeared into his fur and made his way through to a position just behind Yo-yo's left ear. His old pilot position. Back home, he'd been able to steer Yo-yo wherever he wanted to go. But now? After so long?

There was only one way to find out.

"Up, Yo-yo! Up, boy!"

YAP!

Finn felt the whole happy mountain of Yo-yo erupt beneath him as he jumped clean into the air.

"Good boy! Through the door!"

"Don't do anything stupid!" Carla warned, as Yo-yo pushed through the swing doors back into the kitchen.

"What's over there, what's on the other side?" Finn demanded, and Yo-yo yapped and ran joyously through the legs, dodging dropped pans and puddles of soup. Finn clung on happily, riding a galloping dinosaur once again, all the old feelings coming back as they broke through the far doors to hit the Forum.

Directly opposite, Finn could see the arched entrance to the catacombs, which Olga had told them led eventually down to the Caverns.

"Through there, Yo-yo," ordered Finn, and the dog bounded ahead. "Come-by!" he yelled to steer the bounding dog the right way. No one noticed because no one cared about a dog. The ratters were even more invisible than the Carriers, given freedom to roam and licence to kill.

A little beyond the archway was the catacombs door.

"What's in there?" Finn demanded.

He felt Yo-yo rise as he stood on his back legs and pawed at the handle till it turned, the same as he'd done at Grandma's house all his doggy life.

The door swung open – and they were greeted by skulls, set into the walls like bricks, the remains of thousands of ancient monks. Yo-yo whimpered.

"It's all right, boy. Go on."

77

They trotted down the skull-studded passageway, claws skittering across the flagstones. Finn heard a distant hum – mechanical? – coming from somewhere beyond, and footsteps too, ahead of them. *There!*

"Easy, Yo-yo," Finn urged as they closed on the figure hurrying ahead of them. Finn remembered her as the one who'd struck Carla the blow – the Abbot's secretary. Could she be on her way to the Caverns? Where else would she be going?

"Follow the lady. Easy. Nice and slow," ordered Finn.

Yo-yo obligingly padded after her as they wound through the catacombs, keeping at a steady distance. Eventually they emerged at the top of a steep stone staircase.

The secretary was disappearing through an archway far below and the hum was getting louder.

"Down you go, boy."

When they reached the bottom, Finn saw the archway was the entrance to a tunnel into the bedrock. Three burly Siguri stood guard.

"Lie down!" ordered Finn, so that Yo-yo would remain hidden from view. How were they supposed to get through? Wouldn't the Siguri just kick back a dog?

With a squeak, a solution presented itself. A few feet ahead, a brown rat emerged from a drain cover. Immediately, Yo-yo's body twitched.

"That's right, boy! Chase the rat! Fast, boy!"

YAP!

"Hey!" one of the Siguri called in surprise, as a dog exploded out of the darkness. He raised his gun – but just as quickly one of his comrades stayed his hand.

"Ratter! Let him do his job!"

All three stepped aside as the rat sped forth, with Yo-yo snapping at its tail – *YAP YAP YAP!*

As soon as they were clear of the Siguri, Finn called out, "STOP! Let it go! Stay…"

They had entered the start of a natural cave system. For the first time, electric light and not oil lamps illuminated the glassy walls. Then, as the tunnel opened out into a small cavern, came the next surprise—

A monorail! A gleaming steel rail winding down into the heart of the mountain. Four open carts were just leaving the rail's end, the secretary the only passenger, drawn by a humming electromagnetic current.

Finn had left the Middle Ages and walked into the twenty-first century.

"Go, Yo-yo! Follow!"

YAP! – Yo-yo pelted forward and jumped into the last cart, just as it picked up speed.

The descent that followed was, to Yo-yo's mind at least, tremendous fun – carts flying along the rail as they snaked down a crystal flume carved by millions of gallons of water over millions of years; walls worn smooth and streaked in all the colours of a bruise. But the real wonder lay at the end: the twisting tunnel levelled and the carts slowed as the flume opened out suddenly into a huge cavern.

79

Finn was stunned. It was a vast natural cave full of the shapes and shadows of nightmares, a warped and irregular void the size of the CFAC, arc lights bouncing a chromatic cacophony off its weeping crystal walls.

On the bed of what Finn thought must have once been an underground lake lay containers and machinery and equipment of every kind: banks of command computers worked on by dozens of young technicians, bearded hipster types in uniform casual clothing. All of which was remarkable. But what really took Finn's breath away was at the cavern's heart – arranged in a circle were a dozen huge blocks of metal and wiring. Immediately Finn knew he was looking at a great ring of particle accelerators. A Boldklub henge, capable of creating a subatomic magnetic field so powerful it could shrink matter. He'd been in one just like it...

Finn gaped and tried to take it all in.

He had to try and get closer. No dog could wander here unseen and unchallenged. Stalactites and stalagmites formed a spiked perimeter that gave way to a river at the far end of the cavern, a torrent that disappeared into the rock as suddenly as it had appeared.

"Yo-yo, into the woods, boy. Hide!" Finn ordered.

Yo-yo grasped the instruction and jumped from the cart into the calcite jungle. Finn urged him through it, trying to see what he could. But the closer they got to the equipment, the more mystery he found.

In one area were crates and crates of long cables. In another was equipment that looked like subaqua gear: oxygen tanks and futuristic-looking wetsuits bristling with technology. There even seemed to be small surfboards. Most bizarrely of all was an extraordinary beached submarine, a fat steel shark the size of a bus with two thick arms and two giant impeller[5] fists.

What on earth would a submarine be doing down here? Was it something to do with the underground river at the cave's end? And how on earth could they have got such massive components down here?

Whatever it was, Finn thought, the whole place was pure Kaparis. He hadn't just found a Tyro hive – he'd hit the jackpot. But what next? This place would surely have all the communications they'd need to get a message out, but how could he get Carla anywhere near it?

He needed a plan.

He turned Yo-yo round and they started to make their way back through the stalagmites.

Beeeep Beeeep Beeeep – then came the next revelation. An alarm sounded and lights started flashing on an area of the cave floor, then Finn looked up.

There was a gap in the roof of the cavern. A large circular shaft that rose through the rock, manmade, lined with concrete and now illuminated by landing lights.

High above, at the very top of the sleeping monastery, the great dome, apparently ruined, stirred. Exquisite engineering whirred just

---

[5] Propellers with blades extended into a screw shape, usually used in pumps, etc. Especially efficient in viscous liquids.

beneath it and the massive gold hemisphere split in two, the halves cleaving open like a giant Fabergé egg.

Finn urged Yo-yo to stray to the edge of the stalagmites to get a better look and watched amazed as a slice of snow-cloud sky began to expand at the very top of the shaft – then a *wap-wap-wapping* aircraft appeared, blotting out the sky. Finn knew the sound well. Helicopters in whisper mode, coming in to land... Flying machines descending into the mountain.

And there, waiting to greet them on the cave floor, was a reception party headed by the Abbot.

"Hey! Get rid of that dog!" cried a Siguri, spotting them and reaching for his gun.

They had seen enough.

"GO!" ordered Finn. "Home, boy!" And Yo-yo ran for the mouth of the flume and the monorail, just as the carts were starting their automatic ascent.

"In the box! What's in the box!" cried Finn, and Yo-yo leapt.

By the time they made it back to the Forum, handbells were echoing down every passageway, summoning the Carriers and stirring Tyros and tutors alike. *Ding-a-ling-a-ling!*

Finn steered down towards the library in search of Carla. Carriers were streaming out and there was a palpable sense of excitement in the freezing air.

YAP!

Carrier children were appearing from every nook and cranny and hurrying along to the Primo's dais. It was like a fever breaking out.

Carla saw Yo-yo and ducked out of the crowd to intercept him in the shanty shacks.

"Good dog!" she said, giving him a stroke, and picking out Finn like a flea from his fur. Even at nano-scale she could see how wide his eyes were.

"I know what's in the Caverns and it's definitely not cave paintings. There's a Boldklub machine. We *have* to get you down there," said Finn. "This is a save-the-world situation!"

"Again?" said Carla. "Are there phones?"

"There's everything!"

"How do I get there?"

"You can fly or take the train – long story – but you're going to need help."

Carla pushed her way to the front of the Carrier queue at the dais. The Primo and his assistants were snapping out orders, as service bells rang and disembodied voices barked down the speaking tubes.

"Primo! I have to get to the Caverns and I need your help," Carla started.

"Get to the kitchens with Olga," the Primo ordered without raising a blind eye.

"No. Something has happened that's so important the world needs to know…"

"The world has changed," the Primo snapped back. "If you try anything now, you'll kill us all."

"What?"

"The Master is in the mountain."

*On compressed air pads the iron lung slid in stately fashion across the
cavern floor to a side chamber, specially adapted to include a domed screen
array and all the usual support apparatus. The adaptations, as ever, were
the work of eccentric Scots architect Thömson-Lavoisiér, master builder to
the criminal cognoscenti.*

*Inside the iron lung, Kaparis was not just a paralysed hunk of meat. He
was a coiled spring.*

*"Welcome home, sir," Heywood, the butler, said as they docked, inwardly
beaming. They had met in a mental hospital twenty or so years before,
both recovering from nervous breakdowns. It was the place where Kaparis
had forged his cruel ambition, and where Heywood had found a god he
could worship. There was nothing he liked more than to see his Master
happy.*

And Kaparis was happy.

*Home. The monastery and its mountains. He'd always loved it up here,
perched between East and West, heaven and earth, between impossibility
and experience.*

*He cast a reflected eye out of the optical array that encased his head
and took in the great circle of accelerators he'd started building five years
before. Over the course of the day they had been rigged into an entirely*

new configuration and the mathematics of the Time=Place *breakthrough had been incorporated into the control code.*

He could not wait to try it out. The Abbot hovered in obsequious attendance. All it needed was an order.

"Fiat lux[6]," Kaparis declared...

Twenty-two minutes later, a perfect white orb of energy glowed and spun and throbbed deep within the mountain. The bearded young technicians held hands in collective reverence. The noise had been tremendous as it developed, white lightning cracking like candyfloss around the core before resolving into this silent, glowing miracle.

Boldklub. At last. And in a more perfect form than had ever been created – of that Kaparis was sure. The Time=Place *breakthrough meant he'd needed just a tiny fraction of the energy that Al and the Hook Hall team had been using; it also meant it would be many, many times more powerful.*

His eyes flicked to the Abbot.

"Well, what are you waiting for? Get in," he commanded.

The Abbot's eyes nearly popped from his burnt head and he broke into a fearful sweat. But a lifetime's love of bullies kicked in. The Master had chosen him. This was not a privilege to be wasted on an underling.

"Oh Master! I had never in my wildest dreams—"

"Get on with it," snapped Kaparis.

The Abbot walked towards the hot area, paused, then ran and threw himself in. The vortex swallowed him with barely a ripple.

The technicians held their collective breath.

---

[6] Latin for "Let there be light." First words of the Holy Bible.

After observing for a few seconds, Kaparis ordered, "Kill it!"

Power was cut and the orb evaporated into glitter. The technicians blinked and squinted. There was nothing there. No orb, no Abbot.

Yet up close?

"Find him," Kaparis ordered.

The technicians moved forward in a line, scanning the ground with cameras, looking, searching, until—

"Yes!" one cried.

Kaparis flicked to the feed.

There was the Abbot on the floor, astonished, picking himself up to stand just 10mm tall...

At last the path was clear.

Only the tiniest problem remained. And he would soon be dealt with.

The years of waiting were over. Tears, actual salty unfamiliar tears, ran down the much-moisturised skin of his cheeks and his mouth just managed to move and whisper three words: "Quod erat demonstrandum[7]".

He had never felt so alive.

"Heywood? Call the doctors."

---

[7] Aka QED. Latin for "which was to be demonstrated". A term used to show that something has been proved by reason and experiment – last word in science.

PART
TWO

PART
TWO

TEN

"CARRIERS!" the cooks cried out of the kitchens.

"CARRIERS!" the tutors cried from their quarters.

"CARRIERS!" the Tyros cried, just to burn off their excitement.

Even the ratters picked up on the mood and chased each other through the cellars and stores, barking madly, running back up to the kitchens for another fill of fervour and to take in the preparations for the feast.

And through it all Carla searched, in the snatched moments between scrubbing floors, lighting lamps, washing pans, for Santiago. He was their only hope now. He and the dog collar, lost on the mountain.

89

Kaparis... Finn kept thinking. *Here...* Just a few hundred feet beneath their feet. A sitting duck. They had to get word out. But tracking Santiago down without asking the other Carriers, without the risk of one of them telling the Primo, was proving difficult.

Then, amid the chaos, as she emptied a bucket, Carla heard someone shout: "Santiago!"

She turned. A cook was roaring at the black iron furnace at the kitchen's heart, kicking a grill at its base. "Santiago!" Suddenly the fire within the furnace glowed and responded.

"He's underneath!" shouted Finn at her ear. "He must be underneath!"

Carla dumped the bucket and took a chance, ducking out of the fray and heading for the cellars.

There they found him, working the bellows beneath the furnace, sending blasts of air into the fire; a dirty, vital job.

"Santiago!" said Finn, spotting him first.

He scrambled away like an animal when he first saw Carla.

"No! *Angelli!*"

"It's OK. I just want to talk to you," said Carla, softly.

He tried to look away from her, wary.

"I just have to ask you a question. When you found me in the woods – was there anything else with me?"

"In mountain."

"That's right. Did you find a collar too?" Carla mimed a collar around her own throat. "I had a dog collar with me."

Santiago's face corkscrewed in confusion.

"No dog."

"No, but the collar, Santiago. It must be out there somewhere. I can't leave here and I don't know where you found me. But *you* know. Would you look? I need you to help me."

"No!"

"But you are allowed out!"

"Primo says NO," said Santiago. "Not safe for Santiago. The Master is here."

"The Primo cares for you, that's right, but there is something more important out there."

"No for Santiago," he explained. "No padre, no madre. Only Primo."

Watching in Carla's hair, Finn felt pity for him; and connection too – a stab of sweet pain in his chest for his own lost parents.

"SANTIAGO!" a voice yelled down through the hatch from the furnace above. Santiago leapt to compress the bellows and keep the fire in the kitchen white hot.

"Give him the full Grandma," said Finn above her ear. "Tell him somebody loves him."

"Santiago, listen to me," said Carla. "There is more than just the Primo, the monastery, than all of this. There is a whole world of better things out there – there is even love."

Love. Santiago's eyes shone for a second, then he thought better of it and shook his head, certain.

"You are made of love," Carla continued. "Everyone is. The other children love you. You were loved by the old woman who found you in the snow…"

"Witch!" Santiago said and crossed himself.

"And you had a mother and father too, once."

"No! Were jackals!" Santiago cried.

Carla nearly choked on such cruel lies. "That's bullshit. Who told you that?"

"It is written!"

"Where?" said Carla.

"My face," said Santiago, presenting his contorted features.

Carla could have wept. Whatever else they did, they had to try and save Santiago.

"Do it," said Finn at her ear. "Go nuclear."

Carla put her hand in her hair and drew it out again.

"Santiago, out there in the world people know many good things and they can help you, and the Primo too. But right now, we need you to help us."

She pointed her index finger at him. Finn was standing on the end of it, his spike in his hand.

"Look, Santiago, look…"

His eyes almost rolled back in incomprehension at the sight of the 9mm boy.

Finn waved, in a guarded kind of way. Santiago's eyes just got bigger.

"I KNOW IT'S WEIRD, BUT DON'T FREAK OUT!" Finn yelled.

"*Angelli!*" Santiago gasped.

"SCIENCE," Finn replied.

ELEVEN

"The Blessed Monastery of Mount St Demetrius of Thessaloniki," announced Commander King.

The image of the monastery hung in the air on the main screen in the control gallery of the CFAC. Around the conference table were technicians, scientists, engineers and thinkers – the full membership of the G&T – and on a series of screens beyond were the presidents of the USA, France, Russia and China, the chancellor of Germany and the prime minister of the United Kingdom.

"Built by a famously cruel archbishop in the twelfth century – to

93

the glory of God, and as a military outpost on the edge of civilisation. In the years since, it's been Byzantine, Ottoman, Slav, Orthodox, the plaything of a mad Bavarian prince, then Austro-Hungarian, Nazi, Partisan, and finally Communist..."

More images of the extraordinary castle flicked by.

"... The Romanian military used it to test chemical weapons until it was abandoned in 1970, contaminated and out of bounds. Its current owner? A secretive Swiss foundation that went round buying up post-communist curiosities in the nineties."

The classic Zurich picture of Kaparis flashed up on screen. No further explanation was required.

"The peasants speak of a terrible curse on the place and the remote valley it serves, believing the unquiet spirit of Saint Demetrius – a secret brother of Beelzebub – rules the place."

He called up the next shot. An armed Siguri patrol slogging through the snow and looking every inch a paramilitary force.

"If such a spirit does roam the valley, then he's paranoid about security. In 1996 the region was declared an area of threatened wilderness by the UN. It was closed to tourism and development and protected by its own force of rangers, generously funded by the Swiss foundation, which also owns 100,000 hectares around the site. They constantly sweep for radio signals and radar signature and comb the forests for any sign of life."

King called up a series of high-res satellite images of the ruins in more detail.

"There are no outward signs of life, but look a little closer and you find tell-tale wisps of smoke and steam and –" an image of the dome flashed up – "a concealed microwave source that fires bursts of encrypted data at satellites throughout the day."

Another image of the monastery appeared, this one mashed with Li Jun's Minecraft model.

It was a perfect fit.

"I have no doubt in declaring this a Kaparis site and the heart of his Tyro operation," said Commander King. "We need your go-ahead to assemble an assault force. We will also be moving to an Operational HQ in Romania – the National Air Defence Base in Kluge."

Outside the control gallery, in the main body of the CFAC, technicians and military personnel were already dismantling equipment, getting it ready to pack up and ship out. The great hangar doors were open and two RAF Hercules transport planes had started loading. Engineer Stubbs was putting together a tool chest and fretting over spanners; Captain Kelly was assembling a wheelie-bin full of his favourite small arms; while Delta Salazar was preparing her personal F-22 Raptor.

Only Al sat still, eyes closed and meditating, trying to think of a perfect sandy beach, trying to think off-topic, convinced that by 'feeling' his way forward he had made more progress in six hours than he had in the last six weeks.

Back on screen, the Russian president demanded, "What other evidence do you have to support this assertion?"

"Apart from the half-remembered ravings of a brain-damaged girl," added General Jackman, the US military chief and an old sparring partner of Al's.

There was an audible tut from another screen – the comms link to Grandma's six miles away – where the "brain-damaged girl", Li Jun, had fallen fast asleep in front of *Dr Who*.

"Li Jun's recollections are fractured," King responded, "but contain clear evidence of the type of brain programming we think all Tyros are subjected to." He called up a detail of Li Jun's model which showed a series of stick figures with lines leading from their eyes.

"Tyros, just like her."

"What if she's confused it with another of his 'cribs'?" asked the British Prime Minister, employing a word he'd heard his teenage daughter use. "What if it's just a barracks for these ranger types? Before you go in and start killing people, you'd better be certain – *more* than certain."

Al snapped back to the real world. "Nobody is running in and killing anybody! Exactly the opposite. We sneak up, we just... watch."

"Hey, this could be perfect," said General Jackman, suddenly getting a bright idea. "You want intelligence? Send the girl back in there undercover!"

"You will do no such thing!" Grandma protested. "She's at the mercy of post-traumatic stress. Send in the girl! I've never heard anything so ridiculous!"

"Just a suggestion, ma'am," said General Jackman, who hadn't been chastened like that since he'd accidentally shot his drill sergeant in the foot forty years before.

"We will assemble a force but only take action if we are certain of outcomes," said King.

"Twice before, we've had a fix on Kaparis and he's got away," agreed Al. "He is an escape artist extraordinaire. Until we know exactly what's going on, we wait."

"For what?" asked General Jackman.

"For Li Jun to put the pieces together, for a sure-fire way of getting into that place," said Al, adding after a moment, "and for a sign."

"A *sign*? What kind of sign?"

"I don't know yet – it's not strictly rational, it's emotional. But when I get there, I'll let you know," said Al.

Before the General could raise further objections, Grandma interrupted.

"What time is our car arriving?" She was starting to pack a few essentials into a bag. "I hope we'll have a bed each. I hate to share."

Al did a double take.

"Wait a minute... *you're* not coming?"

"Of course. I'm in charge of Li Jun."

"What? No! Who else is bringing their mum?" argued Al. "And anyway, no one's 'in charge' any more – we've got to stop thinking in hierarchies, free up our energy..."

"Nonsense," said Grandma, and she gently began to wake Li Jun.

"Actually, I'm in charge," confirmed Commander King, checking his watch and bringing the meeting to a close. "Thank you for your attention. We'll update hourly."

"Tables! *Schnell!*" One of the cooks yelled midway through the great feast. "Clear the decks!"

Carla followed a crowd of Carriers into the dining hall where the noise struck them like a wave, the air vibrating as three hundred Tyros shoved dirty plates and cutlery down six long refectory tables, a process they yobbishly enjoyed, leaving the Carriers to catch as much of it as they could before the surplus crashed to the stone floor around them.

Carla grabbed an armful of dirty plates and got out quick.

At the head table sat the tutors and, on the remains of an ecclesiastical throne, was the Abbot, reanimated and restored to size, smiling benignly, made idiot by the recent events.

CRASH! Another Carrier collided with Carla and sent her plates flying. As she bent down to gather her load, a great gasp went up, followed by a mighty roar. Finn ran to the back of her head to see what was going on.

The Tyros were all facing one way, focused on one thing. There, blinking to life, hanging in the air like an alien of evil intent, was a ghostly hologram of Kaparis, live and exclusive from the heart of the mountain, his head clad in its pixelating optical array.

"Oh my god..." said Finn, awed at the sight.

A pair of eyes spun round the optical array and took in the scene.

"*Hail, hall,*" uttered the hologram.

The hall responded with a spontaneous warlike "HAIL!"

Finn scrambled back to Carla's ear as she rose to stagger out with her plates.

"Back! Grab something and get back in there!" Finn demanded as they hit the kitchens again. Carla grabbed a jug of water and re-entered the hall, just as Kaparis was incanting, "*I ask mankind for nothing. I ask you, Tyro, for everything. I found you, I formed you, you are my presence, my instrument. Those that have fallen, we honour. Those who have failed, we curse.*"

"AMEN!" returned the Tyros. Finn could see tears in their eyes.

"*Father Abbot, bring forth your new champions.*"

The Abbot, still in awe, stood and began reading a list of names. As each was announced, a Tyro stood, their table-mates bitter at their promotion. Seven were called in this way, then the Abbot added the title "Valedictorian" to a final three: a musclebound beefcake called Barabbas; a towering blonde called Amazon; and a smirking boy called Pan, lithe and nasty, an elfin cut-throat.

"*You are the chosen ones. You are the ones who will undertake the ultimate mission.*"

"This doesn't sound good," said Finn at Carla's ear.

"*For years, I have dreamt of this, have worked for this, every hour of every day. We have struggled and sacrificed much.*"

Beside Kaparis, another hologram glittered to life, *a hologram of Finn—*

"Whoa!" Finn instinctively shrank back into Carla's hair. Shocked to see himself. Beside Kaparis. And at such a scale... frozen with his spike raised to strike, the image captured by a nano-bot somewhere in the Forbidden City.

The Tyros hissed and spat.

"For months we have fretted over Infinity Drake. We were right to. For we must know our enemies to defeat them, embrace those we hate most. We must obsess and seek out every possible weakness, and sometimes, when we do, we discover the most unexpected things..."

As Kaparis spoke, Finn saw a series of scribbled notes begin to float, projected, across the ceiling above him. Notes Finn felt he knew, in a hand he knew. Equations and questions and "L = Place?"

"A breakthrough has been made that will leave our enemies in the stone age."

The hologram of Finn began to fade.

"The future has become clear. History is bunk. It has been rendered irrelevant. The G&T are finished, they have been left behind. Infinity Drake is lost and gone for ever. We can abandon him as he was once abandoned by his father."

Damn Kaparis, thought Finn as his image disappeared altogether.

"I am the future. And I will not desert you."

Damn Kap—

Finn stopped the thought dead as he realised with horror what was happening.

"Get out!" Finn yelled so suddenly that Carla nearly dropped the jug of water.

"He knows I'm here!"

TWELVE

In the library shacks, the Carriers slept, indistinguishable lumps beneath sackcloth and wise old words.

But not Carla. Finn paced and sulked in her hair.

"Don't you see? He's goading me!"

"We don't know anything for certain," she whispered.

"He can't help himself. He's here because of Baptiste," said Finn. "He thinks I'm here – and he's up to something down there! We're going to have to destroy him. It's our destiny."

"*Our* destiny? My destiny is extra cello lessons," said Carla.

101

After walking out on the feast, she'd holed up in the cellars until Olga found her, by which time the show was over.

"Kaparis himself, just the other side of some rock... Do you know what Al or Delta would give to be here now?"

"We've got to try and stay calm, and we've got to try and get some sleep, in case we have to make a run for it in the morning. Don't let him get inside your head," said Carla.

Finn flung himself down in Carla's head instead, in a tuft behind her ear, and lashed himself into place with some of the hair. He closed his eyes, but there was Kaparis, looming large.

"Do you know what he's done to my family? He kidnapped my grandma, he tried to ruin my parents, he's tried to blackmail my uncle, he's tried to kill me – a lot – and he's got this report on my dad," said Finn.

"Or he's forgotten all about you," said Carla.

"If that Boldklub henge is operational, he'll find me in no time."

"How?"

"Nano-radar. He just has to shrink a conventional radar and he'll find me. Everything nano is super-dense. Anywhere out in the open, I'll stick out like a sore thumb."

"Well then, he would have found you already, so either it can't be operational or he can't be looking for you."

"Or he's just a sick bully and he's keeping me dangling and getting ready to pull the trigger any second," replied Finn.

"If he is, then you're giving him exactly what he wants," said Carla. "Stop thinking about him. Relax – that's the only thing that will infuriate him right now. There are only three ways to defeat a bully: imagine them on the toilet; imagine going to the toilet on them; and *never give them what they want!* Now go to sleep."

Deep beneath in the belly of the mountain, the white Boldklub orb spun and glowed, and Kaparis worked his new magic, bringing the future hurtling towards the present, breaking the received laws of physics and recasting them, testing them to the limit, and finding there was no limit to what this technology could now do...

"*Reductio ad infinitum[8]," he breathed.*

He could see a world without end... but he had to start somewhere.

Drake.

"*Bring me my champions."*

FEBRUARY 21 01:58 (GMT+3). C-130 Hercules, Romanian airspace

The C-130 Hercules transport planes began to lose height as they descended to what was about to become the G&T Romanian Command at the National Air Defence Base outside Kluge.

---

[8]   Latin for "reduction to the infinite".

As they touched down, an official reception committee sent by the Romanian president was waiting on the tarmac. While Commander King got out to shake hands, everyone else remained inside the mobile headquarters – technical and military experts brainstorming the options, satellite specialists ordering ground-penetrating radar to overfly the site, drone specialists wanting to create a swarm.

Al offering to give people back rubs.

FEBRUARY 21 02:14 (GMT+3). Airbus A300, Romanian airspace

"Fifteen... fourteen... thirteen... twelve... eleven..."

At a cruising altitude of fifty thousand feet, six members of the équipe bleu of Le Commando Hubert[9] prepared to jump from the cabin of an Airbus A300 airliner travelling at 450mph.

Just eight hours before, Commander Henri Clément had been pulled out of the final of the Declasse cup, Europe's premier fencing competition.

"Ten... nine... eight... seven... six..."

He was joined by five of his top operatives. The Commando Hubert was a strict meritocracy (what had the revolution been for,

---

[9] Special French marine commando force co-opted to the G&T following assault action in Operations Scarlatti and Forbidden City.

after all?) – it just so happened that every member was staggeringly good-looking, with high-maintenance hair, esoteric pursuits, and an appreciation of the very finest food and wine.

"Five... four... three... two... one..."

The target was to be approached with the utmost caution – a HALO[10] drop from a regular commercial flight, modified and fitted with a catapult to spit them clear of the fuselage.

"Zero."

"*Allez!*" said Henri Clément to the drop master, as casually as if signalling to a waiter that they were ready to move on to the next course.

The catapults fired – *THWABOOOINGK!!!*

FEBRUARY 21 02:34 (GMT+3). Carpathian Mountains, Romania-Ukraine border

Santiago made his silent way across the wood. As the ground became steeper, he had to grab at the thick branches and haul himself forward. He was worried about getting caught, but if the Siguri did find his tracks and follow him, he would say he was checking his traps.

Eventually he reached the foot of the cliff and started to pick his

[10] High Altitude Low Opening. A parachute technique used by special forces to avoid radar detection.

way up the ice-slick slope. After a minute or so, he reached the base of the fissure that ran up through the rock like a black bolt of lightning.

Was this the place? "*Si*," Santiago confirmed to himself.

He took off his bow and started to search. He grubbed around in the depths of the fissure, sparking a flint and steel striker for stinging, momentary illumination.

He had to find it. For the angel and the miracle in her hand – the boy he was convinced must be some kind of saint, no matter what he said. Sacred, yes. Not "science", whatever that was.

The Primo would be angry if he found out, but if Santiago could be swift, the Primo wouldn't know.

He could feel a presence in the woods. Had even seen tracks. Had more angels arrived? Nothing surprised him any more. He would have to return and investigate. But now he had to work fast.

The bright moon gave the night a cosmic glow.

The fissure was wide enough to climb right into when you got this low down. It was as if he had walked into the mountain; the two sides might bite him.

Santiago scratched at his flint. The fissure seemed vast and the task impossible. The mix of forest litter and snow would take days to search, but Santiago tried not to cry, tried to keep his eyes open and fixed on the task.

He searched for nearly an hour, moving up the cliff until he was well above the tops of the highest trees on the valley floor. Behind him the silhouette of the monastery loomed across the valley.

Then Santiago spotted something.

A dent in the snow, in a cleft like a basin carved into the side of the rock. He flicked the snow away, just to check, and there was... something.

He picked it up. It was a thing for sure, not a leather collar like the ratters had, like he had expected, but something smooth and made of some other material. And with a thing attached...

"*Angelli?*"

_____

THIRTEEN

FEBRUARY 21 06:57 (GMT+3). Monastery
of Mount St Demetrius of Thessaloniki

Dawn broke across the thousand-mile arc of the Carpathians, catching first the highest peaks, sharp as sharks' teeth, frozen white with a single fleck of gold, as the half-ruined, half-gilt dome of the monastery caught the light.

In the library, Carla woke. Saw giant eyes on a distorted face.

"Santiago!" she said, sitting up. She felt Finn move in her hair.

Santiago nodded, silent and scared. He rummaged beneath his layers and pulled out Yo-yo's strange collar.

"He got it!" shouted Finn.

Carla gasped and touched his hand. "Oh, Santiago!"

Santiago reeled at her touch, disturbed by the electric warmth, and edged away, leaving Carla with the collar. It was chunky, in military green, marked in Chinese, and – most importantly – it had the strange cylinder still attached.

"Switch it on!" said Finn, scrambling down for a better look.

Carla studied it. There was a rectangular button on the side. She tried to press it, but it didn't want to press. She tried harder, tried pulling it.

"Slide it!" said Finn.

"I'm sliding, I'm pushing, I'm pulling – it's not moving!"

"Let me have a look," said Finn.

Carla took Finn from her hair and placed him on the floor beside the strange cylinder.

At his scale, it was the size of a van. He looked at the button – and realised it wasn't a button. It was a cover to protect a handle. A handle that could only possibly be operated by the tiniest of hands.

"Oh, sweet..."

"What is it?"

"I think it's for me."

He pulled the handle. Inside the cylinder, hydraulic pistons released months of stored energy and the whole thing hissed open like a clamshell.

"Oh, wow..." was all Finn could manage, for he was looking at an Aladdin's cave. Tightly packed – in military fashion – was absolutely everything a nano-boy in trouble could possibly need.

The first thing Finn did was rip out a ration pack and sink his teeth into a tube of bolognaise sauce. After feeding on nothing but blood for months, flavour exploded in his mouth and tears stung his eyes.

There was food enough here for days – food for the three of them who had been lost in the Forbidden City at nano-scale, and who Yo-yo had been sent in to find. There was protection too – M27 light machine guns, grenade launchers, flares. But best of all, and taking up ninety per cent of the available space... there was a Bug[11], an X2 Skimmer, sleek and shark-grey.

He pulled a strap marked RELEASE HARNESS and the Skimmer folded itself out of the cylinder.

"Finn? What is that, a bullet?" asked Carla.

"A ticket to ride..." said Finn. "It's Delta's Skimmer."

He jumped into the cab and pressed the twin ignition buttons... *WHOOOOOOOM!* With a sharp intake of breath, the jet compressor at its heart lit and it came to life, floating just a millimetre in the air, soft as a petal, steady as a rock. Finn could have wept.

He did when he saw there was an nPhone[12] backpack on the back seat.

"*YESS!*" he cried, seizing it. "An nPhone! This is it! All we need is a mobile signal and we can text home!"

[11] Aircraft specifically developed to take full advantage of power-to-mass ratios at nano-scale.

[12] Reducing matter collapses the electromagnetic spectrum in such a way that nano radio transmissions cannot be picked up on macro radio receivers and vice versa. An nPhone is a tiny macrophone carried in a backpack with a keypad that allows texting on the regular phone network. It also allows constant tracking.

"What?" gasped Carla, beaming down at him – she'd never seen him so happy.

"I'm OUT OF HERE!" He grabbed an M27 and fired into the air – *DRTDRTDRT!* – and collapsed laughing, delirious with unexpected relief.

"Hey! *Shhhh!*" she said, laughing with him, though there was no one to hear them but Santiago, repeatedly crossing himself a few feet away.

"There's enough fuel in here for hours of flight. I could probably make it to the village!"

"You don't even know what direction that is!" said Carla. "And who knows if that's where the nearest phone signal is anyway."

"Santiago can tell me. And there'll be cars to hitch rides on, trains, people... Real people!"

Finn grabbed the M27 and threw it into the Skimmer cab along with some ammo and provisions.

Carla felt her heart squeeze. Finn was off. She'd protected him for all this time and she was about to lose him, lose the person that was almost part of herself.

"Don't you dare get lost!"

"I won't get lost!"

"Tell them I'm alive," said Carla. "Tell Delta, I mean. Tell her I love her – I love them all – and that whatever they do to save us, they've got to do it carefully! That they have to save the children and—"

"Stop!" said Finn, realising what was going on despite his excitement. He looked up into her eyes.

"Everyone here gets out alive. You especially. For my sake, you have to stay safe. You..."

Finn stalled. How could he say it? *You mean more to me than anything?* Yuk. *You are my blood sister?*

But before he had a chance to decide, Carla broke the look.

A strange sound had disturbed her.

Wacawacawacawacawacawacawacawacawacawacawacawaca...

"What the...?" Finn said, mind racing to place the rising noise.

Carla looked out of a gap in the shacks. She had time to take in two things: Siguri, guns raised, some with nets – and three small birds, closing fast.

Wacawacawacawacawacawacawacawacawacawacawacawaca...

Finn realised what the noise was.

Helicopters. Nano-helicopters.

"Apaches!" shouted Finn.

Then a voice rang out over a loudhailer: "Nobody move!"

Carla gasped. Finn leapt into the seat of the Skimmer.

"GO!" she said.

Wacawacawacawacawacawacawacawacawacawacawacawaca...

Pan, Amazon and Barabbas, each in an Apache attack helicopter, swept in low over the roofs of the library's shanty shacks heading for a bright dot of nano-material at the centre of their radar screens. They were just 9mm tall, their aircraft just 40mm from nose to tail. This they did not find extraordinary.

What they found extraordinary was the honour bestowed on them by the Master.

And the thrill of the chase.

Carla ran through the shacks as grunting Siguri started tearing them apart, scattering the Carriers.

Finn hauled the twin control sticks back and sent the Skimmer into a rocket-like ascent.

It streaked up on the Apaches' nano-radar like a magnesium flare.

"Got visual!" said Pan in the lead Apache as he spotted it.

Finn reached the heavenly ceiling, flipped the Skimmer round to look for an exit, and saw instead a war machine rising at speed, Pan grinning, the 50mm cannon slung beneath the chopper spinning and spitting fire.

DRRRTRRTRTRTRT!

Finn felt the breath of the lethal shells, tearing past and peppering the ancient plaster around him.

He ducked, punched the controls down, and the Skimmer shot back down across the library. Almost blacking out as the seat harness bit into his shoulders and the blood rushed from his brain.

He braked. He had to stay in control. He was way faster than the Apaches, but there were three of them. To prove the point, Amazon was waiting to surprise him…

DRRRTRRTRTRTRT!

Finn rolled out of the incoming fire to skim across the top of the shacks.

113

In the cab of the third Apache, Barabbas locked a Sidewinder missile[13] onto the fleeing blip. He buried the fire button on his joystick and the rocket burst from its launch housing—

BOOOOOOOOOSH! A fierce white streamer snaked across the library. Finn heard the radar alarm, saw it in his rearview, and instinctively he threw the Skimmer hard right.

WOOOOOOSH! He smelt rocket burn as it passed within an inch before smacking – *BAAAM!* – into the stone base of the Primo's dais.

The Primo tried to get a grip on events. The ordered splendour of his mind was rendered useless by the chaos, the crackling fire, the cries of Carriers flushed out of the shacks, the shouts of the astonished spectators.

Get out! thought Finn as – *BOOOOOOOOOSH! DRRRTRRTRTRTRT!* – Amazon and Pan let loose with cannon fire and another Sidewinder.

Finn flipped the Skimmer like a coin and ran for cover, corkscrewing into the shadows, into the shacks, adding to the chaos of their evacuation, hammering through the warren of sackcloth and sticks.

He could out-manoeuvre them in the confined spaces but – *DRRRTRRTRTRTRT!* – he needed a way out. He punched through a rip in a sackcloth roof and emerged into a crowd of Carriers and Siguri.

A great yell went up as Finn slalomed between wide eyes and open mouths. Heads ducked and bodies a hundred and fifty times his size dived for cover.

DRRRTRRTRTRTRT! Barabbas in the third Apache was waiting

[13] Short-range solid-fuel air-to-air missile, relying on infra-red homing for guidance.

114

for him, covering the main passage. Should he evade or take him on? Finn thought of Delta and braced himself.

When in doubt, just point and shoot. His thumb jammed into his fire button.

DRRRTRRTRTRTRT!

Barabbas was still firing as Finn's cannon fire shattered his rotors and chaotic forces instantly tore his chopper to pieces – *BADADOOOOOM!*

One down.

Also an alarm – *Beeeeppeeepppeeepep!*

Finn checked the screen, but there was no screen... just shattered glass. The Skimmer had taken a hit right in the nerve centre. He hit buttons. No weapons. No radar. Great.

Just the flight controls still responsive. Go!

He shot out of the library and up the main passage.

On the dais, the Primo felt a pull at his ankle. "Primo!"

Santiago. Always Santiago. Then another voice: "Help me."

Carla.

They would take the monastery down brick by brick to find her now. It would only be a matter of time. But instinct told him the girl was different, change was coming, the world he controlled was about to crumble. What future lay beyond these walls? What authority?

What to do?

Finn shot into the kitchens pursued by the two remaining bat-like Apaches. They curled after him through the steam, past swinging

115

pots and roasting pigs, past fat cooks roaring at the chaos – 50mm cannon fire ricocheting off pans in tin-pot timpani – *DRTRTRTR TiN TaNG Ti PAP!*

Finn felt the hot breath of burners as he flew through the flame tops.

DRRTRT! – THUDTHUD! – A couple of shells pierced the skin of the Skimmer.

Pan, right on his ass.

Amazon closing.

He dived beneath the worktops and – out of nowhere – *YAP!*

Ratters, incoming.

Yo-yo could smell Finn. Could taste his distress and had sounded the alarm. The ratters had exploded in fidelity – *YAPAPROWRUFFOW!*

Yo-yo leapt and snapped his jaws viciously at the first bird he saw, and narrowly missed pulverising his young master in the Skimmer.

The next dog, Livid, rose like a salmon to take the second. Pan saw a killer row of tusks and a slavering pink chasm and *just* managed to escape the SLAM of his jaws.

Amazon ran into the trailing pack, an ugly-mug uprising of snapping ratters, a freak-show deathtrap – *SLAM SLAM SLAM SLAM!* The last of them, Barrel-Shaped-Fart-Wagon, gave it all she'd got and – *SNAP!* – clipped the Apache's tail with a trailing, slobbering lip.

It was enough.

Alarms sounded and the chopper tumbled over and over, and Amazon braced herself for death.

THUD! – a massive Siguri hand caught her before impact, the shock knocking her unconscious.

Two down.

Finn sped away.

Through his body pumped the blood of the brave. Through his mind ran fruit-machine wheels of options, needs, objectives: top – lose Pan, escape the nano-radar. How?

There.

Mounted on the wall. A set of speaking tubes, each leading directly to a different part of the complex. "Yes!" yelled Finn and he shot into the mouth of the nearest one, into the unknown, into a tunnel that curled and curved and endlessly looped, illuminated by the Skimmer's headlight, accompanied by the screams of its echoing distorting engine. Finn tried not to hit the sides, his mind racing. Could they track him in the tube? Would the radar penetrate? Where would the tube come out?

Suddenly a perfect circle of light ahead expanded and – *WHOOP* – he was out of the tube and back in a room, a different room, with an ancient interior and blackened walls. The High Chapel, holy sanctuary, until...

WHOOP – through the tube after Finn came...

Wacawaacaawacawacaaa...

DRRTRTRRTRTRTR!

Pan.

Finn grabbed his M27 from the back seat, aimed the Skimmer at a small, high window – *DRTRRTRTRTRT!* – shot out the glass, and burst out into a splash of sky.

He gasped. The bright perfect blue. The monastery roofs below, thousands of feet of nothingness above, and a surroundarama of snow-capped peaks.

He was free...

He had no radar or electronic brain, but he still had power. He would outrun the Apache and follow the valley, he would have time and distance then, he would preserve his fuel, he would find people, a road, a boat, anything he could hitch himself to, anything to get to a signal, he would risk it and run, anything was better than this place.

He was free... *ooooooooooOOOOSHSHH! – BAAAAAM!*

The Sidewinder air-to-air missile thudded into the Skimmer's underside and shrapnel ripped through it. Instantly it started to fall and break up, instantly everything around him was in flames.

Finn's ears rang and his body was racked with shockwave pain, his soul shaken. *Stupid*, he thought, stupid radar, stupid no alarm, stupid hope to stop and stare, and now all there was were flames and spinning, spinning, spinning...

THUD. The craft hit a roof and shattered in a dozen directions at once, Finn thrown far from it, burning gold, gold... all he could see was golden flame and the golden sun and... gold.

He was not burning. He was on the half-ruined golden dome, on his back. He raised his head and saw the Orthodox cross that had stopped Baptiste in his tracks...

Wacawacawacawacawacawacawacawacawacawaca...

The Apache blotted out the sun and he passed out.

WACAWACAWACAWACAWACAWACAWACA...

When Finn came to he was in a clattering gale, a blitz blizzard. He forced open his eyes against the wind and saw the dome pass

118

far beneath him. He tried to move, but found he was bound, bound and slung across the nose of the Apache like a prize stag across the front of a hunter's 4x4.

He looked round and saw Pan smirking at him through the windscreen. He was bringing in Infinity Drake, the Master's greatest prize.

"*Oh great,*" was all Finn's brain could think. He had lost the Skimmer, Carla, his weapons, his family... everything.

WACAWACAWACAWACAWACAWACAWACA...

Down they went, sweeping over the great dome and the patchwork terracotta roofs, down through the window at the top of the High Chapel, past the staring eyes of the grimacing Abbot and the whooping Siguri, down and down, as word spread through the Forum and the roars and applause of the hyped adoring Tyros rose to meet them. Down over the head of the Siguri chief as he opened the catacomb doors, down through the skull-encrusted passages, down the flight of steps that led into the depths of the mountain, heading for the centre of the earth, for his destiny.

Down still further, following the twisting line of the monorail as it fell along the natural flue that snaked randomly through the rock, Finn falling in and out of a trance, the colours flashing by – ancient orange and blue and black – increasing his sense of speed, and deepening his foreboding...

Down and down until finally the Great Cavern opened up like the Colosseum before them.

Finn saw the equipment lined up, the weaponry, the personnel. The rushing waters of the underground torrent echoed with the applause of the assembled technicians as Pan rounded the henge of particle accelerators, enjoying the ride, savouring these last moments as he closed inexorably in on the side cavern and Kaparis.

The bulletproof glass screens that sealed the chamber opened.

Finn felt his heart leap and punch the side of his chest.

There was the lung.

There was...

Kaparis.

FOURTEEN

Carla peeked out of the laundry cart.

The infirmary. Cold and silent. She had been pushed there by
Olga and another Carrier.

There were a dozen or so Tyros on gurneys, being drip-fed criminal expertise, information and attitude, NRP probes sticking out of
their swollen, jellied eyes.

The medic on duty was detaching one would-be Tyro from the
machine, irritated with him, pulling off the monitoring equipment
with little care. He drew the blunt edge of a pair of scissors down
the side of the Tyro's body. There was no response.

121

He tutted, then looked up and barked at Olga and the other girl who had pushed in the laundry cart.

"Carriers! To the incinerator!" said the medic, then he turned away towards his office and left them to it.

The Carriers hurried over and stripped the dead body.

A moment later, Carla was out of her basket and had changed into the dead Tyro's uniform. It was still warm... Carla felt the touch of evil, and for the first time understood, profoundly, what Kaparis was.

"Rub eyes, make red!" Olga said.

Carla rubbed at her eyes, Olga adding some dirt, so they looked as sore as the other Tyros' eyes.

When she was done, Olga looked at her, and nodded.

"Go. Don't smile. Whatever, don't smile!"

An hour later, feet marched in robot time out of the Tyro dorms and down through the Forum, down steel and stone and stair.

Stamp Stamp Stamp.

Fifty or so Tyros. The living Will of Kaparis. All but...

One.

Don't smile, Carla told herself, suppressing a grimace of fear and trying to forget how much danger she was in. Everywhere there were Siguri, searching.

A lone Tyro was rare to see, so Carla had emerged from the infirmary and headed for the one place they might go alone – the latrines, the great communal wash-houses attached to the dorms. She hid in a stall and waited till some Tyros came, in between classes, then followed a slender male out and along through the corridors to a lecture hall.

There she found her crowd. No one noticed her. They were too busy fighting each other for space on the benches or manically focusing on the tutor as he discussed explosives.

They were not like any group of teenagers Carla had ever met (apart from the Milwaukee Schools Brass Ensemble). Hungry. Nasty. No eye contact. No flirting. No sympathy. No emotion.

No smiles. She had seen the infirmary. They were neither monsters nor mankind, but base human technology.

Another tutor had arrived and called for the "Senior Cohort". The group she was sitting with had risen and marched out after him.

Carla simply took her place and tried to keep time.

Stamp Stamp Stamp.

Huge doors swung open. What had once been a dungeon was now a gymnasium designed to test Tyros to the limit. There was a climbing wall of broken glass; vaults as high as trucks; a ducking tank to test the lungs; bikes, tracks, weights beyond measure. And in the centre a great drum on rollers, within which many might run side by side.

The tutor ordered the Tyros to halt. He regarded them through slit, suspicious eyes, then revealed: "Infinity Drake is in the Master's hands!"

A huge roar went up.

Finn... thought Carla in the tumult. He hadn't made it. He hadn't made it, and he was going to die. Finn who she had carried halfway across the world, who had saved her. Finn the voice in her head, her best, her biggest friend. About to die. Somewhere deep beneath their feet.

"You, who have failed thus far, now have a last chance to serve Him," the tutor continued. "Barabbas has fallen." There was a collective gasp. "One of you must take his place on what will be the Master's greatest mission on his greatest day. To participate in the resurrection."

Again the Tyros roared, getting more agitated and excited as a group of Carriers filed into the gymnasium, bearing stretchers. What were they about to do? Carla thought, and looked back at the great hamster wheel of the drum. A small figure was at the front of the Carriers. Olga. She caught Carla's eye and shook her head, as if to say no...

The tutor barked: "Start the wheel!"

The sound and sight of the giant revolving drum turned the class into an impatient mob.

It must be some kind of test, Carla thought as it gathered momentum. She got her head in gear. Speed. Endurance. She knew at least she was fast.

Carla ignored Olga. She had to save Finn. She had to win at all costs.

You can do this, she told herself. *You can win. Save Finn.*

"Commence!" cried the tutor.

The Tyros broke ranks and rushed to the drum, Carla with them, into the lion's den.

They leapt in to hit the drum running, to avoid the floor whipping out from under them. Carla's stride met it perfectly, mind and body in electric union, swift feet pounding and climbing the curve as the mob surged in behind her.

Stay ahead, stay at the head of the pack, Carla thought. Straight away she had to hurdle a fallen body as it came down from the top. Other bodies tumbled, splitting heads, breaking bones, being shoved and kicked out of the drum and sent hurtling from the race.

As the mob settled, they were able to jog as one, as a crowd.

Then came a whistle and a roar went up.

And the fight began.

Carla could hardly believe it. At once she felt a hand grab at her as the Tyros began to shove and kick each other.

It was madness; frantic bloody madness.

Carla ducked and hurdled kicks and punches and fought to stay ahead. Her heart pounded like her feet as again and again she had to leap and hurdle the bodies that fell and flailed. It was like spinning in a bloody washing-machine with the door wide open. In a few brutal revolutions the drum was half full.

Carla could not fight, but she could match anyone for desperation. And while she was faster, she could stay just out of reach – but for how long?

SLAM – suddenly gears crunched and the drum stopped dead.

The entire mob was dumped against the drum. Carla felt half a mountain hit her, crushing her into the curve. Stunned, she was late reacting as the drum started to reverse its spin. She only just managed to claw her way up in time to regain her feet and begin running again, this time in the opposite direction, dancing to avoid the fallen as they tumbled past and out.

The drum spun faster with the lighter load, and any weakness, any faltering step, any hesitation was instantly punished. And still the conflict continued. Unnatural alliances formed and dissolved in the blink of an eye as the weak were picked off. Hands clutched at hair, elbows met eyes, shoulders barged, and again and again Tyros fell from the game.

For those that remained, the faster the drum spun, the worse the injuries got. One Tyro tripped and was propelled forward at just the wrong speed and angle and – *CRACK* – his head split as he rolled bloodily out, an unconscious rag.

SLAM – again the sharp change of direction, and – *WHAM* – again Carla hit the drum, those nearest to her driven into her back. But fewer of them now. This time she was straight back up. The drum kept spinning faster and faster, Carla's legs whipping away as more bodies started to fall like mad rain from above. *WHAM* – she was hit by one and fell, felt the world turn, but – *SLAM* – there was another reverse, and this time the forces favoured her and she was bounced back into the centre of the drum and up onto her feet.

On she ran. Faster than anyone. Dodging and skipping the scything legs and the clawing hands. Others were screaming, falling around her. But on the next sudden turn – *SLAM* – no bodies slammed into her.

There were just three of them left: the lithe young man she had followed from the latrines; a goth-like girl, twice her size, with streaming black hair and two handfuls of sharp red nails; and Carla.

She had made it to the endgame.

She had to sprint just to keep upright. It was no longer a fight, it was a race for the line.

Immediately, the lithe young man lost his footing on a slick of blood and with a simple shove from the goth was sent careening from the spinning drum – "*Aiiiieeeee!*"

In her peripheral vision Carla saw five razor-sharp nails flash past as her final opponent took a swipe. The goth missed, but for a millisecond Carla lost her rhythm, her footing, so had to leap into mid-air to recover… then land at full pelt again, just managing to keep pace on the inner skin of spinning steel, to keep running. And running. Her lungs and limbs could barely take it. A minute or two more and there would be nothing left in her.

Run! she heard Finn yell through her subconscious.

Run! she heard Delta urge, driving her on.

Run! she told herself, when all she had left drained into one last breath as she felt herself… fall… and *WHAM* – the world whipped wholly round, the centrifugal force of the rapidly spinning drum pinning her to the sides, squeezing the last fight out of her as it spun. She was a sliding, beaten lump, slipping out, approaching the edge of the drum and who knew what manner of oblivion. Next to her – *WHAM* – the goth fell too, pinned to the opposite end of the drum, so they could see each other, could look into each other's eyes as they were pressed into the blood-slick steel, clinging to the edge,

127

the grip of a single fingertip making the difference, the grip of ten even more...

Not with those nails, sweetie, thought Carla, as the red-tipped fingers of the goth began to snap and slip... Then with a final *WHOOM* and a scream she was gone.

FIFTEEN

Again Finn was plunged into hell.

Surrounded by fire, burning, suffering and gasping for expanding air, Finn desperately tried once more to scrabble up the glass and out of the flame, away from the tip of the blue cone that he knew from so many school science lessons was where the Bunsen burner was at its absolute hottest.

"ARRRRGGGGHHH!" Finn screamed.

"AHAHAHAHAHAHAAAA!" Kaparis laughed.

Kaparis was in heaven. Time and again Heywood dipped Finn,

encased in a test-tube, into the flame so that his boss could listen to his screams and see how long he could stand it.

Just when Finn thought the skin would burn off his back, he felt the heat suddenly relent. Giant white sheets appeared round the wall of the test-tube, the fingers of a giant white glove, and Finn scrambled up the burning incline to the cooler, top end of the stoppered tube.

The smug cliff of Heywood's face briefly inspected him, then he was swung towards the cluster of optics above Kaparis's head and the revolving, revolting eye.

"Oh, you do like a science lesson, don't you, you dreadful little swot! HAAA!"

Finn had never seen such perverse delight.

Above him the screen array showed the Great Cavern. It was now a scene of frantic activity. The extraordinary submarine Finn had seen the day before had been positioned at the heart of the henge of particle accelerators and all the equipment and crates of cables were being loaded onto it. Even stranger, just outside the Kaparis chamber, Finn could see, through tents of thick cellophane, that a state-of-the-art operating theatre had been assembled, with huge lights and an array of medical equipment.

Clearly something big – or extremely small was about to happen.

"BEG ME, DRAKE!" yelled Kaparis.

Heywood shook the tube and Finn slid down the glass, wrapping his hands in his sleeves to stop them sizzling against the glass.

"ARRRGH!" screamed Finn again.

This couldn't last. He couldn't last. He had to throw Kaparis a bone.

"STOP!" Finn cried at the eye in the optics.

"BEG ME, DRAKE!"

"I'M BEGGING!" Finn yelled, without a scrap of shame.

The eye narrowed.

"MEAN IT!"

Mean it? thought Finn.

"Say, I BEG YOU, YOUR MAJESTY!"

"I BEG YOU... YOUR MAJESTY," said Finn.

"AHAHAHAHAHAHAAAA!" roared Kaparis.

This is ridiculous, thought Finn, but every second he was out of the Bunsen flame was worth it. The cackling was interrupted by the Siguri chief, who popped up on the screen array.

"Master, all foot patrols are now in. No sign of the girl."

Carla! She's alive! thought Finn, his heart briefly thumping with joy. What a girl!

The eye narrowed, the pupil blackened.

"Find her!" barked Kaparis.

"Forget it! She left a day ago," yelled Finn. "We're talking about Carla Salazar here. She will be long gone."

"A schoolgirl? Oh, don't worry, we'll find her – probably in bits. We are days from civilisation here, and I am a patient man. You have defied me and defiled my remarkable work, but I was always going to defeat you. Do you know why?"

Finn said nothing. The tube was cooling fast. He had to resist provoking him further.

"Time, you ghastly little sprite. I have it. You have none. Time to catch you, to make you beg. Just as, in time, I will make you ALL beg – your incompetent uncle, your ridiculous grandmother…"

Finn's heart leapt. This was the first word he'd had of his grandma in five months—

"She got away?" he couldn't help blurting…

"I'm GLAD she got away!" roared Kaparis. "She was driving me crazy, the sentimental, meddling harpy!"

Finn's heart could have burst. She was safe! This news was worth all the pain.

"She will be dead once I get anywhere near her! As dead as your mother!"

This was meant to wound, and Finn could see Kaparis look for his flinch. But Finn knew a thing or two about bullies from school – they always struck at *their* weakest point.

"You seem to have a problem with women," Finn observed. "What happened to your mother? Didn't she love you?"

Anger flashed through Kaparis. Anger and an image of a meringue of a woman, always irritated by him, always leaving. He could taste her contempt and smell her cologne.

"SHE WAS ALWAYS TIRED," shouted Kaparis, *"her perennial excuse. So I put her to rest…"* He could see the old woman now, still griping at him as he fed the lethal injection into her arm.

"I always win in the end," said Kaparis, smiling to himself at the happy memory.

132

"You didn't win my mum," yelled Finn. "My dad did."

"You want to know the truth, boy? She was seduced! Lied to! Then she was betrayed!" His eyes spun and found the Ethan Drake report.

Finn looked up.

Intel. report 498090bb – Drake, E., he read as Kaparis splashed the contents across the screen array. Too many pages to take in. Testimony and timings. Scribbled notes and mad diagrams. And photographs. His dad, his mum. Pictures he'd never seen. His parents as happy, normal, young people in love...

"You want the truth about your pathetic father? He abandoned you! He threw himself into that vortex! A suicide!"

"NO!" Finn yelled back. In a family built on love and wonder, it was impossible to believe that his father had abandoned him. According to the only eyewitness, Ethan Drake as he threw himself in had said he had to save his newborn child, save Finn. What that meant though, and what had happened to him, remained a total mystery.

Kaparis pulled up the page of scribbled notes that contained the L = Place? *equation.*

"He was a coward! He saw the answer staring him in the face – time equals place! The breakthrough that made everything possible! Unlimited power! The chance to change the world! But he was too weak to take it! He would rather die than wield that power; he'd rather die than face life with you! You killed him!"

But Finn was blocking him out, reading as much of the notes as he could. The report confirmed most of what Kelly had told him in Shanghai, but not all. Not what Kelly had been told by Al – Al who

133

was still traumatised at having seen Ethan throw himself into the vortex, Al who could never make it all add up.

"No... I get it..."

"*You get nothing!*"

He saw me *in the vortex,* Finn thought to himself. *If time is place, and place time...* What could it possibly mean? He couldn't understand the equation or a fraction of what was in the notes, but somehow, in the most unscientific way, it *felt* like it made sense. His father had glimpsed something, something in the future, his son in danger...

Inside, Finn felt one wound closing over, but just as quickly another opened up as he wished with all his broken heart that he could see Al, speak to Al, to Grandma, and – more than anything and most of all – to his mother. He wished he could be back by her bedside in her final days and he wished he could say, "I know now. I think I can see it. It makes sense. In the end it can make some kind of sense."

He looked up at the picture of her with his dad on Kaparis's screen.

"He went to save me," Finn told her, because he just had to tell someone. "I can find him."

The great eye of Kaparis twitched. "No you can't. HE'S DEAD!"

"If time is place... he could be anywhere..." said Finn, without really understanding, but feeling all the same that this was the beginning of something.

"He's dead!" repeated Kaparis, less convinced, eyes scrawling over the pages of Ethan's notes, the adolescent hieroglyphics. Was there something

more? *Something he'd missed? Panic seized his entire crippled body. Time equals place. The possibilities were too absurd, too endless. He must explore them. But he would need time, an infinite amount of time. He had wanted to keep the boy alive, to dangle him before Allenby, to torture them and him. But if the boy had seen something in the notes already...?*

This was the end.

And the girl... What if the boy was right and the mountains did end up crawling with enemies? Then he would have to leave and start all over again.

If all this was true, then time was scarce, the future so very precious.

His lips pursed in frustration.

Heywood the butler, who knew when his Master needed his spirits raised, interrupted to deliver some better news.

"Sir?" he said, gently raising an eyebrow. "The party of neurologists has arrived."

FEBRUARY 21 14:14 (GMT+3). Intel.
OBS post #4, Valley of the Son of
St Demetrius, Carpathian Mountains,
Romania

Commander Henri Clément of The Commando Hubert flicked open a knife, a lick of silver steel, and began to cut, very carefully, the way his mother had taught him.

He was concealed within a den of banked snow on the ridge opposite the monastery. He enjoyed the extreme environment. He enjoyed the existential loneliness. But most of all he enjoyed the food. For, while crawling through the undergrowth, he had stumbled on a subterranean paradise. Truffles. Three of them, each the size of his thumb.

"*Mon dieu...*" he gasped as the knife released the hypnotising scent. He was about to weep when his eye was caught by a sight so extraordinary he almost dropped the heavenly fungi.

A golden egg. Splitting in two...

He had to blink. Was the truffle not a truffle but some poisonous fungus? Was he hallucinating? The ruined dome of the monastery seemed to be opening like a great golden beak.

Now a helicopter was approaching fast over the mountains. Skimming the peaks – no radar alarm had sounded! And as if this wasn't extraordinary enough – SNAP – movement! A dozen metres ahead, a figure, almost human, a bow across its back, was lolloping out of the snowbanks straight for him...

Henri had three Croix de Guerre[14], but nothing could stifle his scream as he snapped open the emergency comms link to G&T Romanian Command at Kluge—

"*ARRRRGHGHGHGHH!*"

"Shh!" the figure insisted, stopping close enough to kiss him, a magnificent, topsy-turvy fairground face.

---

[14] French military medal awarded for heroic deeds in conflict.

Shh?

"*Blue 4! Confirm?*" Henri heard in his headphones, but he remained speechless as Santiago dug a note out of his layers of rags.

It was written in formal flowing script—

*From: Primo Carrier, Monastery of Mount
St Demetrius of Thessaloniki*

To: The Investigating Authority

Sirs, We wish with all urgency to establish contact...

The great dome opened and the whup-whup-whup-whup *of the radar-cloaked transport helicopter echoed down the shaft into the Great Cavern. The medical party then appeared, winched down in a rescue cage.*

There were three of them, escorted by Siguri. Two of them looked distinctly unamused.

"AHA!" said Kaparis, feeling his mood suddenly lift. "Heywood, put the boy aside -- but not too far! I don't want him to miss this."

The boy must die, thought Kaparis, and soon. He would leave nothing to chance. Not now that he was so close. But before he finished him off, he must let him glimpse the glorious future he'd be missing. He must know that Kaparis had won...

SIXTEEN

Finn felt the world turn as Heywood picked up the test-tube and popped it into a rack on a side cabinet. He had a ringside seat as the glass screen that sealed off the chamber slid open.

"Doctor Leopold and party," announced Heywood, as the visitors entered the chamber.

"Ah! How good of you to come," said Kaparis.

The three medical specialists were led in. Two of them stared at the iron lung and optical array in disbelief, while a third, Dr Thomas Leopold, a hipster prince, beamed. His teeth beamed, his forehead beamed, even his blond hair beamed. Kaparis had identified him seven years earlier as the outstanding neurological medical student of his generation, and a personal weakling. Kaparis had extravagantly funded, corrupted and inspired him ever since to the point where Leopold had become the Splice[15] program's chief technician.

Beside Thomas Leopold stood his former classmate and the woman he most admired in the world, the Indian neuro-engineer Dr Nico Sharma, still wearing the surgical "greens" she had been kidnapped in. Leopold thought her beautiful when angry. She was furious.

Their one-time supervisor, the great neurosurgeon Sir James Tattersfield, glowered at the back, a wrinkled owl of a man in thick-rimmed glasses and full evening dress.

"Dr Kaparis!" beamed Leopold. "May I introduce – at long last! – Dr Nico Sharma and Sir James Tattersfield?"

"I've heard so much about you both," enthused Kaparis.

Sir James stepped forward to interrupt.

"Now listen to me, Dr Kaparis, or whatever you call yourself. Leopold has clearly lost his senses. Call the police and have us released! Immediately!"

"Ah Professor, your famous bedside manner. Well, it isn't your manners I am interested in. It is your expertise."

"We absolutely refuse to cooperate!" said Dr Nico Sharma, raising her chin in defiance. *Like Cleopatra!* Leopold thought.

"My dear, let us hope you're as intelligent as you are proud."

Spinning his eyes across the optical array, Kaparis called up two files, one on Nico and one on Sir James, and opened them over his screen array. They looked up to see their professional lives laid out

---

[15] Nickname for the Exploratory Spinal Loop Interconnect program.

above them in scientific papers, documentary clips, awards and commendations.

"Would you mind explaining what the hell is going on?" exploded Sir James.

The Siguri escort bristled.

"Sir James, you will remain calm," ordered Kaparis from beneath the optical array. *"I have brought you here to assist in an operation that will revolutionise medical science and change the world."*

Sir James scowled. "What nonsense is this?"

"The very 'nonsense' that you yourself and Dr Sharma have spent your careers researching," said Kaparis. *"I'm talking about repairing damaged and severed nerves with artificial nerve fibres: the dream of neuroscience since Luigi Galvani first animated a frog's leg."*

As he talked, Kaparis called up a video of twitching frog's legs, paraplegic patients being tested, and complex technical drawings of medical inventions.

"In theory it's possible; in practice impossible. The problems are threefold. One – how do you tap into the individual nerve fibres to pick up specific signals, then efficiently translate that signal? Two – how on earth can you build something small enough to be practical? Three – how on earth are you supposed to surgically attach such tiny things even if they could be produced?"

"Don't teach us to suck eggs," snapped Sir James.

Kaparis ignored him.

"Dr Sharma, you have managed to transfer two per cent of a signal being sent down a primary nerve via one of your ionic conductors?"

"Two per cent *so far*," insisted Dr Sharma.

"Admirable," slurred Kaparis, *"but not much use if, like me, you fancy popping to the shops, or even just picking up a glass of Château Beychevelle."*

Right on cue, Heywood appeared with a bottle and poured them each a glass of ruby magic. Sir James caught a hint of its aroma and allowed himself a moment of respect.

"Sir, I must stop you. A man in your position hopes against hope for a cure. Dr Leopold has clearly lost his head in telling you we have one. We do not. You have broken the law and gone to extra-ordinary lengths for nothing. We are decades away from any kind of practical breakthrough," stated Sir James.

"Oh yes? Dear Leopold, would you kindly explain what you and the Zurich team have come up with?"

"Yes, Master," said Leopold, bursting to tell all.

"'Master'?" Nico repeated, appalled.

"Yes, Nico, 'Master'. Let us start with the nerve fibre. For years, you have been engaged in trying to capture individual nerve signals? Right? Well, this is what we call a Splice cup."

He took a coiled-up cable, one of the cables that Finn had seen stacked in huge numbers outside, and showed her one of the cups fitted at either end.

"This cup has been designed to clamp on to the end of a severed nerve fibre." He fitted the cup over his fingers to illustrate. "It picks up the electrochemical impulse the nerve is trying to transmit and carries it down one of these cables, made from highly conductive polymer, to the other side of the severed section. What we're going to do," Leopold continued, "is attach a thousand of these cups and

141

cables to either side of the break in Dr Kaparis's spinal column, thus reanimating his entire nervous system. Where *you* have been working, theoretically, to deliver two per cent of available signal, *we* will deliver, in practice, one hundred per cent!"

Sir James shook his head sadly. Poor Thomas Leopold was clearly mad.

"One hundred per cent?" Nico repeated in sad disbelief. "Thomas, this is adness!" She had tears in her eyes for her old friend.

"Don't be such a fool!" barked Sir James, wanting to bring this nonsense to an end. "Even if these things could be manufactured at the appropriate scale, you would never be able to attach them!"

Leopold pointed through the bulletproof glass into the Great Cavern, to the submarine at the centre of the stone circle of particle accelerators. The hold doors of the craft were still open and, lying in them, packed tight like spaghetti, were hundreds and hundreds of Splice cables, each ten metres long with a connector cup at each end.

"But don't you see? Everything is ready aboard the *Vitalis*, Sir James," said Leopold in awe.

"What on earth do you mean? Who are you going to fit them to – a giant?"

"HAHAHAHAHA!" exclaimed Kaparis. *"Oh my dear professor! Of course we're not going fit them to some giant – hahahahahahaaaaa! We're going to shrink YOU."*

"What?" Sir James whispered, uncomprehending in the laughter that followed.

Laughter from Kaparis. Laughter from Leopold, who looked as

if he was about to go totally doolally. Obsequious smirking from Heywood.

"You are all quite mad! Call the British Ambassador!" he demanded.

"Shrink?" Nico demanded of Leopold.

"Yes! A miracle!" said Leopold, his eyes shining.

"Quite," said Kaparis, recovering. "Here's something I made earlier."

And with that, the chamber door hissed open and a small bird flew in.

Wacawacawacawacawacawacawacawacawacawaca…

A tiny helicopter. *One of those remote-control toys?* thought Nico. But then it landed on top of the iron lung. And two toy soldiers got out… They were no more than a centimetre tall. And human. And moving…

Nico gasped.

Sir James held his breath.

"Say hello, Tyros."

Pan and Amazon, the two tiny figures from the surviving Apache, met the eyes of the doctors. Amazon, 10mm tall and proud, strode forward as if on a catwalk. Pan simply cackled up at their giant disbelieving faces.

"Pan! Amazon! To your places!" Kaparis ordered, and the two tiny Tyros climbed onto a Petri dish offered by a technician which was then taken out into the Great Cavern.

"What have you done…?" whispered Nico, overcome by fear and fascination as they were carried past.

"Impossible…" said Sir James, feeling each of his sixty-eight years of age.

"It's called the Boldklub process. And this is only the beginning. Thanks to my latest breakthrough, we now have the ability to shrink you to just a hundred-thousandth of your normal size."

Even though Finn had had a perfect view of what had unfolded, just like the doctors, he struggled to believe what he had heard.

"One hundred thousand times…? What is he talking about?" he said aloud.

The way Al had explained the Boldklub process to him, you'd need such huge amounts of energy to get anywhere near microscopic scale that it was practically impossible… But Al had also once told Finn that it wasn't because Kaparis was so evil that made him dangerous, or because he was so intelligent. He was dangerous because he was so *imaginative*. Maybe he had made the breakthrough he was boasting of… and maybe this operation – the cables, the submarine, the doctors – had been behind his pursuit of the Boldklub secret all along…

But how on earth was it all going to work?

He didn't have to wait long to find out.

"Leopold, do kindly talk us through what is to happen. I would hate to run out of time."

"Of course, Master," said Leopold. "First, let us look at the injury site," he announced, and he called up an X-ray that, despite the passage of time, caused a stab of pain and self-pity in Kaparis.

"In 2000, Dr Kaparis undertook an experimental medical procedure designed to enhance his physique and extend his life, under the care of his then-wife, Dr Ondine St Emmanuel de Morales."

Kaparis gritted his teeth as a picture of the extraordinary Ondine flashed up, a Latin-American beauty beyond compare -- dark-skinned, head thrown back, demanding attention, magnificent right to the tips of her sharpened green nails.

"This involved injecting the stem cells of panthers into various sites across his anatomy. The extraordinary result was that Dr Kaparis and his wife became forty per cent stronger. Cell analysis showed they were actually getting younger. But then some sort of temporary insanity in his wife -- possibly a side-effect of the treatment -- led to a domestic dispute that ended in a near-decapitation."

"She was a most unreasonable woman," Kaparis managed to explain. He blinked away a flashback of falling against the sword. Of the blood. Of his inability to move... Ondine...

"As we can see from the X-ray, this resulted in a fracture in the spinal cord at the top of the neck, between the first and second cervical vertebrae -- so high that Dr Kaparis now lacks automatic lung function, a condition, ironically, known as 'Ondine's Curse'."

Kaparis twitched.

"The spinal fluid is clear and tests indicate nerve cells on either side of the wound are healthy and responsive. The rest of Dr Kaparis's body has been constantly stimulated by electrodes to maintain perfect musculature, and by spending his life in a negative-pressure ventilator, or iron lung, his chest cavity and all internal organs have remained in perfect condition."

Leopold tapped at the keyboard and called up a 3D holographic CAT scan of Kaparis to illustrate and animate his plan, an electric green body that hung in the air like a diabolical mannequin. Leopold hit a key and a point of light appeared in the scan's left thigh.

"Ever since Dr Kaparis discovered the Boldklub process, we decided this procedure was theoretically possible. Two years ago, we began developing and perfecting the Splice hardware. One year ago, we began to plan in detail the operation. Now, here, today, it will come to fruition. The Splice cables and all personnel will be loaded aboard the medical-support craft *Vitalis* and shrunk via the Boldklub process to a scale one hundred thousand times their actual size."

Nico let out an uncomprehending curse. Sir James just stared.

"Once at scale, the craft will be injected into the femoral artery and fed via a tiny tube, a cannula, through the arterial system into the neck, as close as possible to the injury site."

As he spoke, the point of light moved and an animation of the whole operation played out on the hologram.

"Once in the neck, we will pilot *Vitalis* through the local arterial system until we reach the intervertebral foramina, where we shall anchor. We shall then leave the craft and Sir James will lead us into the spinal column."

Sir James's owl eyes almost bulged from his head.

"The submarine's atomic reactor will be emitting a radioactive pulse, allowing it to be traced in real-time by particle detectors. Manipulation of this pulse will allow the craft to contact us using

Morse code. In addition, we will carry radioactive flares in case we get lost in the bloodstream. Simply set one off and you will be evacuated by hypodermic needle. Once we're in the clear spinal fluid, it will be much easier to navigate and to work. Dr Sharma will be in charge of the distribution and arrangement of the connectors between the two sides of the wound."

"What?" Nico said, the power gone from her voice.

Leopold picked up a Splice cable again.

"To give you some idea of scale, we will be around 50 microns tall. A blood cell is usually about 5 microns in diameter. A nerve fibre is less than a single micron thick – just perfect for one of these cups to clip on to."

He pinched the body of the cup and clipped it on to his fingers again.

"But… there's a thousand of them?" whispered Nico, wondering if this was all a dream and she was going mad.

"We plan to be on site for ten hours, making one hundred connections per hour. We'll have a staff of ten to help us – the two nano-colleagues you've already met, plus eight more crew members drawn from the senior Tyro group."

He grinned and gestured outside. There, being escorted into the Great Cavern, were eight more Tyros.

"Each crew member has been trained and programmed specifically for this mission, and should be capable of fitting twenty cables per hour," Leopold continued.

"More than enough time," insisted Kaparis.

Leopold turned to Nico and Sir James, trying to transmit his joy to them.

"Just imagine!"

Imagine... thought Finn, trying to digest the implications. Kaparis paralysed was bad enough. The thought of him fit and able and evil was too much to bear. He had to do something – sabotage the mission, get word out, anything. But from here? How? Could he even be in a more difficult position?

He watched the new Tyros filing in.

He'd messed up. Why did he stop to admire the view when he'd reached free air in the Skimmer? Why didn't he—

Wait... Carla?

There she was – unmistakable at the end of the line of Tyros.

Oh no...

Carla as a Tyro? She must be looking for him. His heart bulged. What a girl. What a sister. What a trooper.

What a mess.

What was she going to do?

The holographic animation showed the nervous system of Kaparis coming back to life.

"By the time we've finished, the spinal cord will be linked by a thousand new fibres," said Leopold.

"The repaired spine will be even stronger than the original," added *Kaparis.*

"And then what?" asked Sir James, who had now passed into a state of utter bemusement.

Leopold hit a key to start the homeward journey on the animation.

"We all return to the support craft and navigate back to the neck for cannula extraction. Thereafter we will return to our normal size in time for a celebration breakfast – with Dr Kaparis in full attendance!"

"A celebration…? Breakfast…?"

"Yes. We're going in tonight."

"Tonight?"

"Speed is essential, and so is your presence," said Kaparis. "If I may cut to the chase, you will both be rewarded. Ten million dollars is on deposit for each of you in Swiss bank accounts."

"Never! This is madness! If you think for one moment—" started Nico, then halted as live CCTV footage of her husband and two young children came up on another screen… They seemed to be enjoying themselves, dressing up in odd costumes in some kind of grand hotel.

"I have also, as a precaution," Kaparis explained, "invited both your immediate families to be my guests for forty-eight hours. They think you have set up a surprise Murder Mystery weekend for them. Let us hope there will be no actual murders to spoil the fun. There won't be, of course… not if you do your duty. You will soon be free and very rich…"

"More than that…" interrupted Sir James, his voice shaking as he stared at the operation playing out again on the hologram. "We will have conquered nature itself."

"Yes..." whispered Leopold, delighted to see the old surgeon catch the fever.

Nico kept staring at the live feed of her husband and children.

"You cannot be serious..."

"Deadly," confirmed Kaparis. *"Everybody remembers the first men on the moon. Well, this is our Apollo. You, those first heroes. The first beneath the skin. The first to make a man walk again."*

Leopold took Nico's hands in his.

"Think what this could mean, the possibilities of this technology, of true nano-surgery!"

Sir James's old eyes shone with wonder. Thomas Leopold grinned like the schoolboy he always would be. Nico opened her mouth to protest, but the sight of her little boys stopped her. She must save them. Any thought beyond that was unbearable.

"This isn't just medicine, this is history!" proclaimed Sir James.

A tear rolled down Leopold's cheek.

SEVENTEEN

FEBRUARY 21 16:52 (GMT+3).
C-130 Hercules, G&T Romanian Command,
National Air Defence Base, Kluge

Alive...

Grandma wept.

Delta Salazar stepped forward to grab the microphone and demand confirmation, her heart choking on the words. *"She's there?"*

In the overcrowded, and now overexcited, temporary G&T HQ in the hull of the transport aircraft, full of technicians and soldiers trying to coordinate events and process incoming information, it was difficult to make sense of what she had heard.

Carla... Alive...

"She is being taken to the Great Cavern. To the Master," said the distorted voice of the Primo over the comms.

Delta dropped into a chair in shock.

The note from the Primo which Santiago had handed to Henri Clément had been digested immediately. Henri had given an LPI[16] data-burst communications device to Santiago to take straight back to the monastery.

Li Jun had been shown a picture of Santiago and the shock of recognition had broken a dam in her mind. Suddenly they knew the whole social structure of the monastery, the tutors, the Tyros, the Siguri, the Carriers. She even remembered "a cave".

As is so often the case, thought Al, *a tiny breakthrough opens the floodgates.*

Soon after the LPI comms link had been opened between the Primo and Commander King, three facts had been established.

First, Carla Salazar was in the monastery and hiding at grave peril among the Tyros.

Second, Kaparis himself was in residence in a secret cavern beneath the mountain.

Third, there were "little people" at large and Carla Salazar apparently had one of her own.

"One of *our* own..." Al corrected.

He had never experienced such intoxicating, delicious relief. He

---

[16] Low probability of intercept.

was so elated he thought he might actually float off. Only his mother, weeping across the cabin, held him to the earth.

"He's alive!" said Al.

"I know... I think... I think I'd been blocking it all out," said Grandma, holding back tears. "I think I'd been preparing for the worst, and now to know he's just a few miles away..."

"I know," said Al.

"Well, it's just too much. I must act, I must do something!"

"We will, Mother, I promise. Just as soon as we get more information—"

"No, *I* must do something," his mother interrupted, "or I'll lose my mind. I've left my knitting at home."

"You've got plenty to do! Just keep working with Li Jun. There's more she can tell us, I'm sure. Do anything you can to jog her memory, do any crazy thing you think might work."

"He's alive," Grandma repeated, anchoring herself in those words.

Al squeezed her hand and turned away to find Delta right in his face. For a fraction of a second he thought she might kiss him. Instead she said, "Send me in. At nano-scale. Take me back to base. Shrink me and send me in."

"You know I'm not reshrinking anybody till I know it's safe. Besides, he has nano-radar and— Ow! You're breaking my hand!"

Delta reluctantly released her grip on Al, but still tried to fry him with her eyes. "She's my *sister*."

153

"I know, and for her sake you've got to undertake your most testing mission to date."

"What?"

"Do as little as possible. If we run headlong at this, it's just going to get a lot of people killed. We have to find a back way in. A trap door. A trick. Meditate, free your mind. Seriously. It's done me the power of good."

She snarled and stomped off.

Over the comms link, the Primo was seeking reassurance. "Commander King, the greatest care must be taken to protect the Carrier children – they will fight, but—"

"Our raid, when it comes," said Commander King, "will be perfect in its execution. You need not be concerned. You are already surrounded by some of the most sophisticated killers on the planet—"

Listening from his snowdrift, Henri gave a modest shrug.

"...But right now, an attack is not imminent. You will of course be warned when one is."

The possibility of an armed raid, a gas attack, a siege, had already been discounted. They needed to know more, much more. They had Carrier help now, but as for how much time they actually had, who knew...

"So what are you going to do?" asked the Primo.

Amid all the emotion, Al felt his way forward. They needed agency inside the castle. A spy. He looked across the cabin and found the answer.

Cometh the hour, cometh the... child.

FEBRUARY 21 18:07 (GMT+3). Great Cavern, Monastery of Mount St Demetrius of Thessaloniki

Any minute now, thought Carla...

She had waited for an opportunity to look for Kaparis, to look for Finn, but so far, with each moment that passed, she seemed to be getting further and further from a moment alone.

After winning the final place on the Tyro team, she had been taken down through the cave system to join the other seven elite Tyros waiting like zombies for the mission to begin. The Great Cavern fitted Finn's description exactly, right down to the extraordinary submarine they were led towards. They entered through airlock doors in the huge hold, which was full of cables that had been loaded onto racks. They were led past the REACTOR ROOM and on through another steel door, marked CREW, and into the crew compartment. One side was lined with bunks, recessed like tombs, while the other was laden with subaqua kit – air tanks, helmets, utility belts packed with all kinds of tools and gadgets, and propulsion units like hoverboards.

The Tyros began to strip and put on fluorescent yellow wetsuits, at which point Carla began to seriously wonder what she'd got herself into. She had no choice but to copy them and soon found herself lying on her bunk in a wetsuit, saying nothing, thinking. *Any minute now...*

A technician was coming like an air hostess along the line of bunks to make sure they were all comfortable. *Weird*, thought Carla.

In the centre of the crew compartment Carla could see a spiral staircase leading up to the glass canopy and the bridge. It didn't seem like anyone was up there. Maybe she could—

The technician gripped her arm as she reached Carla's bunk.

"Good luck!" she said, and Carla felt something sting. She just had time to register the hypodermic pen in the technician's hand before everything went happy white and she passed out.

The three neurologists were led out to be put through a crash course in nano-physics and the mission particulars. As they walked away, Finn saw the two reflected eyes on the Kaparis optical array swivel round to fix on him.

Kaparis said nothing, turning things over in his mind until he came to the appropriate conclusion.

"Raffles," he said to Heywood. "I wish to dine with Raffles."

Raffles? *Raffles who?* thought Finn.

He didn't have to wait long to find out.

Heywood returned with a glass tank.

Oh great... Finn thought.

Hudson had one just like it, a vivarium for Dweezel, his pet snake.

Heywood put the reptile tank on top of the iron lung so that Kaparis could see it directly, then plugged in its heat lamp.

There was Raffles in all his glory. Six lethal, starving inches of Uromastyx lizard.

SCHCHHHHHHWHWHWWWWWWWWWWWWWW...

The air was violent noise as they dropped through the darkness at 120mph.

Hudson clung on, partly through primal fear ("I've never jumped out of a moving plane before!"), but also because his drop buddy was Yvette Dupuis of Commando Hubert, the most beautiful woman he had ever seen. Let alone been strapped to. Despite the fact that she took absolutely no notice of him whatsoever, and perhaps because of this, he knew he would love her for ever.

On the altimeter round her wrist the digits spun downwards – 12,000... 11,500... 11,000...

SCHCHHHHHHWHWHWWWWWWWWWWWWWW...

Through night sights, Yvette picked out the blinking infra-red landing light.

"*Trois, deux, un...*"

"*Oeuuoooo...*"

WHACK!

The chute deployed and the harness bit. They went from 120mph to 12mph in two seconds flat and Hudson spent the remaining few metres of the drop vomiting into a paper bag.

Yvette drifted to a perfect halt beside Santiago and Henri.

157

Santiago regarded Hudson, the "special agent". He seemed an unlikely saviour. But who was he to question the ways of the Primo or the Investigating Authority?

"Hut-sun?" said Santiago.

Yvette decoupled Hudson, and he wobbled forward on weakling legs, handing over his sick bag.

Santiago took the bag and examined it. Was it a gift? Was it magic sick? He pocketed it for safekeeping, then took a set of sackcloth Carrier rags and started to dress him.

"Quick, Hut-sun! Quick!"

The sun swung across the sky, fell, and the day died, as it always did for Kaparis, with grand operatic warbling.

> "... O della madre mia casa gioconda
> La wally ne andrà da te, da te..."

What a voice, what a woman...!

When Maria Callas hit the high notes, the test-tube Finn was trapped in – now clamped and suspended just above Kaparis's head – threatened to burst.

> "... Nè più la rivedrai!
> Mai più, mai più!"

Kaparis gurgled like a baby. What a way to go!

Heywood finished preparing his favourite meal. Le caviar Beluga dans une mousse de champignons – *a dozen tiny spheres of the finest caviar wobbling atop a foam of matsutake mushrooms – and carried it over on the tip of a long lab spoon.*

"Waft, Heywood! Waft!"

It had been his delight to wave every treat he was consuming past Infinity Drake in order to torture him -- and past Raffles, poised in his vivarium on top of the iron lung, in order to drive him to a frenzy of hunger. Raffles followed the spoon with mad swivel eyes, thwapping his whip-like tongue against the glass as it passed. The foulest creature ever to stalk the deserts of Niger, he had somehow evaded security in their Saharan base and crawled into the heart of the complex, where he'd been trapped. Kaparis had admired the lizard's pluck and the elegant dismemberment of his prey, and so instead of being killed he'd been kept on as staff and got brought out to amuse the Master as and when required.

And he was most definitely required now.

The culinary treat completed its journey as it was fed through the optical array and deposited on Kaparis's fat grey tongue.

"It looks like spit with black bits in it!" shouted Finn. *"I hope it improves your breath!"*

"To think you shall never know the heavenly pleasure of higher things," Kaparis replied. *"Never drink the finest wines, never experience the music of Wagner, never complete the mile's run. Oh, the sunsets you will never see. No one will ever be kissed by you, or know your heart's song. You will be like Peter Pan. Except no one will be told your story – or even remember*

you by the time I've finished with your family and friends. You will exist in my memory alone."

Finn shuddered at the thought. He had no plan, and by the look of Raffles he had nothing left to lose. But he still held onto one slight hope, and it lay just beyond the lizard's cage. But how to get there?

A hipster technician appeared on the screens above. One of Kaparis's eyes twisted on the optical array and glared at him.

"Yeah, hi," drawled the technician. "The accelerator is – like – ready to rumba?"

These relaxed young friends of Leopold's were all – like – very competent, but extremely irritating to have to listen to. Idiots, with rising inflection.

"What?" Kaparis spat back.

"The technical staff wish you to know we're approaching completion," Heywood translated.

Kaparis took in the Great Cavern overview on another screen. The last component of the accelerator was being pushed into position around the submarine. Five years of research, design, plotting, criminality, massive investment, and diabolical action were coming to fruition.

He took it all in. The electrostatic hum of the particle accelerators as they began to power up. The tented operating theatre. The technical data now cascading down his screens... Infinity Drake trapped in his test-tube.

It was all undeniably fantastic. And so was he. He deserved this.

This was Kaparis's time.

Finn watched his lips twist like struggling slugs.

"Double power to the core!" Kaparis ordered. "Begin the countdown."

"Sir, we should be making our way down to the operating theatre," counselled Heywood.

"Yes, yes, just one last thing..." said Kaparis.

Finn felt Kaparis's eyes roll round the optical array and zoom in on him.

"Dinner time!"

FEBRUARY 21 21:55 (GMT+3). Monastery
of Mount St Demetrius of Thessaloniki.
T minus 20:00

Far above, Hudson felt just like he did every time he had to do a reading in assembly. His throat was tight and dry. His heart thumping. Should he pretend to faint? *No, pull yourself together, Hudson,* he told himself. This was not reading aloud a few paragraphs on Sir Ernest Shackleton, this was a save-the-world situation.

He had been whisked across the valley, smuggled into the extraordinary castle and taken straight to the Primo, who had traced his features while some malnourished, fearful children looked on.

"They sent *you?*" the Primo had said eventually.

"I'm the only kid they've got," Hudson had replied.

Whatever their misgivings, the die was cast. They had to put their hopes in him.

"We've got to get you into the Great Cavern," the Primo said.

An hour later, Hudson found himself crawling through the narrow roof space above the Abbot's High Chapel, making his way through the fabric of the ancient buildings in the wake of Santiago, little Olga, and half a dozen other Carriers.

The creeping and crawling ended beneath the great false dome, where a climbing frame of structural metalwork and powerful hydraulics was suspended above a thousand-foot open shaft.

It was onto this climbing frame above the abyss that Hudson was now urged.

"Come, Hut-sun!" Santiago whispered and led the way.

Hudson took a deep breath and began to climb to the bottom edge. Sound echoed up from far below. They could make out structures, even see activity, but they were too far away to make any sense of it.

Which is why the other Carriers had brought the rope.

And why one end of it was tied round his waist.

"*Uno, duo, tres?*" asked Santiago, secured to a rope of his own.

Hudson gulped. The Carriers looked at him, little bony faces expectant in the gloom, somehow in awe of him.

"Crumbs," said Hudson, and he stepped off the frame, letting himself dangle on the rope, the Carriers taking his weight via a pulley.

Get a grip, Hudson, he told himself again, as he held the rope as tight as he could.

Santiago ordered the Carriers, "*Vite!*"

And down they went, into the darkness above the Great Cavern.

"Bravo, Hut-sun!" cheered Santiago.

If Yvette could see me now, thought Hudson.

The lid of the vivarium opened and Raffles stirred, flicking out his evil pink tongue, suspicious.

"No!" Finn cried, but it was great-glass-elevator time again, as Heywood picked him up and tipped the test-tube upside down into the bottom of the lizard's tank. Raffles, the size of at least a T-Rex to Finn, became extremely interested.

Except there was a problem. Finn wasn't coming out of the test-tube. He had managed to wedge himself across the curve at the tube's base, his half-melted sneakers giving a good grip against the glass.

"Come on, man!" yelled Kaparis.

ZIPASH – out shot Raffles' lasso of a tongue and Finn felt it slap and stick against the glass.

THWACK – Heywood bashed the tube against the corner of the tank to shift him.

"Arrrghhhhh!" Finn shouted as he shot down the steepest glass incline and thumped out into the sand.

163

He got up. He was surrounded by glass and sand dunes – and a very hungry lizard, its head alone the size of a double-decker bus.

ZIPASH – the tongue lashed out again. Finn dived and it slapped the side of the tank beyond him. He got up and did the only thing he could do – run.

"HA!" laughed Kaparis as he saw a tiny cloud of dust shoot across the sand.

Quick as a flash, the lizard was after Finn on mad clockwork legs. Finn ran for a mock-ruined temple in the sands ahead. *ZIPASH* – the tongue clipped his right shoulder like a punch as he ducked it, hitting the sand ahead like a lightning strike. Before Raffles could reel it in and fire again, Finn made it to the temple.

"Come on, Raffles!" said Kaparis, mindful of the time.

Finn hid behind a pillar and tried to think what next. He was in a glass box full of sand, his only cover this ridiculous mock temple and a bleached wooden stick. There was a hanging heat lamp and, where the flex entered the tank high above, there was a tiny gap, but even if he could get up there without being eaten, even if he could squeeze through it, they were hardly going to just watch him escape. The only other features were a water bowl and lizard poo.

ZIPASH – Raffles' tongue whipped round the corner at him.

He needed a disappearing act, and there was literally nowhere to run. But still he ran, falling back as ever on the three pieces of advice his mother had given him on her deathbed.

Trust yourself. Be yourself. And – the one he found most useful at times like this – *just keep going.*

He had to think of something radical. He had to think fast. He threw himself forward to try and bury himself in the sand, but he couldn't dig himself in fast enough, and anyway, he thought, they'd simply pick him out again in no time.

Then he saw something.

In the sand in front of him, near where he'd first been knocked from the test-tube – a shard of glass, no more than a chip, that had been bashed off the top of the tube.

It was nothing. But to Finn it was a hand axe, a dagger... it was something. He scrambled across and grabbed it.

Kill the dinosaur. Great. How? What did he know about dinosaurs?

ZIPASH – Finn scrambled behind the water bowl for safety.

They were related to birds...

Birds... Of course! A disappearing act—

Finn ran hell for leather towards the stick of wood which was propped across the back of the tank.

ZIPASH – Raffles spotted him and this time scored a direct hit, the tongue wrapping round his leg like a living rope, but Finn kicked back and broke its grip. He ran on and leapt up on to the stick. He had to get this right. He had to get height. He climbed and ran up it. Giving it his all.

Raffles hissed below and opened his great jaws to show his dagger-like teeth. Finn had been in a mismatch like this once before. Against a bird many times his size...

Remember being swallowed by the bird, he told himself. *Just avoid the teeth and you'll be fine. Think beyond the mouth; think soft flesh and stomach. Think about Carla. Do it for her...*

"There! Get him! Get him!" roared Kaparis.

The time was now. Finn closed his eyes, took the deepest breath he could, and, pretending to lose his footing, he fell – or rather dived – through the air... straight into the open jaws of Raffles – SCLUMP!

"YEEEAAHSHSHSHSSS!" roared Kaparis, *savouring the moment.*

As Finn was sucked down, down into the belly of the beast, the last thing he could hear was:

"HE'S DEAD! INFINITY DRAKE IS DEAD!"

EIGHTEEN

26... 27... 28... 29...

Deep in the eternal darkness of the lizard's guts, Finn counted to try and stay sane.

30... 31... 32... then he could count no more. The acid liquid that engulfed him, burning his skin, was too much – he had to get out. Months before, he had kicked the gullet of the bird that had swallowed him and been expelled. So with the lizard, it was surely a matter of scaling up the stimulus. He took the shard of glass and dug it into the flesh around him, ripping at it. The flesh tightened

167

so hard he thought he would be crushed to death, then – *HUUUUUUCCCK* – suddenly the world seemed to explode as he found himself propelled into the air in a bloody projectile of vomit – *THUMP* – to land, skin still burning from the acid, in the sand beneath the heat lamp.

Behind him, Raffles looked, as far as a lizard could look, freaked out.

Ahead, he could see Kaparis and his lung being slid out of the chamber and down to the operating theatre, surrounded by technicians and medics.

Finn scrambled up and leapt up into the water bowl – *SPLASH!* – to rid himself of the acid. Then he looked out of the tank, out along the top of the iron lung to see if it was still there...

And it was.

Hope.

In the shape of the 40mm Apache helicopter Pan and Amazon had flown in on.

YES! Finn leapt from the pool of water and ran back to the bleached wooden stick at the back of the tank. This time Raffles ran to cower in the furthest corner.

The heat lamp was high above, but maybe, if he could get to the very top of the bleached stick...? He ran up the main trunk of it, then took to all fours to pull himself along a twig that branched off, thinning as it rose. Its tip was the highest point beneath the lipped edge of the conical shade.

Wobbling, he pulled himself to the end of the twig. Once there, he manoeuvred himself till he was perched on the tip, like a diver on the edge of the highest board. He could feel there was some give in it. Some spring.

He took the deepest of all breaths, thought of Carla... and jumped once – twice – three times – then LEAPT up and out and *just* caught the hot-lipped edge of the heat lamp.

It swung wildly, but he was wild himself. He hung on and clawed and hauled his way up the hot, steep side of the shade, until he made it to the flex it dangled from.

From there, it was a short shimmy up to the smallest of all gaps between the flex and the access hole in the lid of the tank.

Raffles watched with some relief as Finn squeezed his way through, and out.

Kaparis looked up. The six members of the second specialist medical team he had hired from Zurich were around him. This one was a crack surgical team who would perform the external part of the operation and was led by the incurably greedy surgeon known to Kaparis as the Big Swiss Cheese.

"Permission to open the lung and begin the procedure?" the Big Swiss Cheese asked.

"Get on with it," said Kaparis.

169

He took a deep iron lung breath and held it.

KERCHUNK – *three clasps were released* – HISSSSsssss – *air pressure equalised and the lung was opened. Despite being unable to "feel" anything, this procedure always disturbed him. His optical array disappeared and suddenly he was robbed of 360-degree vision. For a moment, he was properly exposed, all but naked. His body had been kept in perfect condition over the years of his paralysis, but now it had nothing to keep him alive but a single held breath.*

Then he felt the hissing, the positive pressure mask come down over his face, and he was able to breathe again.

To live again, he thought, as he had for years, not as slave to one kind of machine or another.

Beneath the mask he actually smiled.

FEBRUARY 21 22:11 (GMT+3). Great Cavern,
Monastery of Mount St Demetrius of
Thessaloniki. *T minus 04:28*

Finn dropped down the side of the tank and sprinted to the waiting Apache, thinking *please, please, please start...*

He leapt into the cab and looked at the controls. It was enough like the chopper that Delta had given him lessons in back in England for him to understand what was what. He flicked a series of switches, hit a green button and—

WwwhooooshshshsSSHSHSH...

The turbine screamed to life and the rotors turned.

He had no fear of being overheard. The henge was beginning to roar.

On screen, the two nano-Tyros – Pan and Amazon – were being placed on two full-size bunks inside the submarine *Vitalis*. The rotors above Finn were turning faster and faster.

Wacawacawacawacawacawacawacawacawacawacawaca...

The technicians in the henge sealed the iron doors of the *Vitalis* and ran for the safety of the perimeter as white lightning began to whip and crackle around the core.

Finn had seen many hot areas created and this one was no different. The lightning would become a continuous arc, then expand into a shimmering ball of perfect light.

And Finn knew that no one could tear their eyes away from such a spectacle.

Wacawacawacawacawacawacawacawacawacawacawaca...

FEBRUARY 21 22:14 (GMT+3). Monastery of Mount St Demetrius of Thessaloniki. T minus 01:29

The noise coming out of Santiago was one thing.

"*Ouuuuwuuuuwuuuuwwuuwwuuu...*"

171

But the noise rising up the shaft towards them from the Boldklub henge as it powered up was something else.

Hudson had recognised the stone circle of particle accelerators at once, but the light and noise was freaking Santiago.

"Ah... aaaaaAAHHH!" he wailed, stressed to the pit of his being and desperate to signal to the Carriers in the dome to pull them back up. He reached for the flashlight, but Hudson stopped him.

"It's OK! It's going to be OK! I know what this is!" he insisted.

They would have to report straight back to the Primo, but first Hudson had to identify whatever was at the centre of the henge.

It looked like some kind of submarine, but how *could* it be?

They had to take a closer look.

FEBRUARY 21 22:15 (GMT+3). Monastery
of Mount St Demetrius of Thessaloniki.
T minus 00:23

As the power indicator turned from red to green on the Apache, Infinity Drake maxed out the thrust and pulled back hard on the stick.

In the operating theatre, Kaparis was surrounded.

The surgical team in green scrubs worked as a seamless unit to prepare him.

The cannula was taken from its sterilised sheath and placed opposite the incision site on his thigh.

Outside, the accelerator had reached tipping point.

WOOOOOOMMMMMMMMMMM!

Dangling above, as the screaming of the henge reached its fever pitch, Hudson got a view of one of the technicians' screens. On it were faces, bodies, strapped into vibrating bunks. Obviously the crew of the submarine in the core.

Then he saw a face he recognised. A face he knew from a thousand briefings.

Carla Salazar.

The crucial moment had arrived. All it needed was the final order.

"Ready to commence Boldklub sequence," said Heywood, bent over his boss.

173

He lifted for a moment the mask that was forcing air into Kaparis's lungs.

"DO IT," ordered Kasparis.

A switch was thrown. Power surged.

WOOOOOOMMMMMMMMMMM!

FEBRUARY 21 22:15 (GMT+3). Monastery
of Mount St Demetrius of Thessaloniki.
T minus 00:00

Wacawacawacawacawacawacawacawacawacawacawaca...

Unseen above the electromagnetic maelstrom was an attack heli-copter the size of a baby bird.

Finn pushed the craft on as the world beneath flashed magnesium white – *WHOOOOOM!* – and the crazed hoop of energy resolved into a perfect orb of white light.

The hot area.

Finn had been there before. He would go there again. There was no way back but this. It wasn't complicated; it was a fairy tale. He had to rescue Carla. He had to kill the giant or die himself. And Infinity Drake did not fear death, for in it lay all the possibilities of oblivion, of communion with the love that brought him into being, with his mum and with his dad.

He put the helicopter into a drifting trajectory that would eventu-ally see it crash into the river at the back of the cavern.

Then he opened the cab and stepped onto the weapons' hard mount in the fierce downdraft.

Wacawacawacawacawacawacawacawacawacawacawaca…

He meant to throw himself out. Instead, he dropped. Simply fell. In shock.

Hudson?

Hudson??

Hudson???

Hudson was dangling with Santiago just a few metres above him, staring in rapt fascination at the spectacle beneath.

It could not be, but it was.

Hope, Finn thought as he felt himself hit the edge of the perfect light, the perfect end.

In an instant, it possessed him and his mind flashed ice white.

PART
THREE

PART
THREE

NINETEEN

"OOOOOOOoooooaaa…"

It wasn't an animal sound, and yet it wasn't quite human either.

It's me, realised Finn.

His eyes opened.

White. Absolute. Solid seamless white with no depth or perspective.

He pulled himself up. He blinked into it. As he did so, the white above turned a smudgy surreal grey. More white ebbed away as he found his feet and mind, and the "ground" he was standing on revealed

179

itself as rough glass – endless trenches and ridgelines of crystal, a raging sea caught and frozen.

Distorting through the waves, he could see a dark mass. He walked along the trench he was in and then scrambled up a ridge twice his height. Strange waves of pressure buffeted him. Shockwaves? Sound waves? He was still in a daze.

Then, from the crest of the ridge, he saw the *Vitalis* lying on its side like a great beached whale, perhaps a hundred metres away – at a scale of 1:100,000.

Finn slid down the ridge and tried to run across the chaotic terrain, leaping and sliding as best he could. The misty grey sky brightened. He felt more shockwaves drumming his chest.

As he approached, he realised he was on the same scale as the submarine – everything in the hot area must have ended up at the same scale, no matter what size they had started out. It felt weird, to be *relatively* normal.

He wondered if anyone inside would be conscious. Or even alive. Would he be spotted? Surely the technicians would have a ready way of finding the craft – some sort of scanning microscope?

Just get on board. Unnoticed. Stow away, somehow. Sabotage, somehow. Kill the giant.

That was as detailed as Finn's plan got.

If Hudson was here, then surely Al must be near... Commander King... All of them.

Just keep going.

Finn reached the side of the *Vitalis* and the door of the hold. It was a garage-sized door that ran half the length of the vessel – he had seen it open, seen them loading in the cables. He found a raised button and struck it with the heel of his hand – *KER-CHUNK*. A hydraulic lock fired and the door gaped open.

Yes!

The hold was full of racks. Hundreds of bundles of Splice cables strapped to them. Before Finn could take in anything else, he felt a shockwave hit his back. He looked round.

Water exploded towards him.

Finn dived in and hauled down the hold bay door as – *SLAM* – the force of water struck it, knocking him across the hold, but also – *CHUNK* – slamming it shut again.

Chaos. He was thrown around the racks, the water he'd let in sloshing and soaking him as tornado turbulence took possession of the *Vitalis*.

But within a minute, the vessel became steadier, much steadier. And, after all the chaos, silence.

He could hear himself panting.

He took stock. There were two portholes, like observation panels, through which light filtered. He was soaked, but the hold was only ankle-deep in water. The Splice cable racks filled most of the space, but also gave him a place to hide.

At one end of the hold was a series of hatch doors. Finn sloshed over to the first of them and a stencilled sign identified it as AIRLOCK A.

Airlock?

181

He looked at the big hold doors he'd jumped through, and it all made sense. The whole bay would have to be flooded so that they could float out the cables.

They're going to flood this whole place, he realised.

There was a wheel on each of the hatch doors. He turned the wheel on Airlock A anticlockwise, the hatch door opened and he climbed through into a smaller chamber. There was another door on the opposite side. Another wheel. Slowly, he turned the wheel, opening the hatch into the main body of the *Vitalis*.

He didn't move but listened hard. He could hear the whirr of fans, small digital beeps – the vessel's computers coming to life. But what about its crew? He could hear no movement.

He dared to step through and into a passage that led past the reactor room towards the door marked CREW. He listened again. Nothing.

He opened it slowly and peered in.

There were the Tyros and the doctors in the bunks, laid out in their high-tech tombs as still as stone. And there was Carla…

He walked to her in a trance. He could hardly believe it. She was… his size. He'd never seen her like this before. She was at once the most familiar and the most strange thing he'd ever seen. She was… normal. He was about to try and shake her awake when he thought better of it.

If this is freaking me out, she's bound to lose it too, and she might wake the others.

He registered all the equipment stowed on the wall opposite. Then the spiral staircase in the centre of the quarters.

Finn climbed up it and emerged in the great glass bubble of the *Vitalis*'s bridge, a dome of movement and light filtering through the water they were suspended in. He presumed they were in some kind of vessel being transported across the Great Cavern, but the shapes and shades were too indistinct to know for certain.

At the centre of the bridge on a raised dais was a chair for a pilot with dual joysticks and a fingertip control panel, the kind of ultimate gamer chair Finn had always craved. Around it, on screens, the craft was already coming to life, its computers beeping and flashing and running tests. Everywhere data ran. A message flashed up – "REACTOR SYSTEM SECURE: OPERATIONAL". Gyroscopes whirred, an autopilot engaged, and outside the blades of the two great impellers turned and angled to stabilise the vessel.

At the back of the bridge was another steel door. Finn opened it and found himself in an engine room, full of gyroscopes, a turbine, and the electric motors that projected power down complex couplings and gears to the great arms of the beast. Another hatch at the back of the engine room led back down a ladder to the airlocks.

When he returned to the bridge, he saw an image on the principal screen. The outline of a man had appeared, a man made of red and blue lines, lines that branched and dived ever smaller, and Finn quickly realised what he was looking at.

It was a roadmap of Kaparis.

It snapped him out of his reverie.

He had to stop this.

The crew. He must incapacitate them. But how? Murder them in their beds? The thought made him sick. But he had to do something...

"*Urrrhh...*"

A groan. From below.

Finn ran to the spiral staircase. One of the Tyros was stirring, groaning in semi-conscious distress.

Finn had to hide. But he also needed to know what was going on. He noticed an intercom panel. One of the buttons read HOLD.

He hit it and dropped back down into the crew quarters. He grabbed as much kit as he could before any of the Tyros could fully wake up – then he shot back out to the hold.

By the time he was through the airlock, he could already hear abrupt Tyro voices over the intercom channel he'd left open.

Finn looked at the kit he'd managed to get out: a fluorescent yellow wetsuit, a tank of liquefied air, a helmet and a utility belt – and one of those hoverboard things too. He prayed it would be everything he'd need, and cursed himself for not grabbing some kind of weapon.

Louder voices came over the intercom as people climbed up to the bridge, voices that Finn recognised.

"Are we 'Go' for the Splice mission, Number One?" It was Leopold. Finn could hear the self-satisfaction in his voice.

"Yes, Herr Doctor. Systems tests complete. Crew complete."

Pan.

"Send the following message to the Master," said Leopold.

"*Vitalis* awake... all well... we beg to honour and serve the Master."

Pan tapped out the message on a device linked to the nuclear reactor, varying the radioactive signature of the craft to create a series of dots and dashes that could be detected by the surgical team.

...- .. - .- .-.. .. ... / .- .-- .-. .- -.- . / .- .-. .-.. .-. / .-- . .-. .-. / -.... . --.
... / .... --- -. --- .- -. / .... . .-. .-. . / --- .- ... - . .-.

Anyone could respond to events, anyone could react. Shaping events was quite another matter, and it was the business Kaparis was in.

Life was to be conquered, not revered.

Drake was dead. He, Kaparis, was surrounded by his dedicated medical team. And the Vitalis was about to enter his bloodstream and embark on its mission. Within hours, he would be able to feel again. He would be resurrected. There was no sign of any move by Hook Hall. They would do nothing in haste, even if they did find the girl. The fools! He was supreme.

The eyes of the Big Swiss Cheese surgeon appeared over him.

"There are no contra-indications. We are ready to begin."

Kaparis flicked his eyes to Heywood, who understood he had to lift the mask.

HISSSSSSSSS...

"Fiat Kaparis,"[17] croaked the old devil.

TWENTY

The operation began.

A 10mm incision was made in the patient's upper right thigh and the femoral artery was exposed and punctured. A very fine cannula tube was inserted and fed up through the torso, past the heart, through the top of the chest and into the neck,[18] then more slowly, it was twisted and turned through ever smaller blood vessels until it finally

---

[18] More precisely, take a right into the femoral artery, then turn left up the iliac artery, then left again up the descending aorta. As you approach the heart, take the third exit on the right and follow the subclavian artery for a short distance before taking another right into one of the vertebral arteries.

reached its destination between the first and second cervical vertebrae, or back bones, where the blood vessel was so narrow it could go no further.

The whole journey took six minutes. About the same amount of time the Big Swiss Cheese spent in his Porsche driving to work every day.

"In position," he declared. "Launch the *Vitalis*."

The phial of saline solution containing the microscopic craft was attached to the end of the cannula...

FEBRUARY 21 23:29 (GMT+3). Body of D.A.P. Kaparis

Movement. A sudden change in the light. Finn had his face pressed against the small porthole, trying to make out what was going on.

"This is it!" he heard Leopold exclaim over the intercom.

"We're being attached to the cannula. We're going in..." said Sir James with reverence.

"Crew to stations! Strap yourselves in!" he heard Pan bark.

They must be in for a rough ride. Finn looked around. There were no seats, but the cables were held on the racks by cargo straps. Finn released one and wriggled under it to lie alongside the cables.

Just in time.

SLOOOOOOOOOOOOOOOOSH! The *Vitalis* lurched, spinning in

a hundred directions at once, struggling, its turbines and impellers crying out as some unstoppable force, some incredible turbulence, thrust them into instant total darkness – then blinding red. Finn clung to consciousness as lights sprang on around the craft as it fought to control the energy singing through its structure.

SLOOOOOOOOOOOOOOOSH! Through the porthole, Finn saw walls of red glass flashing past – the red silk lining of an endless spinning tunnel...

All eyes watched the monitor as the nuclear trace – picked up as a distinct blue spot by the scanner embedded in the operating table – made its way directly up the tiny cannula through the arterial system until it was deposited exactly where it was required, high in the neck.

The surgeon withdrew the cannula and the blue dot stayed in place. He had parked the Vitalis *in just the right spot.*

"There," he said, beaming. "All better."

"Idiot..." Kaparis muttered beneath his mask.

But nothing could defeat the euphoria he now felt.

He even felt moved to say a few words.

He made eyes at Heywood to lift his mask and Heywood obliged. HSSSSSSSSSS...

"Thank you, ladies and gentlemen..." he started, looking around at their eager faces.

Then he felt his mood turn (and there was nothing he liked more than a sudden change of mood). They were pleased as punch in their moment of triumph. And what had they done? They had performed a function under his instruction. All the organisation and inspiration, all the genius, had come from him. If he should be thanking anyone, it should be himself.

So, just to let them know who was really the hero here, who could truly command life and death, who was paying their life-changing fees, he added: "You may kiss my hand."

Sweat beaded on their brows. Then, one by one, they bent to brush their lips against his lifeless fingers.

Dhu-dhu, dhu-dhu, dhu-dhu, dhu-dhu, dhu-dhu...

Finn came round with his head still spinning as the *Vitalis* finally levelled out.

While his mind and body recovered some sense of balance, he noticed the light through the portholes was now a steady red. He loosened the cargo strap and got up to take a better look. He could barely believe his eyes.

Red...

It was as if they were part of a thick shoal of fish. He had once been to an aquarium with his mum. In one of the rooms, you walked through a tunnel of glass beneath a tank full of tropical fish. That was exactly what it was like now. But red...

The giant shoal of fish were up close, touching the porthole, as if inquisitive, and the craft was floating free, going with the flow, being part of it. But Finn knew that what he was looking at weren't fish. He knew because he'd had to draw them, colour them, label them, and look at them through a microscope in a biology lesson the year before at school. They had a distinct form, like a frisbee, and he knew they were suspended not in water but in a translucent plasma.

"Blood cells..." Finn said, aloud, to confirm he wasn't dreaming. "We're inside him..."

He felt a strange euphoria. Over the intercom, he could hear technical chatter as the Tyros returned to the bridge, but also manic laughter.

"Corpuscles!" cried Leopold.

"Magnificent!" said Sir James.

"Dear Nico, I present to you the eighth wonder of the world," Leopold declared.

"Or rather, blood vessels leading to the gap between the first and second cervical vertebrae," said Sir James almost in a whisper.

"No, this can't be..." Nico began, but could not continue, her voice suspended in awe.

Finn pressed his face to the porthole as the *Vitalis* eased along the blood vessel, caught in the blood flow. The red frisbees were streaming past, urged on by an unseen force – *dhu-dhu, dhu-dhu, dhu-dhu, dhu-dhu, dhu-dhu* – the beat of a heart, the essence of Kaparis. Among the red blood cells were occasional whites, floating like baby blankets among the hurried fish: the body's own Siguri, there to protect against invaders. There were much smaller sponges in the mix too – *platelets,*

Finn remembered, whose job it was to plug gaps and form clots.

Gaping holes appeared in the walls of the tunnel as they sailed by, sucking blood cells into them, branches of smaller arteries that led off to who knew where, each with a place in some great scheme. As they drifted close to them, Finn could see that the waxy arterial walls themselves were a mosaic of millions of tiny cells. It was inside-out brilliant engineering, just one tiny part of one human body, on a planet spinning on the outer edge of an insignificant galaxy, billions of years old...

Dhu-dhu, dhu-dhu, dhu-dhu, dhu-dhu...

Life – so little, yet so much. Finn felt dwarfed by it all, and his heart ached for Al to be there, for Grandma, for anyone else to see this with him—

A line of thought that snapped as he remembered. "Carla!"

Carla stayed in her bunk, trying to control her fear. Where were they? What was going on? She dreaded to think.

No! Don't dread, don't think, she told herself. *Just try and control your breathing, just try and stay alive. Do what they do. And don't smile...* Though admittedly smiling was now the very least of her problems.

Finn heard the *Vitalis*'s impellers whine as the vessel turned 180 degrees and held its position in the flow in a particularly narrow part of the blood vessel, the shoals of red frisbee fish having to squeeze past its bulk.

"Coordinates achieved. Firing anchors."

Tzzzzot – Tzzzzot – Tzzzzot – Tzzzzot –

The hull twitched as anchor lines shot out of the *Vitalis* and pierced the rubbery walls of the blood vessel. Servomotors whirred as the lines were automatically tightened. Directly ahead was the entrance to a branching artery of a good size, easily big enough to swim through.

"There it is – AE347567," said Leopold.

"My God..." said Nico.

"God had nothing to do with it," said Sir James.

You want to try arguing that one with my grandma, thought Finn in the hold.

"Kaparis has brought us to this point," said Leopold.

And you want to try arguing that *one with my uncle Al.*

"And we are here to serve him. Come. Let's get started," ordered Leopold.

"All crew: check helmets, tanks, valves and power status," said a Tyro voice.

They're coming, Finn thought. He jumped down to retrieve the kit he'd stolen and started to climb into it.

"Shall we go through?" said a smiling Leopold, leading his two medical colleagues down from the bridge.

The Tyro crew were releasing themselves from their bunks and beginning their equipment checks. They wore bright yellow wetsuits and Nico thought they moved like robots; all apart from one girl who seemed scared and whose hands shook as she fumbled with an air regulator. Pan and Amazon, the lead Tyros, were the only ones that seemed to have independent intelligence – of the cruellest sort – and they were kitted out in fluorescent green wetsuits like the medics. Pan noticed Nico staring and scowled back.

"We are at the narrowest navigable point in this intervertebral artery," explained Leopold, pointing out their position on a screen, a tiny channel between two bones in the back. "From here on in, we must swim through the foramina to reach the spinal cord."

"Swim?" said Nico.

"Using the scoot," he said, detaching one of the hoverboard-like units from its rack. It was like a fat snowboard, with a grilled intake at the front and jet openings at the back.

"Just clip your feet in and tip forward and they drive jets of plasma through the unit. Very simple. Now you know why I gave you both a hoverboard for Christmas!" laughed Leopold. "But don't be nervous. We will guide you anyway – and it's only a short distance to the spinal cord."

Leopold turned to his old tutor.

"Sir James, I would like to give you the honour of breaching the blood–brain barrier. It's vital that we make the smallest practical incision using one of the laser scalpels…"

He took what looked like a bazooka of some kind from a rack on the wall.

"Just enough to get us through one at a time, and of course to feed through the cables. This is precisely why we needed you on the mission. Hopefully, the bleed into the spinal fluid will be insignificant."

"It would be an honour," said Sir James. He regarded the laser scalpel and tried its weight. "A clean incision in the meninges, the barrier that protects the spinal cord, should allow an opening that will close in on itself, like an elastic curtain. The body's natural structures should do the work for us."

"Exactly," agreed Leopold.

"But what about its natural defences?" said Nico. "We'll be attacked by antibodies at once, then those white blood cells will move in and we'll be consumed or trapped within minutes."

Leopold laughed.

"Oh, we thought of that. You can see already no antibody has stuck to the *Vitalis*. That's because a small positive electrical charge is being carried through the hull. This prevents the antibodies attaching, and so they don't send out any alarm to the whites. The wetsuits all carry a battery pack –" he indicated a black unit the size of a paperback book on the utility belt – "which will send a similar charge through the suits. There's enough power in each of these to repel antibodies for up to twenty hours. Also, the system allows us direct communication. As long as two parts of our suits are in direct contact, we can converse through headsets in the helmets."

Nico watched as Leopold and Sir James donned utility belts and checked their helmets. When she made no move to do the same, Leopold looked at her with incomprehension. Sir James was less understanding. He grabbed a belt and thrust it at her.

"Don't be a fool. You have been invited to take part in a miracle. This is the future!" Sir James was convinced; insistent. "Just imagine the capacity for good. Imagine the thousands who may walk again, the tumours we can starve of blood. We are the pioneers in a medical revolution!"

"Do you really think this man has good intentions? Have you even thought that far?" said Nico.

Before Leopold or Sir James could answer, Pan stepped between them. He had heard enough. "Disobey, Dr Sharma, and your children will suffer." He nearly spat into Nico's face.

"Now wait a min—" Sir James began.

But Pan snapped. "No more talk. Action!" He almost punched the utility belt at Nico, who had no option but to swallow her pride and put it on, while Sir James, because he was too ashamed to meet her eye, quickly put on his mask instead. Only the nervous Tyro girl whose hands had shaken dared look at her.

Listening at the intercom in the hold, Finn thought, *Talk to Dr Sharma.*

He still had no plan, but at least he had a list:

1. Save Carla.
2. Talk to Dr Sharma.
3. Sabotage the mission.
4. Kill the giant.

The details he would have to work out along the way.

Dhu-dhu, dhu-dhu, dhu-dhu, dhu-dhu.

TWENTY-ONE

"**C**rew to airlocks," crackled the intercom.

Finn grabbed his helmet and stuck it on. Surely, with so many Tyro crew members on board, he'd go unnoticed? He flicked a switch on what he presumed was the battery and heard a click in the speakers in his helmet. As his visor began to steam up, he turned a dial on the regulator and fresh air hissed in to clear his view.

The last he heard from the intercom before it automatically shut off was: "Flood the hold."

Straight away, valves clicked open and liquid began to roar in.

At the back of the cable racks Finn checked the seal on his helmet and tried not to panic. He had no choice but to hunker down in the rising plasma. It was soon over his helmet and, a few moments later, the hold doors began to open with a whirr. As they did, illuminated by lights all over the craft, red blood cells poured in, bouncing around every nook and cranny like dumb, insistent creatures with a life of their own.

Dhu-dhu, dhu-dhu, dhu-dhu, dhu-dhu.

Finn grabbed one. Squeezed. It was like a slimy sponge. His wonder ceased with the metallic *CLUNK* of the first airlock opening.

Three bright yellow divers emerged, Tyros, and got straight to work, each releasing a bundle of ten or so Splice cables from the racks. More airlocks opened and more Tyros swam out to do the same. Each had a scoot on a short tether attached to their ankles. When they were ready, they clipped their feet into their scoot and propelled themselves out of the hold into the bloodstream, into the artery itself. They leant into the force of the flow and the scoots came to life and held them steady, angled like ski jumpers in flight, trailing thick cable tails, happy to ignore the soft pummelling they were getting from the oncoming cells.

Straight away, Finn got a familiar urge.

I want a go...

Dhu-dhu, dhu-dhu, dhu-dhu, dhu-dhu.

He clipped his feet into the scoot he'd grabbed, and attached a bundle of cables to his belt.

The airlock opened again and the last of the yellow Tyro crew emerged, this time with five green figures: the three medics, plus Amazon and Pan. The medics huddled and tested their scoots while Pan corralled the crew using a laser pointer. Amazon attached a line to her belt from a set of reels marked UMBILICAL COMMS TETHERS, laying a guideline from the *Vitalis* to their destination.

Out in the stream, one of the yellow Tyro crew struggled to control the scoot, like Bambi finding his feet, flipping a full 360 degrees.

Carla! thought Finn. Should he do something to help her? But before he could move, she'd read the power dynamics of both blood flow and scoot, righted herself, and was holding her own among the Tyros. A natural. *Delta would be proud*, thought Finn.

As the three green medics eased out of the hold to join them, there was some more instability and a rush to assist Sir James, who seemed in danger of careering off downstream.

During the confusion, Finn floated out to join the Tyro crew.

Dhu-dhu, dhu-dhu, dhu-dhu, dhu-dhu.

As soon as the stream hit him, he angled the scoot. Immediately, it whooshed and responded, threatening to whisk out from under him, until he threw his shoulders forward to balance the forces and gain some stability. At first, he was washed too far back, but he angled his feet to increase the thrust and edge forwards, steadying himself as best he could at the back of the pack of yellow Tyro crew members, acutely aware each would happily kill him.

Immediately beyond the lights of the *Vitalis* was utter, gaping darkness, and out of this darkness rushed the red cells, like fat confetti, the artery walls full of forbidding dark potholes where smaller blood vessels branched off.

Leopold touched Pan and gave him an order. He waved forward

two of the crew with his pointer and they led the way, switching on arc lights that illuminated the mouth of the target blood vessel. Another wave of Pan's laser and they were ordered to follow him as he went in first. The medics came immediately after, then the Tyro crew members, all in a line, trailing their cable tails.

One of you is Carla, Finn thought, but he couldn't risk approaching her now. Instead, he entered at the back of the line, following the narrow snaking path ahead. Behind him, Amazon closed in, bringing up the rear with another arc light, trailing the tether line back to the *Vitalis*.

Down the blood vessel they went, in single file, carried by the flow, all the while the walls around them closing in till they were like surfers riding a tube, curling round the slick arterial skin as they twisted and turned. The bright arc light was making the membrane translucent, so Finn could see the press of other vessels, black and sinewy, in the flesh beyond. Down and down, Finn having to focus against panic as the ugly tunnel tightened still further. Then, suddenly – light and space. Relief.

The tunnel had opened into a much larger space, an interface chamber with a ghost-grey membrane of some kind, a great thick curtain that attracted the blood cells. As if in a frenzy of worship, the cells pressed themselves against it and changed in colour and form, their redness dulling in a moment as oxygen passed out of them before they fell away to drain out of the veins, dark and spent.

Finn saw the medics holding each other's wrists, discussing something. Then he saw the laser scalpel brought forward by Pan, bigger than a rifle. One of the medics, the old surgeon, Sir James, braced it against his shoulder.

Everyone backed away as Sir James took aim and pulled the trigger.

FZZZZTZTZFZTZZTZZTZTTTTTTT! An intense beam of light appeared at the tip of the device and boiled the liquid plasma it shot through, sending out blooms of bubbles. But the surgeon kept the electric-blue blade steady, and ran it down a section of the membrane, cleaving it along the grain of tight grey cells. Then he stopped and let the bubbles and debris drift off in the flow. Gently, reverently, he parted the curtain at the gap and slipped through into the unknown.

Leopold followed, then Nico, then Pan. One by one, trailing equipment and cables, the Tyros followed suit. Finn felt the grey membrane pressing tight against him, but he pushed on through to emerge into yet another world.

A crystal-clear ocean trench. The spinal canal. They were deep within Kaparis now, near the injury that so defined him. Beneath them, about twenty metres or so away at their scale, lay the great grey-black snake of the spinal cord, suspended in the clear spinal fluid by ligaments that ran like anchor lines to the walls around them. Following the line of green and yellow figures that scooted ahead of him in the arc light, Finn looked along the vast snake to the wound itself.

A great cluster of gnarled flesh and bone seemed to have burst through into the perfect ocean and then set like lava down one half of the canal, and while clear spinal fluid passed easily around it, the great snake itself was cut clean through, its two severed sections ten or so metres apart, both sides held firmly in place by the web of ligaments, or else fused to the landslide of scar tissue.

With barely a pause, the medics led the party down into the gap. The two circular sides of the crevasse, the ends of the severed spinal cord, were huge, the size of cricket pitches, and the cut ends of the nerve fibres that ran through it swirled in different patterns of grey and white, like letters running through a stick of rock. Each grey nerve fibre was barely the thickness of a thumb and there must have been thousands on thousands of them facing each other across this abyss, unable to connect.

This is it, Finn thought. *Journey's end.*

Suspended just a few metres ahead of him, stunned in the silent chamber, one of the crew members had stopped.

Carla.

He wasn't going to get a better opportunity.

Here goes nothing, he thought.

He eased himself forward on the scoot, reached out... and touched her.

"Whatever you do, do not freak out!" he said.

She spun round and her eyes grew so wide they almost burst.

"*What...?*" He heard a gasp like a choke, then she grabbed hold of him, almost convulsed in shock.

"*WHAATTT...?*"

"I said DON'T!" hissed Finn, looking around nervously at the others, but no one seemed to have noticed.

Carla's body buzzed with the shock of it, the impossibility, the joy too. In the depths of her despair, in the deepest pit, he had found her. And he was...

He was bigger than her! It was like she had never seen him before, had never met him, yet she knew him absolutely – not a face on a screen, not a voice at her ear, but whole and real. She wanted to burst into tears of absurd joy.

"I found you..." she said.

"No, I found *you*! I followed you and crashed the party," said Finn, grinning at her. She had a hold of his arm like she would never let go.

Amazon spotted them and angrily waved them forward with her pointer.

They started towards the other Tyro crew.

"One of the medics, the woman..." said Carla.

"I know," said Finn. "She's not one of them. We've got to get to her, sabotage the mission, then get out of here."

"How?"

"I don't know yet – just copy what the others do and we'll try and get close to her."

Finn! It was really him. She couldn't believe it. *Don't smile*, she reminded herself, just in time.

As they rejoined the main group, Dr Leopold lifted a cable off the back of one of the Tyros and unfurled it. He took the Splice cup at one end of the cable and clipped it on to a severed nerve fibre at the dead centre of a dark carpet swirl of endings on one face of the cord, then he scooted across the chasm to the corresponding swirl on the opposite side.

He looked at Sir James, then at Nico. Then with a mad laugh inaudible across the abyss, he drove the end of the connector into the corresponding nerve fibre.

LEDs along the length of the cable leapt into life...

FEBRUARY 21 23:52 (GMT+3). Great Cavern, Monastery of Mount St Demetrius of Thessaloniki

"ARRRGH!" Kaparis cried out, in shock and... pain.

The surgeons wondered for a moment if he had suffered a heart attack.

He might as well have. His soul shook. Every hair on his head stood on end.

It was as if part of his left leg had been hit with a hammer. And he felt it... felt the pain subside to a warmth, an abstract mysterious joy. Life. HSSSSSSSSS...

Heywood saw his terrible face contort in ecstasy beneath the mask.

"I am REBORN!" Kaparis raved. "My left leg!"

The Big Swiss Cheese yanked the sheet up. There was the left calf muscle, tight as steel.

"Command it!" the surgeon insisted.

"Move!" went Kaparis's brain, *and an electrochemical command shot down his spinal cord – all the way.*

The muscle twitched.

It was the surgeon's turn to scream.

"IT'S WORKING!"

Santiago dangled above the henge, silent, mesmerised like Hudson.

They had seen the submarine disappear, consumed by the hot area. They had seen technicians move in with a massive microscope with robot arms that had picked something up from the centre of the particle accelerators.

Did it contain the submarine? Did it contain Finn and Carla?

"Closer!" Hudson had urged, and Santiago had flashed the instruction up the shaft to lower them just a few feet more.

All eyes were on screens, the technicians and Siguri in awe.

The robot microscope was wheeled into a temporary tented structure composed of sheets of thick translucent plastic; at its heart, a figure lay prostrate on an operating table.

"*Diablo!*" gasped Santiago.

"Bloody hell," agreed Hudson.

Hudson didn't *know* what was going on. He could guess, but they had to *know*, and they had to tell Al.

"Just a little closer," he whispered to Santiago.

TWENTY-TWO

Deep in the vast intraspinal crevasse, the reconnected nerve fibre
sparkled.

Dr Leopold scooted a loop-the-loop, while Sir James shook his
head in wonder.

Nico couldn't believe it. To operate at this scale... The possibilities
cascaded through her mind. The potential was huge. She saw cables
running through bodies ill with multiple sclerosis, she saw children
with spinal injuries walking again – running even! Never having to
see a doctor again!

And then she thought of her own children running. And she remembered where they were. Where she was. And who she was inside.

The flick of a supervising laser, wielded by one of the senior Tyros, called her to action.

The Splice cable bundles were being offloaded by the Tyro crew and collected in a tethered bale. Half the Tyros were unfurling cables ready to start work, the other half were heading back to the *Vitalis* to fetch more, scooting along the tether line that Amazon had laid and which led all the way back to the ship.

Dr Nico Sharma felt a hand touch her arm. It was Leopold, his eyes shining.

"Now do you understand why I brought you here?" He opened his arms as if to offer her the strange new world. "Isn't this the most stupendous thing you've ever experienced?"

But Nico didn't know what to think or what to say.

"Where do you want them to start?" asked Leopold. He handed her a laser pointer and gestured towards the Tyros. "They are yours to instruct."

Nico looked at the vast surface of the spinal cord, at the cross-section of nerve endings she'd studied all her working life and knew so well. There were relatively few cables compared to the thousands of nerve fibres, but, as long as the key connections were in the right place, the brain could fill in the gaps. The logical thing to do was to distribute the cables evenly by structure and function, following the patterns on the faces of the severed cord.

She selected a pattern she knew controlled the motor function of the arms and put her hand on the first crew member.

"Start on this swirl here –" and she indicated the precise spot with her laser – "and run your cable to that swirl over there," she said, indicating the swirl on the opposite side of the crevasse.

The swirls looked exactly the same... almost.

The Tyro did her bidding and connected the first Splice cup as directed, as Nico scooted along the line of Tyro crew, issuing the same order.

Leopold watched her, and slowly the scales fell from his eyes.

At the end of the line, the last Tyro shocked her by speaking back. "Dr Sharma, please don't freak – we're not Tyros – we're on your side."

Nico felt alarm. What was this? Had she been found out? She looked into the Tyro's eyes. They were bright, desperate. Another Tyro, the clumsy girl, touched the first, so that all three of them were linked somehow. Instinctively, she knew these two weren't like the others.

"Make it look like you're giving us instructions," said the boy.

She took the Splice cup Finn held and pretended to show them something as he machine-gunned information.

"My name is Infinity Drake. This is Carla Salazar. We got caught up in this a while ago. We're in as much trouble as you are."

"More," said Carla.

"We have to stop this," Finn continued, while out of the corner of her eye Nico saw a pair of green shapes swimming towards them. "We've got to figure a way out of here and we somehow have to booby-trap the body, and I figured that as you're a doctor you'll know what to do, see? Dr Sharma?"

She glanced up as the pair of green figures closed in.

"I understand," she said quickly. "I've already started, but now it's too late."

"Too late?" Finn began, as Nico pushed away, breaking contact with them just as Amazon seized her and Pan swooped in to cut the short tether running from her ankle to her scoot. Then he took the distress flare and knife from her utility belt.

"What are you doing?" Nico said.

Finn and Carla backed off, trying to read the situation.

Leopold arrived, gestured at the cables Nico had ordered to be attached, then touched her arm. "I fought so hard to get you on this mission," he said. "Both of us know this is sabotage."

Nico tried to play dumb. "I don't know what you're talking about..."

"You're connecting the nucleus proprius to the dorsal nucleus," he said.

Nico protested. "No, this is the nucleus proprius."

"It's really not that difficult to study a spinal cross-section," replied Leopold, flatly.

"If you think you could do my job, why drag me into this in the first place?"

"Because you're special, Nico. But not *that* special." He gripped her arm, hard. "This would have cost all of us our lives, our families' lives. Not to mention the damage to the patient. As a doctor, you took an oath to do no harm..."

"Don't talk to me about right and wrong!" said Nico. "Can't you see you are in the pay of a madman?"

"You think the man who gave us *all this* should suffer?" Leopold paused to contemplate his own question a moment. "I wanted you to be part of it. To see it. Ever since we met at the institute in Zurich... I've loved you."

Nico shook her head. "No. We're friends, you're not in love. You don't know what love is. Don't tell me you've thrown your life away for that," she said.

"Maybe I have..." said Leopold, hurt. "I've waited so long for you to see the real me. I've given you everything, even this. And if you can't see how extraordinary this is, how extraordinary Dr Kaparis is, then that makes you very ordinary indeed. So thank you, Nico, thank you for setting my heart free."

Leopold suppressed tears of self-pity, then ordered Amazon to take her back to the *Vitalis* and lock her up. Then he turned away and started to disconnect the Splice cables that had been misplanted on the nerve endings, like the arrows through his heart.

Amazon regarded Nico through eyes narrowed to gimlets of hate. Pan scooted up behind her. They exchanged a few words.

Finn and Carla watched from the cable bale. They saw Amazon grab Nico and scoot with her back up the guide line.

"We've got to follow," said Finn.

There were enough Tyro crew members coming and going for Carla and Finn to drift up after them without being noticed. But what were they actually going to do?

They rose out of the crevasse into the great body of spinal fluid in the canal above. Carla was already thinking ahead. "If we can get back to the *Vitalis* with her, we could try and rescue her and take the ship."

"And do what?"

"I don't know!" she said for both of them.

Ahead, Amazon was forcing Nico back through the cleft in the canal lining, back into the bloodstream, a plume of red cells escaping to pollute the fluid as it opened.

Finn and Carla waited a few moments, then parted the cleft and wriggled back into the bloodstream themselves.

There were no arc lights at this point and the atmosphere back in the red blizzard was menacing. They could only see by the lights on their helmets. Beyond them, the lights of Amazon and her prisoner were disappearing back the way they'd come earlier, through the intervertebral gap.

"Come on," said Finn.

The heartbeat soundtrack had returned too – *dhu-dhu, dhu-dhu, DHU-DHU, DHU-DHU, dhu-dhu, dhu-dhu* – punctuated by spikes of pressure, and a kind of distant whale song...

"ARRGHHH! ARRRRRRRAAA!" Kaparis cried out, struggling to contain
the pain as more connections were made.

He made no sense now, just noise, only breaking from his suffering to
scream no at any suggestion of a pain-killer.

He was a god made flesh, and each nail hammered through him was
a miracle.

"ARRGHHH!"

Dangling just a few metres above him, Santiago flashed his signal
light back up the shaft.

And down they went again.

Santiago began to whisper mad prayers. But Hudson finally had
a good view of one of the screens which so fascinated the technicians.
On it was a 3D model of a man. At its neck, flashing away, was a
green light.

Hudson had seen enough. "OK. Up, Santiago!"

Santiago flashed the signal, and they began to rise again, escaping
in jerks, back up finally towards the roof. Hudson reached inside his

rags and took out a pencil and paper. He scribbled a note. When they reached the dome, runners would have to take the news to the Primo and the authorities as soon as possible. When he finished scribbling, he thrust the note at Santiago, but as he moved, he felt his glasses begin to slip down his nose...

No! He snatched his hand up to catch them before they fell – and caught them, just.

But, unbalanced, he spun, once, a full 360 turn at the end of the rope. It was a small movement in the Great Cavern, and they were so nearly out of the light. But not quite.

"ALARRRRRM!" screamed a voice from below.

Suddenly, there were a hundred eyes on them, and yells, and rifles loading.

"Shoot them down!"

DRTRTRRDT!

Bullets whistled past them. The Carriers in the dome hauled as fast as they could. But not fast enough. Bullets tore through the ropes.

In a hunter's instant, Santiago flipped the bow from his back and whipped an arrow from his rags, piercing Hudson's scribbled note. As the pair began to fall, he drew back his arm and – *THWAMM!* – fired the arrow directly up the shaft, before – *WHAAAAMP!* – the two of them landed on the tented cellophane roof of the operating theatre.

Kaparis cried out in fury.

"Bum," said Hudson.

TWENTY-THREE

Dhu-dhu, dhu-dhu, dhu-dhu, dhu-dhu...

Finn leant forward to scoot up the blood vessel, pursuing the distant lights further up the narrow channel, trying to keep steady in the turbulence. He glanced back at Carla's helmet light bobbing just behind him.

The channel became wider until they could see arc lights ahead at the end of the tunnel. They had reached the larger artery where the *Vitalis* was anchored.

Emerging into its flow, they braked just upstream of the moored

213

submarine. A couple of Tyro crew members were hauling on more cables as Amazon approached the vessel with Nico.

Finn grabbed Carla's arm.

"Let's try and rescue her in the airlocks, where no one will see," Finn said. "Then we can tie up whoever's on board and—"

"Wait. Look!" interrupted Carla, pointing.

Finn turned and saw that instead of going towards the airlocks, Amazon was taking Nico up and over the submarine, dragging her off into the darkness of the blood flow beyond.

"Why are they overshooting? Where's she taking her?"

The last they saw was the flash of a blade as Amazon drew a knife.

"She's going to kill her!" said Finn.

As one, Finn and Carla kicked round their scoots and fired themselves down the artery. They shot over the *Vitalis* and made out two lights dancing in the darkness beyond.

Dhu-dhu, dhu-dhu, dhu-dhu, dhu-dhu...

"There!"

They closed in on pure struggle. Amazon swiping wildly with her knife as Nico fought for her life, kicking, clawing, digging her thumbs into any soft flesh.

Wham! Wham! – Finn and Carla hit them, throwing themselves into the fray, adding to the chaos.

Amazon screamed in uncomprehending fury as Carla grabbed her from above. Finn tried to grab her knife hand, but she ripped it free again, narrowly missing slicing off his arm. She threw Carla off her helmet and realised it was now three against one.

Relishing the challenge, she scooted round 360 – *WHAM* – straight into Nico's midriff, winding her and sending her flailing out into the flow. Carla flew after her.

Finn was left to deal with Amazon. She raised her knife and he could see her screaming *"DIE!"* As she lunged at him, it was his turn to spin 360 – *SMACK—*

His scoot hit steel. Amazon's knife was knocked from her grasp.

Both dived for it, fighting as they raced to grab the knife that flashed like a fish in the flow, just out of reach in the helter-skelter blood slide that was washing them down the twisting, forking, narrowing arteries, ever further away from the *Vitalis*.

Amazon was stronger, but Finn was faster. He grabbed the spinning hilt of the knife and turned back into the struggle just as Amazon tried to whip round to ram him with the scoot – *SHTUMP!* In the chaos, the blade in Finn's outstretched hand ended up buried not in the Tyro's flesh, but in the battery pack on her utility belt – *FZZT!*

It flashed as it shorted out, and straight away – *schlip, schlip, schlip* – fibrous material, short lengths of milky, translucent rope seemed to whip out of nowhere, covering her, strangling her, as she tried to fight back at Finn.

Antibodies.

There was no more charge in her suit to keep them away. Finn stopped fighting and struggled to get away as the immune system closed in on Amazon. First the whipping antibodies, then, out of the gloom, white blood cells swooped in like ghosts to surround and suffocate, enveloping her in moments, turning her into a wriggling cocoon.

Finn watched, horrified – this was no way to go – but before he could do anything, a muffled explosion from within the cocoon called a halt. Amazon's air tanks had ruptured. The struggle was over. And there was no time for guilt.

Dhu-dhu, dhu-dhu, dhu-dhu, dhu-dhu.

Where was he?

Dhu-dhu, dhu-dhu, dhu-dhu, dhu-dhu.

He was being swept down a narrow blood vessel. All he could see was darkness at first. He tried to steady himself on the scoot, then – there! Two lights swung out of the gloom, coming towards him, Carla trying to stabilise Nico on her own scoot. He grabbed them as they were sucked into a smaller blood vessel, which was immediately blocked by the great snowball sarcophagus clot of white cells and platelets that had formed around Amazon.

They found themselves trapped against it, gasping.

"The whites!" said Nico, as more flapping whites rushed to join the others.

"It's OK," said Finn, pointing back at the clot. "They're coming for the dead Tyro. She lost her battery."

"No! We must get away! Get out!" said Nico.

Finn and Carla followed doctor's orders and jammed their scoots into action, each grabbing Nico by an arm to haul her back up along the artery, but they ran straight into a blizzard of white cells and platelets.

"Where are they coming from? Where are all the reds?" asked Carla, as more and more flocked out of the gloom.

Scooooghghghghg – Finn heard the strange sound and looked down.

"What's happening?" The grill intake of his scoot seemed to have sucked in dough-like white cells and jammed. He tried to claw them clear as – *scooooghghghghg* – Carla's scoot jammed too.

Visibility was down to just a couple of metres.

"Just swim! Crawl! We've got to get out of here!" Nico urged.

They swam as hard as they could, further and further into the slowing, blinding, thickening snowstorm of white blots.

"Faster!" gasped Nico.

"What's happening?" cried Carla, as the blood became a white, hot porridge.

"It's the immune system! It's gone into overdrive!"

FEBRUARY 22 01:21 (GMT+3). Lubecki Salt Mine, Romania

The nearest cavern of any size near the airbase in Kluge was in a disused salt mine six miles south of the city.

Grandma and Li Jun had gone there under police escort. On arrival, they donned hard hats and were lowered into an eerie manmade void ten storeys deep.

When she reached the centre of the silent cavern, Li Jun asked for the lights to be switched off. Once they were in total darkness, Grandma felt Li Jun take her hand. The utter blackness was hypnotic, and another door opened in Li Jun's mind.

217

"I remember..." she said.

It was in Siberia, or Switzerland, or the Andes... The secret bases had blended into one, but wherever it was, she was present at a long, late meeting between the Master and the crazed architect of his top-secret HQ, Thömson-Lavoisiér.

The plans for the conversion of a Great Cavern were discussed, and as the details started to come back to Li Jun, she rapidly sketched the basic layout – the henge, the control plant, the command chamber; everything she could remember.

The sketches were zapped straight back to King and Al, and although they were too late to help Hudson, they at least gave the authorities a sense of the size of the task they faced if they were going to attack.

When Li Jun had finished, Grandma was pleased. It had been a successful trip and Al would be pleased his lateral-thinking approach had again borne fruit. She asked for the lights to be turned back up. But then Li Jun stopped her.

"No! There's something else, Grandmother..." she said, squinting back through time. She wasn't done yet.

She saw her recumbent Master. She saw his Scots architect describing his plans, spit flecking his thick beard. She saw Heywood serve them whiskey. She heard them talk about the building and about other things too.

"What things?" asked Grandma.

"About the Master's wife. She was called Ondine..."

TWENTY-FOUR

FEBRUARY 22 02:59 (GMT+3). Body of D.A.P. Kaparis

Finn, Carla and Nico were stuck. Exhausted. Sweat poured off them.

The white cells had congealed into such a thick, hot custard that they were being cooked with every forward stroke. Soon they ceased to be swimmers and became miners as they were dragged further and further down into the mass of cells.

They couldn't possibly keep it up, they'd die of exhaustion. Nico stopped them first.

"Don't give up – we've got to reach the edge. But just stop a moment. Rest…"

"The edge of what? What's happening?" asked Carla.

"It's an inflammatory response. The immune system. It can't identify what it's being attacked by, so it's going into overdrive to isolate the dead Tyro. It's cutting off the whole area. Crushing it and cooking it. Sending in these cells to die and set like concrete. Forming an abscess."

"How far away are we from the edge of it?" Finn demanded.

"Depends... If the body thinks it's a blood infection, it will bury us deep," said Nico.

"What can we do?" asked Finn.

Nico, sweating in her helmet, looked empty of energy and ideas.

"If we can reach the outer edge, we could burst it," she said.

"Burst it?"

"Just like a balloon," said Nico. She thought again of her children, of them playing. There was no way she was going to take this lying down.

"C'mon, kids. Let's dig!" she said.

They began to dig, like moles, like ancient miners buried alive, dragging themselves through the hardening clay, the walls pressing in on them, harder and harder, the heat boiling them in their suits, their air tanks dragging them back, away from life.

Finn tried not to think about the crush, the claustrophobia. As long as he kept moving, as long as his limbs felt they were propelling him forward, he could keep it at bay. But over the next ten, twenty minutes, the digging became useless, the abscess harder, hotter. And soon the three of them were straining for nothing, stuck fast and pressed together, in their own hell.

"This is no good. We can't go any further..." admitted Nico. Then, "Wait, what about your flares?" she said, suddenly hopeful.

The radioactive flares! One of those would get them out. It would also see them removed – resized – and then... killed in front of Kaparis.

But anything was better than this.

"Mine was taken away," added Nico.

Finn checked his belt. Nothing.

And Carla checked hers.

Nothing.

"I guess the Tyro crew don't get issued any flares," concluded Finn.

For a long while none of them spoke.

FEBRUARY 22 03:43 (GMT+3). Carpathian Mountains, Romania-Ukraine border

Movement!

Henri crept from his hole.

Since the comms link to the Carriers had gone down, all watchers had been on high alert. Was the fault technical, or was it more sinister? If it was technical, surely they'd send Santiago across the valley?

Just then, he saw a figure tacking up through the trees on the winding hunter's trail. But this wasn't Santiago. This creature didn't lollop and bound like an animal. This thing was smaller and darted forward in fits and starts. Faltering.

When it stopped altogether, Henri drew his machine pistol and slid expertly down the slope. He ended up standing over a small injured ragged girl.

"Angel…" Olga breathed, and held out a note to him, her hand shaking.

FEBRUARY 22 03:47 (GMT+3). Great Cavern, Monastery of Mount St Demetrius of Thessaloniki

Kaparis was exhausted too. Sweating. The hours of pain, the overkill of sensation was taking its toll.

The Big Swiss Cheese repeated a test he'd been trying for the last hour. He placed a soft ball in Kaparis's right hand. "Once again. Try and squeeze the ball, sir."

The ball trembled in Kaparis's hand. His blood pressure climbed.

"You can do it, Master," said Heywood in an anxious whisper.

Then the ball simply rolled off his open palm and hit the floor.

"ARRGGHH!" Kaparis roared in frustration.

He had been warned he might require years of physiotherapy and rehabilitation, but he had dismissed these concerns out of hand. He was a man of will and of science.

Across the operating theatre, Hudson and Santiago hung from the arms of the Siguri, heads beaten and bowed. Again and again, the questions had been the same: "Who was in the shaft with you? Who sent you? What were you doing?" And again and again, Santiago wailed and Hudson said nothing.

Kaparis felt hot. Outraged that the G&T had got so close – with an idiot bespectacled schoolboy (Hudson instantly recognisable after months under surveillance). There must be a whole conspiracy against him. He would root out and destroy every last bit of it. He would lay waste to every Carrier – then flee.

But not yet. Not when he was so close.

Hot, hot, hot. He couldn't think straight. He wanted to close his eyes and, at the same time, he wanted no part of such weakness. He roused himself and made Hudson and Santiago his most heartfelt pledge.

"As soon as I can move these hands, you will be the first I destroy. I've killed Infinity Drake and I'll kill you and that ghastly hunchback too!"

Hudson felt his heart jump. Was this true? Was this a taunt?

"Doctor?" said one of the Big Swiss Cheese's nurses, trying to get his attention. "Look!"

The nurse pointed to Kaparis's neck. The soft flesh beneath his chin had begun to swell.

Kaparis was so hot, he decided to close his eyes, just for a little while...

Just then, a message came through from the Vitalis.

-.-. .-. .. .-- / -- .. .. -. --. / -- --- - .. ...- . / ..- -. -.- -. ---
.-- -. / ...- .. - .- .-.. .. ... / - --- / .. -. ...- . ... - .. --. .- - .

"Crew missing... Motive unknown... Vitalis to investigate..."

"What's that supposed to mean?" asked a puzzled technician as the surgical team went to work to bring Kaparis round.

Finn... thought Hudson, and felt himself relax again.

The three of them could hardly move now, helmets pressed together in the burning hell of it.

"We must keep going," Nico told them, but reality was setting in as hard as the abscess they were trapped in. They were giving up.

Finn felt bleak, crushed.

They said nothing, nor did they try and move. Finn could see the air regulator readout projected against the inside of his helmet: 47% LCA[19] REMAINING. APPROX. 125 MINUTES.

Three hours. Three and a half.

He had come all this way, Finn thought, all the way across the top of the world, to fulfil an unwanted destiny, to kill the giant...

Now the giant was killing him.

[19] LCA = liquid compressed air. Improved power-to-mass ratio at nano-scale allows more air to be stored in a standard tank than at macro level.

TWENTY-FIVE

FEBRUARY 22 04:00 (GMT+3). C-130 Hercules,
G&T Romanian Command, National Air Defence
Base, Kluge

"She was his second wife and her name was Ondine. She was a
South American beauty and an evolutionary biologist. They met at
a genetics conference in Chile, where he no doubt spotted her as a
perfect fit for his theory of superorganisms[20], one of his chosen few."

---

[20] A superorganism is a group of individual organisms that gather together to better
ensure their survival (e.g. an ants' nest, coral reef, human society). As a young scientist, Kaparis developed a theory that superorganisms worked to serve a few special
individuals (such as himself). In 1993, in a lecture given in Cambridge, his theory was
demolished by Finn's father, Ethan Drake, who pointed out a simple mathematical
error in the statistical method.

225

Grandma was back in the Hercules nursing a mug of tea and telling a love story.

"They were the perfect couple, fabulously rich, hugely intelligent; she as poisonous and hurtful and wilfully cruel as he. They could have had anything their hearts desired. Yet, they wanted more."

Because they knew so little about Kaparis's marriage, and because they were so tired, Al and Commander King were hanging on every word, as was Delta, and the world leaders, up on the screens.

"If you can't improve on perfection, what do you do? Try and preserve it. They set off to try and stay young for ever. Ondine thought she had found the answer in panther stem cells. Injections started. At first it worked. Both Kaparis and Ondine showed improvements in strength, stamina and physique, but then side-effects kicked in. Ondine experienced mood swings and became insane. At some point, she tried to escape from the Kaparis ancestral home. He caught her and there was a struggle. In it, whether by accident or not, he crashed into the wall, onto two crossed swords and a shield of bloodied falcons – the family crest – and one of the swords cut deep into his spine. Ondine was imprisoned by his staff in the Great Cavern beneath the Monastery of Mount St Demetrius, while doctors in Geneva fought to save Kaparis's life. As he recovered, he thought only of revenge, but before he could take it, Ondine somehow managed to escape, disappearing into thin air. It was only when she resurfaced in Brazil a year later, making threats and issuing taunts, that his butler managed to track her down and murder her. Then

Kaparis had her family murdered and every record of her and of the marriage destroyed."

"Charming story, charming man," said King.

"A love story?" said Al.

"Yes –" said Grandma (who had been head nurse in the UK's top criminal psychiatric facility) – "in its way. Some people can't help but turn love into hate. It's an alchemy of sorts."

As they spoke, teams were still scouring official records in South America for any remaining detail.

"Maybe it gives us something we've been looking for, for a long while," said Al.

"What's that?" asked Delta.

"An Achilles heel. A weakness," said Al.

Grandma agreed. "Right next to his heart."

"Given the guy's rap sheet," General Jackman interrupted on screen from the US, "do you really think the murder of one ex-wife is going to make a blind bit of difference? And what are we going to do? Call him up and kinda allude to it in conversation?"

He had a point. The story was just that, and of no immediate use.

Al sighed. "Well, it's another piece of the jigsaw at least."

Further discussion was interrupted by a technician with an urgent message.

"Sir! Blue 4 has Carrier contact and intel from Hudson!"

There was a rush back to the screens and a video feed of Hudson's note, in a hastily written thirteen-year-old's scrawl.

Finn Carla SUPER-NANO INSIDE KAP!!! Doing op with docs, fixing spine! DO NOT DESTROY KAP BODY!! Cavern guarded - 50? Techs and Siguri. Hurry! xox

---

FEBRUARY 22 04:18 (GMT+3). Great Cavern, Monastery of Mount St Demetrius of Thessaloniki

Kaparis, when he occasionally regained consciousness, just saw eyes, masks, faces. They were crowded around his head, examining his swelling neck and attaching new instruments.

"What? What is it?" *spat Kaparis.*

"A blockage – a thrombosis," *said the Big Swiss Cheese,* "caused by an abscess, I should think."

"You THINK?" *Kaparis yelled, as everything went black.*

And again he passed out.

The Big Swiss Cheese ordered a nurse to prepare an anti-inflammatory drip, an antibiotic, and a plasminogen activator. "We'll use them in that order – to reduce the swelling, attack any bacteria and dissolve the blockage. If they don't work, as a last resort we can always try and blast it with ultrasound."

"ARRRRGH!" *Kaparis woke violently as yet another connection was made in his spine. The surgeon watched his blood pressure climb.*

"I'm afraid I'm going to have to insist on a sedative," he told Kaparis while he was still conscious, turning away to prepare it. "Your heart has had far too much for one day."

Kaparis exploded – "NO!" – and his arm shot from his side and seized the errant surgeon by the neck. Kaparis gasped. Even in his fevered state, he realised something significant had happened...

He had moved. It was not his conscious mind but his subconscious that had made the breakthrough. His rage had restored the connection between mind and body.

The Big Swiss Cheese choked because he couldn't breathe.

"HAH!" Kaparis cried in delight, before his hand dropped as he once again fell unconscious.

FEBRUARY 22 04:22 (GMT+3). Body of D.A.P. Kaparis

34% LCA REMAINING. APPROX. 91 MINUTES

"Freshly cut grass," said Finn.

"Gasoline," said Carla.

Nico screwed up her nose at this.

"Curry!" said Nico.

"Curry," agreed Finn.

They were onto favourite smells.

"Baking," said Carla.

"Seaside chip shop," said Finn.

"Babies' heads," said Nico, and her eyes flooded again.

Finn and Carla looked down, waiting for her to manage her emotion.

To avoid talking about the inevitable, they talked about anything at all. Finn and Carla knew far too much about each other after so long on the road, but Nico was new. They made her list her favourite films, books, TV shows, sandwiches, sweets and treats. They talked about ideal holidays, the perfect Christmas. They made her name the seven dwarfs. They laughed and made a genuine connection with her in a way thirteen-year-olds never usually did with thirty-three-year-old neurosurgeons. Nico was more like a favourite teacher, but out of school – a teacher you finally got to know.

But then she would remember her children – Ronny and Raj – and her eyes would fill with impossible tears, and Finn and Carla wouldn't know what to do or say because Nico was back in the grown-up world and may as well have been on Mars.

Then she would stop. Recover. And they would start again. Talking as if the future existed. When they all knew it was disappearing fast. Pressing in as hard as the yellow scum they were trapped in.

Crack... CRACK... cra-ck... cc-crack...

In the absence of wool and knitting needles, Grandma wrung her fingers and cracked her knuckles.

More and more world leaders came online, to watch Al pace, and to watch Commander King cogitate, his eyebrows rising and falling independently as he went through the mental motions.

The whole operation had been jolted awake by Hudson. There was no stimulant like fear. The base had gone on high alert. Every soldier, every part of the operation, had been ordered to prepare for immediate action.

And in the face of all this frantic activity? Al paced. Incapable. In shock, and angry – at the situation, at the terrible options, at himself.

"He's cracked the codes..." Al kept muttering, trying to take in the enormity of what they had learned. He could hardly believe it. Kaparis must have found a way through Ethan Drake's notes, he must have reached the secret heart of Boldklub. And now he was able to shrink whatever he liked to any size he liked and who knew what else might yield from the breakthrough... It was unimaginable. But worse, much worse... Finn...

"He's crackers and he's... he's crackers and he's cracked the codes... and Finn..."

"What's he saying now?" asked the German chancellor.

"It's about the codes again, Madam."

Commander King had heard enough.

"We have to start making some decisions. If Kaparis is having his spinal cord reattached, then I suggest we make a move sooner rather than later, before the operation has any chance of success."

"We have to stop him. Now. We agree on that. But how?" said the British prime minister.

"Do we go in all guns blazing at dawn?" asked General Mount, his military chief.

"That would be suicide – if we assume they are fully prepared, heavily armed and fanatical," said the president of France.

"That's why we wanted to play a long game," said Commander King. "We wanted to make sure we'd covered every angle. But with Hudson taken, with this last message..."

"I will drain him, I will drink his blood..." muttered Delta, fully armed. She hadn't got this close just to let her sister die. "I will stop his heart..."

"There may never be a better time to strike than now," said the prime minister. "The messenger said the Carriers have been locked up and are awaiting their fate. Surely only Kaparis can determine that. And if he's not yet out of this operation..."

"The Primo said specifically, 'The Carriers will rise up on our command'," General Mount pointed out.

"The Carriers are *children*," Grandma scolded from her chair.

"Most of the Tyros are barely in their teens and the Siguri are hired hands; they will know when they're out of their league. If we drop three thousand guys out of the sky on them – believe me, it's going to be over pretty soon," said General Jackman from the White House.

"But with us taking how many casualties? Two, three hundred?" said his boss, the US president.

"That can't be worth it," agreed Commander King. "And yet, look at what Kaparis has achieved in an iron lung... Imagine him running wild – with Boldklub."

"Imagine a lot more than a few hundred casualties," agreed General Jackman.

The fate of the entire operation – and who knew what consequences – hung in the balance.

And everyone was aware that Al had so far said nothing.

Not that Al cared. Al was still deep in his own mind trying to compute the fact that Finn, his beloved boy, was somehow trapped deep within the body of the most evil man on earth. His new philosophy had backfired. What a useless hippy he had been. He'd hung loose and let it all happen, and look what had happened. Kaparis had made a great leap forward that Al couldn't begin to understand, and Finn was microscopic...

Was it too much for him to think about? Too personal? Maybe it was? Maybe there was no way round this problem, rational or irrational. All Al could think to do was scream *HELP*...

"Is he having 'feelings' again? Is he going to share them with the group?" asked an irritated General Jackman.

Grandma watched him too, but the more trouble she sensed he was in, the more she relaxed. She had found that in moments of crisis good people returned to their values, to what they really knew.

Her value was unconditional love.

"Al," she said, "whatever you decide will be right."

Commander King raised an arm to stop anybody else interrupting.

"You were born to do the most difficult things," she continued. "That's why you attract these decisions, because only you can make them, only you are big enough in brain and heart."

Al stopped pacing and looked at her.

"Really? And when you've reached the end of your intellect, the end of your emotion and hoodoo – what do you do, Mum? Do you stick or twist?"

"I am your mother, you are my son. I trust you. You know what to do."

He opened his mouth to object, to say no, her trust was misplaced, he didn't know what to do. To tell her that he didn't have any more ideas, that he'd reached the end of the line. But something... something about that word. Trust...

And a thought, simple and powerful, slapped him hard across the mental space. Finn. He trusted Finn. Just as his mum trusted him, he trusted Finn, absolutely...

Maybe he wasn't required to come up with every answer. Maybe he just had to pass on the baton. To trust Finn. Finn, who'd defeated a doomsday bioweapon; Finn, who'd defeated a nano-bot army; Finn, who had the secret heart of a lion whatever size he was.

Finn would be the one to get them out of this. Of course he would. Al didn't know how, not one clue, but he knew there was no one better placed than Finn.

All Finn needed was... help.

So, what to do? Al turned to the assembled brains and world leaders.

"We ride at dawn."

FEBRUARY 22 05:09 (GMT+3). Great Cavern, Monastery of Mount St Demetrius of Thessaloniki

Kaparis's mind flexed just beneath the surface of sleep.

He seemed to have muscles everywhere now, spikes of feeling that had been driven into his body as if he was a pincushion. While his subconscious was fighting to make sense of it all, his conscious mind was simply trying to wake up.

The more he could feel, the worse he felt. One moment freezing and shaking, the next burning hot. And his neck. The pressure. It was as if he was growing another head.

He began to hallucinate. His mother on a golden horse trailing endless

hair. Infinity Drake expanding to enormous scale, ready to crush him underfoot...

"Snap out of it!" he told himself.

"He's not responding," he heard from somewhere far above him.

FEBRUARY 22 05:10 (GMT+3). Body of D.A.P. Kaparis

16% LCA REMAINING. APPROX. 43 MINUTES

After a long period of silence, Nico began to sing some kind of nursery rhyme in Bengali, a children's round, like "London's Burning", but beautiful.

"We're not going to get out of here, are we?" Carla said.

Finn ignored her. He had to. He tried to flex his feet and create some more room.

Nico had said they must be near the surface of the abscess or the pressure wouldn't be this great, the material wouldn't be this hard. And the heat...

"We have to tell each other what we love. Our favourite people," said Nico.

Finn didn't want to look at her, he didn't want to think about it. This was all too much like it had been when his mum was dying.

"Love. That's all that will be left of us. Don't you want to leave that behind inside him?" she said.

Carla instantly saw the logic. It was their best revenge.

"I love my sister and my stepmother and... my brother Finn," said Carla, her voice cracking as she stared at him with liquid brown eyes. "Though it's so weird seeing him for real and in the flesh," she said, and he laughed.

"Weirder than being 9mm tall and living in your hair?" asked Finn. "Weirder than *this*?" And it was her turn to laugh.

"Now you," said Nico to Finn.

"I love my grandma and my uncle Al and – my sister Carla," he said, returning the compliment. "I love Stubbs and Kelly and Delta. I love Yo-yo. Christabel the vicar. The Queen – I love everyone, really."

"And your mother and father," said Carla.

"Yes, of course. But I'll be seeing them."

"What do you mean?" said Nico.

"I don't know – no one does – what's on the other side of life," said Finn.

Nico's eyes filled with tears again. She didn't have to even say who she loved.

"I just want to hold them and kiss them and talk to them one more time –" Nico said, and she looked at Carla and Finn as if they were her children – "I love you, I am so proud of you, you are the best, most wonderful things that ever happened to me. I want you to fill the world and never be sad, because I love you."

Carla was crying now too.

Great, thought Finn. This was what it was like at the end of his mum's life. He hated this bit. It could go on for days. All he felt was guilt for not joining in.

"Your boys wouldn't want you to cry, especially the older one," said Finn.

Nico laughed in recognition.

"Boys are totally ridiculous," Carla said.

"If you could talk to your mum, if you could go back and tell her all the things you wish you'd said, what would you say?" asked Nico.

"I wouldn't have to say anything," Finn said, "because *I know.*"

"You know what?" asked Carla.

"That I'm never alone. That she's with me. Always."

Nico bit her lip and leant her head against the visor of her helmet where it touched his. Finn and Carla did the same.

"All for one," said Finn.

"And one for all," they replied.

FEBRUARY 22 05:15 (GMT+3). C-130 Hercules, G&T Romanian Command, National Air Defence Base, Kluge

Technicians hit buttons, military commanders started barking orders and finalising battle plans. Suddenly, all was action after Al had given the dawn command.

All except for Grandma, who sat, murmuring "I am your mother... you are my son...?" and going over an idea that had occurred to her the moment she had said the words to Al, turning it this way and that, seeing if it made sense whichever way she looked at it.

Five minutes later, she found Li Jun in a bunk in the main hangar and woke her.

"Grandmother?"

"Li Jun, you must get up, dear. We're about to take off, we're about to attack. But first you must tell me – you must try and remember – what else Kaparis said about Ondine before she tried to run away. Why did he think she was going mad? Did he say anything else, anything at all?"

"No, Grandmother, only..."

"Only what?"

"Something I didn't understand, or didn't hear properly."

"What was it?"

"He said to the architect, 'She didn't just drive me up the wall, she was eating them'."

"She was eating the walls?"

"Yes. It makes no sense, Grandmother."

"Or perfect sense..." said Grandma, and she hurried off to make a phone call to Brazil.

TWENTY-SIX

"He's not responding."

It was becoming a mantra. The first time had been after the anti-inflammatory drip had gone in. The second after the antibiotics. Now it was the turn of the plasminogen activator – the clot-buster, drain cleaner.

Kaparis could see the faces of the surgical team swimming above him. He had once seen the edge of life. There had been nothing but the open-mouthed screams of his victims. And snarling panthers. And Ondine. He had recovered and sworn never to return.

"Do something!" he managed to demand through his delirium. It

240

brought him round and he saw Santiago. Hudson beside him. Twin idiot tormentors.

Kill, *he thought. That will cheer me up. That will break the fever.*

"Bring... me... the... fool..." *he said.*

As the Siguri dragged Santiago to Kaparis, Hudson at last began to crack.

"Stop! I've told Commander King everything. They are coming. You must surrender or die."

Kaparis gasped in laughter and locked his hands awkwardly around Santiago's neck.

"You think I am not ready for Commander King? People like me always win. Because we deserve to," *he said.*

"I'll tell you anything you need to know – just let him go!"

Kaparis laughed again and Santiago began to choke... splutter...

This wretched creature, *he thought,* the antithesis of all that I am... Kill... Yes, kill...

Kaparis passed out and his hands released, letting Santiago slump to the floor, choking.

"He's lost consciousness again. Heart rate dropping!"

The Big Swiss Cheese and his team dived in to save Kaparis. Hudson could feel the tension rising in the room, the first tendrils of panic.

"Get the clot-buster!" snapped the surgeon.

Hudson knew all about panic. As a nurse hurried to fix up a bag covered with toxic warning marks onto the drip stand, Hudson said with quiet assurance, "Give up."

The surgeon turned.

"Save yourselves. This place is surrounded. This man is going to die and there's no way you're going to save him."

The eyes of the Big Swiss Cheese and the surgical team were, for a moment, fixed on Hudson. Then –

Click.

As one, the eyes of the team turned to the source of the noise. Heywood had pulled out a pistol and was levelling it at the head of the Big Swiss Cheese. "Save him or die."

The nurse finished connecting the bag of pink liquid clot-buster to the intravenous tube, and squeezed.

FEBRUARY 22 05:40 (GMT+3). Body of D.A.P. Kaparis

5% LCA REMAINING. 13 MINUTES. CRITICAL!

Finn was so hot he was delirious. They all were. The words had stopped. They had said all there was to say. They were exhausted and waiting for death.

Nico's eyes closed.

Finn let his own lids drop, just for a moment, and from somewhere in his mind's eye he saw a faint, uncanny sparkle... Was this death coming? No... It looked to him like the sparkle from a Spharelite stone, the stone that had once hung round his neck, that had been the only thing left in his father's lab after it had burnt down, part of his experiments, part of himself. When you scratched it, it sparkled.

Spharelite...

He gasped and took a huge breath, snapping awake. And as he did so, the heartbeat beyond him seemed to shift gear from distant jungle drums to a cacophony—

Dhu-dhu, dhu-dhu, dhu-dhu, DHU-DHU-DHU-DHU-DHU-DHU-DHU-DHU...

He wondered if his air had run out and if this was his own heart, if this was his end.

But Carla could hear it too. "What's happening?"

Nico's eyes sprang open. "They're trying something!"

Spharelite, thought Finn. He did not question it, he did not try to make sense, he just thought: *I must not go without a fight*. And so for one last time, he clenched his right fist in the cramped space and drew it back the few inches he could. And he reached out one last time, for the sake of it, from death to life and life to death and back again.

He thumped the meat of his fist against the tomb, against fate, and with all his might...

Thud... Thud...THUDPOCCCCCCCCCOOWWWWWWW!!!!!

The world exploded.

"ARRGGHHgggggggghhhhh!" Finn screamed, as the shockwave burst through them and through the surface of the detonating abscess.

"ARRRRGGGGGHHHHHHHH!" Nico and Carla screamed, as they clung to each other, the hard pus shattering around them as unleashed tension propelled them away from the abscess core into a liquefied blur of swollen tissue...

Nico rebooted from emotional wreck to highly trained medic in less than a second.

"IT'S BLOWN!"

"IIIIIIII KNOOOOOOOOW!!!" Finn yelled in cathartic ecstasy as they slowed to a halt in a confusion of water, random cells and – red blood cells.

"Find fresh blood!" shouted Nico. "Find an artery! All roads must lead back the way we came, they have to... Just find a blood flow and swim against it!"

But where? They were in a grim ocean of debris. Only one thing appeared clearly – the projection on the front of Finn's visor:

3% LCA REMAINING. 8 MINUTES. CRITICAL!

But they were free.

Finn grabbed the scoot where it still dangled from its tether at his ankle and ripped away the lumps of white goo that blocked its intake, as if picking its teeth. Carla did the same, while Nico frantically searched for fresh blood, looking every which way.

"THERE!"

2% LCA REMAINING. 5 MINUTES. CRITICAL!

Dhu-dhu, dhu-dhu, dhu-dhu, dhu-dhu.

It's like those deep-sea diving films, thought Finn, *those ocean trench explorations.* The swollen tissue was a soup, crowded with debris, jet black beyond their headlight beams. But Nico had spotted it – fresh red blood cells rising like smokestack from somewhere deep beneath.

244

Carla and Finn with Nico between them spiralled down around the smokestack until they found the billowing source. It was like a magma-spewing vent on the ocean floor. A blood vessel blown open by the exploding abscess and not yet sealed.

"That's it! In there!"

Finn and Carla, getting used to the three-legged race they were in, bowed their heads and angled their scoots and shot straight into the snowstorm of blood cells.

2% LCA REMAINING. 4 MINUTES. CRITICAL!

They bounced off the walls of the open blood vessel, felt the pressure increase, and found themselves back in the game, back in the arterial system, scooting up against the flow of blood, flying up the tight wriggling pink-white tunnels they'd been washed down so long before, into the blizzard flow of blood cells, the clear plasma a joyous relief after the clouded inflammation, as they twisted and turned until suddenly—

SWOOOOOOOOOSH!

They emerged out of the tunnels into one of the big pipes, the larger blood vessels where surely, if they just kept going...

"Follow the red brick road!" Nico urged them, her mind beginning to drift as the oxygen levels began to fall. Finn could feel his own heart thumping as it fought to squeeze every atom of oxygen from his tanks.

"GO!" agreed Finn, starting to panic—

1% LCA REMAINING. 3 MINUTES. CRITICAL!

"I can't..." Carla mumbled. He could hear her panting. If she lost consciousness...

"JUST KEEP GOING!" he cried, yelling his mum's words, urging Carla on with all his heart as they steered out into the largest artery yet.

"This must be it!" Finn shouted. He dipped his head and pointed his toes and led them speeding on into the darkness, into the flow, into more red, into unconsciousness, stars now beginning to appear before his eyes, and—

THUD.

They hit the artery wall, the shock waking him up.

"Light!" yelled Carla.

They drove forward once more, their heads ringing and their vision contorted, fixed on a single expanding eye, a searchlight, and – around it – a body and two huge arms.

The *Vitalis!* The mother ship had found her young.

Carla and Nico passed out as the mighty impellers eased the vessel round in the stream, her hold doors opening to scoop them up.

FEBRUARY 22 05:56 (GMT+3). Great Cavern, Monastery of Mount St Demetrius of Thessaloniki

Back... Back he came, rushing back, his mind clearing, the nightmares floating away... The gargoyle faces, the panther child, the curses and hisses of the dead and undead... all gone.

"BP 120 over 49 falling, heart back under 120, temperature reverting to normal," reported the nurse to the Big Swiss Cheese as Kaparis started to come round.

"We've done it…" the surgeon said, sweat pouring off him.

The fever had broken, the moment of maximum danger had passed.

"You can put that away now," he barked at Heywood, still holding the gun. "We've saved him." The gun was slowly lowered.

"Sir!" interrupted a nurse, pointing to Kaparis's chest. It was no longer rising and falling in a mechanical pattern, in time with the cycle of the ventilator. It was rising and falling of its own accord – almost fighting against the ventilator.

"Take off his mask," ordered the surgeon.

They unclipped the breathing apparatus.

HISSSS… The chest continued to rise and fall.

"He's breathing independently. We've done it!"

An eye popped open. "I think you'll find I've done it…" Kaparis said, *his first freely spoken words in more than fifteen years.*

"Yes… Master," whispered the surgeon, in awe.

Kaparis felt a whole continent of new sensation… of new being. He felt the cool sweat running down his body. He felt his lungs fill and deflate. He felt like a creature washed up on a beach.

Reborn.

TWENTY-SEVEN

FEBRUARY 22 06:02 (GMT+3). Body of D.A.P.
Kaparis

Deep in the patient's neck, Dr Leopold surveyed the night's work. The great crevasse between the two severed sections of spinal cord was lit up like Christmas, a glade of glittering cables, swaying like seaweed in the crystal-clear fluid.

The last of the cables was about to be deployed.

Sir James scooted over, exhausted but in a similar state of wonder. He grabbed Leopold's hand, shaking it in emotional congratulation.

"This is the resurrection, this is the light!"

*

SSSSSSSSSSSSSSSSSS – air gushed into the airlock. Finn ripped off his helmet and gulped, gasping at the cool, fresh, life-giving air. Sweet oxygen, knocking sense back into him.

He hauled up Carla and Nico, tearing at their helmets, willing them to breathe. Both were deathly pale. He beat at their sternums and slapped their backs, trying to pummel them back to life.

And there was life left in them, just. They began to splutter and take desperate shallow breaths.

"COME ON!" Finn yelled, as the waters subsided around them. "BREATHE!"

They groaned. He didn't know which one to help first. He was in a blur of panic. He had to bring them round before...

Tschchht—

The wheel on the airlock turned and the door automatically opened, spilling the three of them into the body of the *Vitalis*. Finn thumped open an emergency medical panel and pulled out a mask. Oxygen began to flow. He jammed it onto Carla's face—

Tschchht – the door of the next airlock opened.

A fluorescent green spectre emerged and barked out an order to the bridge.

"Return to base," said the pilot's voice over the intercom.

"Roger," said Pan. Their most unlikely saviour. He had emerged from the airlocks when they were in the hold and shoved them straight back inside.

Finn slumped to the floor and pretended to recover. The moment

Pan saw his face, he would be finished. Pan grabbed the hair at the back of Carla and Nico's heads to check they were still breathing.

"Where's Amazon?" Pan demanded. "We've been patrolling every hour!"

Finn took a gasp for effect. "She's dead."

Carla groaned as she regained consciousness. Finn knew he had to talk before she gave them away.

"Her battery failed. The body attacked her," said Finn.

"Why didn't she use her flare?" demanded Pan.

"She panicked," said Finn. He could feel Carla's eyes on him, figuring out what was going on.

"Panicked?" spat Pan in disgust. "She did not accept death for the Master?"

"No."

"Scum!" barked Pan, and slammed his helmet against the airlock door. The shame of it! His eyes bulged in psychic pain. Then they lighted on the prone green form of Nico. The prisoner.

"Amazon had orders to kill *her*!" His face became a snarl and he raised his helmet again, ready to dash it against Nico's head.

"NO!" ordered Carla, and Finn jumped across Nico's body to protect her.

Pan hesitated for a fraction of a second... Processing shock at their disobedience. Processing the face he was looking at... Infinity Drake's face...

Pan's whole body became a snarl, a downward killing force led by the helmet—

Tzzzzot – *Tzzzzot* – anchor lines fired from the hull of the *Vitalis* as it docked. The craft twitched, Pan rocked, and Finn kicked out to ensure – *SMASH!* – the helmet missed his head and crashed into the metal floor.

"Vitalis *secured...*" came the pilot's voice over the intercom.

"ALARRRRRM!" cried Pan. As Finn instinctively struck out – *BAM* – Pan clipped him hard with the back of his helmet. Finn felt his eye scream and his head slam against the floor. Pan appeared over him and shot an iron hand down to snap around Finn's neck.

"Ag... Uc..." Finn tried desperately to breathe. The pain in his Adam's apple was excruciating.

BAM – relief came as Carla slammed into Pan like a tornado of hair, knees and nails. Finn kicked himself free just as the Tyro pilot jumped down through the engine-room hatch. With a kick, he sent Carla flying. Now it was two against two.

Finn saw red, roared up from the floor, and in a desperate play-ground scramble managed to butt the pilot and headlock Pan. But Pan was pure wire, pure brainwashed Tyro strength, and he dug claws into Finn's face to prise himself free.

"Arrrgghhhhhhh!" Carla screamed as – *SLAM* – the pilot shoved her into an airlock, spun the wheel and threw a locking bar across to open the valves and flood the chamber.

"No!" cried Finn, but – *BANG* – Pan caught him with a karate kick to the side of his head. Time slowed as he flew sideways, seeing stars... Then speeded up again as he hit spent air tanks. *SLAM.* Finn grabbed one and with a great grunt of effort lifted it, and swung.

251

Hard, heavy metal arced through the tight space – *WHUCK* – clipping the pilot on the point of the jaw. In a sickening instant he was down, and out cold.

Pan ran back to the crew quarters. For one triumphant moment, Finn thought he was on the ropes... but then he reappeared. With a harpoon gun.

He raised it like a rifle, and pointed it square at Finn. With only a second to think, Finn grabbed the dazed pilot and raised him as a human shield. Pan gave a bark of laughter and simply fired – *KSCHHOOOOOTD!* – *WHAM!* The harpoon shot straight through the midriff of the stricken pilot. Finn felt hot steel skim the right side of his belly and he dropped the pilot in shock.

This is the end, Finn realised, *he's going to kill me*. But his blood was up and he didn't care. In fact, he'd never felt more alive. He flew at Pan, just as Pan swung the butt of the harpoon gun – *WHACK*. Finn took a savage blow and hit the floor.

Pan appeared over him, and raised his harpoon butt again to bring it down and finish Finn off.

Then from nowhere – *WHAM!* – an air tank smashed into the side of Pan's head, almost knocking it off.

Finn looked across.

Nico... Still a little dazed. Still amazed at what she'd just done.

"Quick!" shouted Finn, and dived for the airlock. He unlocked the wheel and spun it in reverse to let the air back in. Pan was struggling up again, staggering back, determined to fight on to the death, wanting more, but for the moment as harmless as a drunk.

The airlock opened and out spilled a spluttering, swearing Carla, a little mermaid gone bad. Finn then grabbed Pan and shoved him into the airlock in her place, delighting in kicking his desperate hands from the riveted frame and – *SLAM* – banging home the door. The wheel spun and he threw the locking bar across, leaving Pan to his fate.

"Come on!" he said, and the three of them climbed up to the bridge.

Beneath the great glass bubble, glorious in the *Vitalis* lights, was the endless flow of surging blood cells. But they could also see, emerging from the entrance to the intravertebral foamina, a line of fluorescent yellow and green figures; the returning Tyro crew and two medics, making their way back to the mothership and about to discover they were locked out.

"We can't kill them," said Carla.

"They've got the radioactive flares. They can get out," said Finn.

"And what about us?" asked Nico.

Finn turned and jumped into the pilot's chair, trying to figure out the controls, dual joysticks set into the armrests, fingertip panels and screens cascading data.

"What are you doing?" asked Nico.

"We need to get out of here, before *they* get in," said Finn, as concerned Tyros started scooting up to the glass canopy, signalling to them to open the airlocks.

"Stay out of view, Nico," warned Finn. "We can't let them know you survived." Nico ducked back down the stairway.

On his screens, Finn saw the Tyros outside had managed to open the airlock and release Pan. He would live. Finn felt a pang of regret, but also, *Better out than in.* He gripped the twin joysticks and nudged them forward. The *Vitalis* lurched, nearly knocking Carla off her feet, as it strained against the anchor lines. The Tyros at the glass stopped trying to signal and instead started hammering and threatening. Even Leopold popped up to stare through with disbelieving eyes at Finn.

Finn shoved the joysticks forward again, and again the craft kangarooed on the spot.

"Let me have a go!" said Carla, all but kicking Finn out of the hotseat.

CRACK CRACK CRACK CRACK! The Tyros were now smashing something against the glass canopy.

With a curse and a prayer, and trusting the instincts of her flying-ace sister, Carla scrolled through the screens.

CRACK CRACK CRACK CRACK!

"Quick!" shouted Finn.

"Just have to figure out how to – aha! – disengage the anchors." She touched a hyperlink and – *Tz-Tz-Tz-Tzoot!* – at once the four anchor lines were released.

For a moment, the *Vitalis* drifted, then as Carla eased the joysticks forward, the mighty craft *SWOOOOOOSHED* off at maximum thrust, leaving Leopold, Sir James, Pan and the Tyro crew tumbling and struggling in the receding darkness.

"Now what?" said Nico, emerging as the *Vitalis* shot away up the artery.

"We kill the giant," said Finn.

PART
FOUR

PART
FOUR

TWENTY-EIGHT

Kaparis writhed and twitched like bacon frying in a pan. Every attempt at movement was trial and error, but he was getting a grip.

In addition, his perfect, cooling mind was putting together the events of the past few hours. Logical actions and solutions were presenting themselves.

If Hudson was here, the G&T would not be far behind. That said, it would be suicide on their part to attack this fortress: the terrain alone would defeat them. Although, it would be a delight to witness... But then the world, which had till recently been a clam, was now his oyster. He intended to skip through every meadow, splash in every puddle… He must escape. Now. They must not get any closer.

"Heywood! Prepare the escape vehicle."

"Yes, Master," said Heywood, and he immediately left the operating theatre.

With great effort, and to general astonishment, Kaparis rolled onto his side, then raised his head.

The surgical team stood round in awe. Hudson and Santiago rightly cowered.

He would take the Hudson boy with him. A hostage. Keep him alive until he was well clear.

Outside the operating theatre, Heywood hit a red button and a panel opened in the rock wall of the Great Cavern. Behind it was a Polaris ballistic missile, adapted as an escape vehicle. Kaparis had bought a dozen of them at the end of the Cold War and they had proved invaluable. The missile slid out on tramlines while a launch ramp was hurriedly assembled.

Inside the theatre, Kaparis braced an arm against the operating table and pushed. Too hard – he was propelled from the bed. But before he could hit the floor, his arms and legs fired reflexively outwards and he clung on… He hung for a moment, half on half off the apparatus, like an orang-utan.

Instinct. Another breakthrough. Don't try, he told himself, just be. Your brilliant subconscious mind will unscramble the signals.

The surgical team helped him into a sitting position.

"I can sit!" he said, looking down at his dangling legs like a delighted toddler. He even managed to bring his hands together for a single clap, provoking nervous laughter.

"Heywood!" called Kaparis.

The dutiful butler returned and, eyes shining, extended a splendidly tailored arm towards his Master. Kaparis gripped it and slid off the operating table onto his feet. Balance sensors in his inner ear fired signals down his new spine and he tipped his weight forward... to stand.

Kaparis, giddy with new sensation, lifted one leg, swung his hips, and put the leg down. A step! Two!

"AHAHA!" he exclaimed. He could walk! He would run! He would drink a waterfall and eat a horse! He would dance across mountains like a singing nun!

But not just yet.

"Sir..." said the assistant surgeon, noticing a blip on a monitor.

Kaparis was still connected to a dozen machines, trailing wires.

"What?"

A particle scanner was held over his neck.

"They're on the move."

On screen, Kaparis saw the green Vitalis marker travelling down his neck. Then his eye was caught by bright white specks that began to appear at the old injury site.

"Distress flares!" snapped the Big Swiss Cheese.

What were they doing?

"Get them out!" ordered Kaparis.

The team sprang into action and laid him down.

Something had gone wrong. What? He could not let this happen – he would not, not after all he'd been through. He must act. Now.

"And fire up the hot area!"

"Kill the giant?" said Carla.

"As soon as we leave Kaparis's body, he's going to kill us, one way or another," reasoned Finn. "If we can stay down here, we can keep him occupied until the G&T gets here – or maybe we can even stop him altogether."

"And live in his rotting corpse till the cavalry show up?" said Carla.

"You got any better ideas?"

"How are we going to do it?" Nico asked.

"*I* don't know – *you're* the doctor. You must kill people all the time?"

Nico turned to take in the blizzard of blood cells hitting the dome. *Dhu-dhu, dhu-dhu, dhu-dhu, dhu-dhu.*

After only a moment's thought, she came up with a plan.

"The pacemaker."

"The what?"

She located the *Vitalis* on a 3D arterial map and then shifted the view to zoom in on different areas of the beating heart.

"We're halfway down the main vertebral artery," she explained, "the blood supply to the spine. If we follow the flow, we'll get back to the heart – an organ so important it has a little brain of its own,

260

the pacemaker, a nerve bundle that tells it when to beat. If we can get close enough to it via the coronary arteries, we could swim out and cut through the nerves with a laser scalpel to shut it down."

"Genius!" said Finn.

"Simple," said Nico.

Carla, at the controls, put her foot down.

Dhu-dhu, dhu-dhu, dhu-dhu, dhu-dhu.

In the Great Cavern power began to throb around the henge of particle accelerators.

The Big Swiss Cheese had plunged a hypodermic needle deep into Kaparis's neck, guiding it expertly into position before slowly drawing out the white flecks he could see on screen.

Kaparis had to remain absolutely still. Though he wanted to scream.

The Swiss Cheese removed the needle, chock-full of blood.

"Gotcha!" he congratulated himself, and handed it over to be rushed to the centre of the henge. But the green dot on the screen just kept on moving.

"What's it doing!" barked Kaparis.

"Vitalis approaching the subclavian artery!" shouted the surgeon's assistant.

"It's heading for the heart!" the Swiss Cheese realised. "Work!" he shouted at Kaparis.

"What?" spat Kaparis.

"Your heart! Work, sir! We need to get it pumping…"

Dhu-dhu, dhu-dhu, dhu-dhu, dhu-dhu.

As it swung into the subclavian artery, the *Vitalis* shook. The force of the flow was tremendous.

Carla gripped the joysticks and tried to keep a steady course, tried to ride the storm.

Finn and Nico held on and watched their progress on screen. They were barely moving against the flow.

"Can we go any faster?" asked Finn.

"We're almost at maximum," said Carla.

A nuclear power indicator showed they were about to tip off the green scale into the red.

"Increase the power. Take us into the red," Finn said.

Nico looked at the map. "He's right. We've got no choice."

"OK, taking it up," said Carla and pushed a power slide all the way up – *WOOOOOOOOOM!*

Power bloomed through the craft, the impeller blades becoming a blur as the craft surged forward into the river of blood, heading for its source.

DHU-DHU, DHU-DHU, DHU-DHU, DHU-DHU, the heart seemed to hammer back.

Nico watched the power indicator climb into the red.

"It's working!" said Finn, following the progress of the flashing dot as it moved down the chest towards the next major turning point...

"They're nearly at the aorta!" the assistant surgeon reported as an oxygen tank rose and fell.

When ordered to "work" to increase his heart rate, Kaparis had grabbed the nearest thing to hand, and was now repeatedly bench-pressing the tank above his head.

Kaparis began to sweat.

The aorta. The main road out of the heart. Highway number one.

"Faster, sir!"

DHU-DHU, DHU-DHU, DHU-DHU, DHU-DHU.

The aortal flow hit them like a hurricane, like being pummelled by a million fists. The blood cells were no longer distinct, but a blur, a red glow. Finn clung to the pilot's chair for dear life.

Every fibre of the ship's being was straining. What would go first? Would the engines fail? Would the glass canopy shatter?

Carla kept her eyes fixed front and drove them on into the abyss. Nico held on and prayed.

The aorta was miles wide at their scale. But if they could stand it, if they could just make the turn into the coronary artery at the mouth of the heart...

Beep beep beep beep beep beep...

Danger lights started flashing on the screens. Overheating lights.

"What's that?" screamed Carla.

"The engines! They're hot as hell!" yelled Finn.

Then came another siren.

NEEW-eu- NEEW-eu- NEEW-eu- NEEW-eu- NEEW-eu...

Carla looked down. A yellow radiation hazard symbol. Flashing up at her.

WARNING MELTDOWN! WARNING MELTDOWN!

Nico took one last look at the map. They were stuck halfway down the aorta and nothing was going to drive them further through the flow.

"That's it!" she shouted. "We're not going to make it!"

Carla killed the power and raised the impeller arms, as if in surrender, and the ship was instantly blown back by the flow, the blur of red becoming a billion cells again.

DHU-DHU-DHU-DHU-DHU-DHU-DHU-DHU.

And they became part of it. The endless remorseless flow.

"You've done it, sir! You've done it!"

Kaparis was exhausted.

The increased heart rate had flushed the craft back around his body. Currently it was travelling down his left arm. The Big Swiss Cheese was hurriedly preparing a large hypodermic needle.

Kaparis flicked his beady eyes from the position of the Vitalis *on the 3D map of his body to the henge outside.*

WOOOOOOMMMMMMMMMMMM!

The crazy energy in the core resolved into a perfect throbbing white orb of pure light. Boldklub had been achieved. The hot area. Now it was only a matter of time and quantum physics. No one had even been reduced to a one hundred thousandth of their actual size before. And certainly no one had ever been brought back.

In a few seconds, the Boldklub cycle ended and power was cut to the henge.

The orb dissolved into a billion sparkles. And there, at the centre of the core, he saw it. A pile of bodies in fluorescent green and yellow wetsuits, slithering and steaming, full-sized and... alive!

"Leopold!" he barked, as he saw him lift off his helmet.

The technicians ran in and pulled an exhausted Dr Leopold from the wet heap.

"Master..." he managed to say. "It's Drake, Master! Infinity Drake!"

"There's no way we're going to get into the heart against that kind of flow," said Finn.

They were listening to the ticking, cooling engines, letting the blood flow take them, giving the *Vitalis* a rest.

"Wouldn't we go back round through the veins? Don't they go back round to the heart?" asked Carla.

"Yes, but on the wrong side," said Nico. "To get back to the red half, we need to go once through the heart on the blue[21] side, round

---

[21] Blue – shorthand for the deoxygenated blood carried in the veins, to distinguish it from the red (oxygenated) blood, although in reality "blue" blood is a dull red.

to the lungs, then back again to the red half, trying to make an impossible turn as we get spat out, praying the heart doesn't crush us in the ventricles along the way..."

KDOOOOOSH!

Suddenly a wall of silver slammed straight into the flow ahead of them, the force of the arrival sending a shockwave through the ship as – *CLANG!* – the *Vitalis* bounced off it.

"What the hell...?" yelled Carla, pumping the controls.

"Get us out of here!" said Finn, getting there first. "It's a needle! They're trying to suck us out!"

Carla fired the impellers to turn 360 and thrust back up the flow, but suddenly they were being sucked down the steel cliff, backwards, into the black mouth of the tip of the hypodermic.

"GO!" cried Nico.

Carla slammed the joysticks forward and gave the engines everything she'd got, the ship again shuddering against the force of the flow, being dragged ever faster back into the void until, just as suddenly as it started... it stopped.

"It must be full!" realised Nico, as the massive steel shaft completely withdrew.

"They missed! GET OUT OF HERE!" yelled Finn.

Carla reeled the *Vitalis* round and sped off in the direction of the flow.

"Which way?"

"Any way!"

"Damn. Missed," said the Swiss Cheese, holding the full phial of blood.

"Incompetent!" snapped Kaparis.

The Swiss Cheese took up another needle.

Damn that Drake, *thought Kaparis.*

"Wait!" shouted Finn as they sped away through the arteries. "Kill the engines! Kill the reactor! They can only trace us because of the atomic signal. Shut down the reactor, or we're sitting ducks!"

Carla killed the engines and began to slap everything off on the control screens.

Nico saw it first – REACTOR SAFETY SHUTDOWN – and hit it.

Instantly the lights died.

The world around them flicked from red to black. Inside the bridge there was total darkness and silence for a moment—

Just *dhu-dhu, dhu-dhu, dhu-dhu, dhu-dhu.*

The Swiss Cheese paused before he broke the skin.

"Where has it gone?" demanded Kaparis.

"They must have switched off the reactor."

"FIND THEM!" yelled Kaparis.

The *Swiss Cheese* plunged the needle in anyway.

KDOOOOOSH!

The *Vitalis* shook again as the needle burst into the flow. Again they felt a change of direction, but as the auxiliary power units kicked in and dim emergency lighting returned, they could see no steel.

"Missed!" said Finn.

In a few seconds, the flow returned to normal.

KDOOOOOSH! went another needle, but this time further away.

"I think it worked," Finn dared to suggest, as they drifted on down the artery.

Kaparis examined the pincushion that his lower arm had become.

"You butcher!" he yelled at the Big Swiss Cheese.

Drake, Drake, ghastly Drake! How had the impossible been allowed to happen?

TWENTY-NINE

Dhu-dhu, dhu-dhu, dhu-dhu, dhu-dhu.

Blood ran over the bridge of the *Vitalis* like lifeless mud, a sea of dead jellyfish.

They had been tossed and turned back through narrowing blood vessels until, somewhere in the flexor carpi ulnaris muscle, they had bounced off oxygen-hungry tissue and drained into a vein.

"What happens now?" asked Carla.

"We're in the veins, deoxygenated, being pumped back round to the heart and lungs," said Nico.

"Will we make it through the heart?" asked Finn.

269

"Depends how much the craft will take," said Nico.

"Options," said Finn. "Can we make it to the pacemaker?"

"No. We'll never make the turn. We'll be spat out on the red side like a bullet from a gun," said Nico. "Right now, we don't have much control, but we can keep drifting round the entire system, as long as we don't fire up the reactor."

Dhu-dhu, dhu-dhu... DHU-DHU, DHU-DHU.

The three of them gripped the pilot seat harder as the turbulence increased.

"Hang on tight! This must be the heart!" said Nico.

DHU-DHU, DHU-DHU, DHU-DHU, DHU-DHU.

All at once, thunder seemed to break around them, blackness and violence and noise. Everything shook and Finn was thrown up against the glass canopy, but in a heartbeat – literally – they were through it.

Finn ended up winded on the deck, but the jolt had given him an idea...

"The reactor," he said, "it was overheating...".

"So?"

"So what happens when a nuclear reactor overheats?"

"It explodes?" said Nico.

"Right," said Finn.

"Like a nuclear bomb?" said Carla.

"Something like that... It's got to do some damage anyway," said Finn. "We could trap the craft somewhere, run it on full throttle till it explodes, while we get away."

Above, their world was changing again. The cells rushing past were springing back to bright red life as they pushed through the lungs, picking up oxygen.

"That's the craziest thing I ever heard," said Carla.

"But it could just kill him! If we pick the right place to do it..." said Finn, thinking hard.

"The brain!" said Nico, slapping the console. "We'll head for the brain. We can hide there anyway – and we can switch all the systems back on, as no one's going to go slamming needles through the brain. As long as we stay inside his skull, we're safe. And if we do blow the craft up, then we can do some real damage there too."

"Great! Let's go!" said Finn. "What are we waiting for?"

"We're waiting for this..." said Carla.

DHU-DHU, DHU-DHU, DHU-DHU, DHU-DHU.

"Hold on tight – we're going through the heart again. On the red side," said Nico, as the *Vitalis* raced down the pulmonary vein back towards the heart. They had to act fast.

"Switch on the reactor and fire the engines!" Nico shouted over to Carla. "Slow us down as we exit!"

"COPY!" shouted Carla, and she gripped the controls as they hit the heart.

DHU-DHU, DHU-DHU, DHU-DHU, DHU-DHU...

The engines screamed and the impellers were a blur as Carla did everything possible to hold the *Vitalis* in the manic aortal blood flow.

"Hold fast!" yelled Nico, focused on the map, as the green dot was forced up the aorta. "Any second... NOW!"

"They're back!" yelled the Swiss Cheese as the green light flashed to life on the circulatory hologram, the green dot swinging out of the aorta into the subclavian artery, riding the curves and currents like a spacecraft sling-shotting around a planet.

"Needle!" demanded Kaparis.

The Swiss Cheese wielded a new monster needle capable of penetrating the sternum.

"Allow me!" said Leopold, staggering in and swiping it off him.

As the dot slowed in the subclavian artery to swing into the carotid that led up to the brain, Leopold let out a bellow and drove the needle down through Kaparis's chest like a stake through the heart of a vampire –
"ARRRRRRRRRGH!"

The needle missed and the green dot was pumped straight up the carotid artery at speed.

"It's heading for the brain!" yelled the assistant surgeon.

"DAMN YOU!" roared Kaparis, as he watched the green dot fly north.

"Nearly there!" yelled Nico.

All was red rush again. Carla steered as best she could, trying not to hit the walls, as Nico, at the map of red lines, shouted out directions.

"We're past the jaw! OK, let's pull over... hit a side road!"

Carla swung left and found the wall of the mighty blood vessel. At the first opening she found, she shot the *Vitalis* forward, then swung it round 180 to stabilise it in the flow.

"Are we there yet?" Finn asked.

"We're there yet," said Nico, struck by the absurdity of it all. "We're in Kaparis's brain."

To Finn, it didn't look that different from anywhere else they'd been – just a blizzard of blood in the headlights. But the idea of it…

"What do we do now?" asked Carla.

Finn smiled. "Let's mess with his head."

Dr Leopold, the Big Swiss Cheese and his surgical team, the Siguri – even Heywood – all quailed. They had seen Kaparis angry before, very angry, but then he had been trapped in an iron lung, with not even his head visible beneath its optical array.

Now they saw the full ghastly range of his presence and his expression, the anger of his entire being, twisting and twitching with rage.

"GET IT OUT!" Kaparis foamed.

The Swiss Cheese had to come clean.

"If we stick a needle directly into your brain, we'll do far more damage than a dozen Infinity Drakes."

"You, sir, do not know DRAKE!"

Heywood had already been to check the chamber and confirmed the nano-scale Apache had disappeared. Somehow, Drake must have escaped the belly of *Raffles*, boarded the helicopter and flown it into the hot area, to hijack the mission.

Kaparis had already ordered the lizard to be shot.

"Leopold!"

"Master?"

"What could they do to me?" he demanded, suddenly gripped by mortal fear. "What damage?"

"None, Master."

"What?" said Kaparis.

"Don't worry, sir. As soon as they open the airlocks, they will get a nasty surprise," said Leopold, and beamed.

23% LCA REMAINING. APPROX. 64 MINUTES

In the hold of the *Vitalis*, Pan breathed. He had taken the air tank from the first Tyro crew member to reach him in the airlock. He had clung on in the hold as the craft shot off with the hold doors open. Then he had allowed himself to be shut in.

He had waited, listening – listening oh-so-hard for any sign of activity at the airlocks, willing Infinity Drake to come out. *Come out, come out, wherever you are...*

It was no longer just duty. It was personal.

All he had to do was hate, and wait.

THIRTY

FEBRUARY 22 06:50 (GMT+3). Carpathian
Mountains, Romania-Ukraine border

It was snowing again. Not heavily, just enough to obscure the advance.

In his snow hole, Henri Clément packed the last of his kit. The Commando Hubert members had been ordered to new positions, with instructions to target the timber wheelhouse.

Already Henri's mouth was watering. He savoured fine violence in the same way he savoured fine wine. Around him the forest teemed with silent killers. Nearly a thousand special forces, ground troops from five different countries, were converging on the monastery, on skis, in Arctic camouflage, and from all points of the compass.

At Kluge airbase, a twenty minutes' flight south, airborne troops were being assembled, supplied, drilled and briefed.

FEBRUARY 22 07:04 (GMT+3). Body of D.A.P. Kaparis

Finn headed for the airlock.

Dhu-dhu, dhu-dhu, dhu-dhu, dhu-dhu.

They had parked the *Vitalis* high in the arterial system, in as narrow a place as they could get into and still turn the craft around. Already an indistinct whale song vibrated through the hull – sounds filtering into the brain, from the outside world, through Kaparis's ear.

Exactly where Finn was heading.

Before they blew up the craft and killed Kaparis, or disabled him, or whatever it took to stop him getting away, Finn wanted to say goodbye and let him know who was about to pull the trigger. Carla and Nico had been reluctant to go along with this part of the plan, but both knew, with Finn and Kaparis, it was no longer rational. It was personal.

Nico checked the guideline comms link console and activated it. "It's live to the bridge. It says there's four hundred metres of tether on the drum, just enough to get you to the ear."

"Don't let go of it!" insisted Carla, helping him on with a new tank of gas. "And make sure you come back! We haven't come this far just to lose you to a bit of name calling."

Finn unhooked the lock bar on one of the airlocks.

"I promise. I just want to get close enough to deliver a personal message."

He still couldn't get over Carla at this scale. She looked doubtful.

"Carla! I'll be OK."

He locked on the helmet, checked the regulator and the scoot, then closed the airlock door. The blood-side valve opened and in a moment the chamber was flooded with warm plasma.

He opened the door into the hold. It was spooky in the dim light, the framework of empty cable racks like a skeleton. He pushed himself through the liquid to the reels of communication lines, the umbilical tethers. Line #1 was already gone, so he attached Line #2 to his belt.

"OK, I'm on. Open it up."

"Got it," replied Carla from the bridge.

With a whirr, the great hold doors began to open. Red light appeared and blood cells poured in. By the time the doors were fully open, he was already outside and balancing in the bloodstream on the scoot. He swerved round so that they could see him from the bridge.

"Take the third blood vessel, the narrowest one," said Nico over the comms line, pointing out an opening in the artery wall. "Follow it all the way down and you should reach the hard labyrinth in the inner ear. Good luck."

With a final wave, Finn switched on the light attached to his helmet, angled the scoot and powered through the blood flow into the vessel. In the hold, the umbilical tether unspooled from its reel, whizzing round as it played out its line.

And an unseen figure swam past into the open airlock...

FEBRUARY 22 07:14 (GMT+3). Great Cavern, Monastery of Mount St Demetrius of Thessaloniki

With an effort of will, Kaparis sat himself up on the operating table, swiping off the high-end medical equipment attached to him.

He felt magnificent. Heywood draped a silk dressing gown over his shoulders. "Sir, the escape vehicle is ready," he reported.

Kaparis looked over at Hudson. He would still need the boy as a hostage until he was certain.

"Good. Bring the boy. And bring something to pick up signals from the Vitalis."

The Siguri had not picked up any definite sign of attack from the G&T yet, but Kaparis expected that if they had the guts, which he very much doubted, Allenby and King would attack at dawn.

"Prepare the Siguri and every Tyro for the assault. The Master expects every man to fight to the death, to the very last drop of blood."

"And the Carriers, Master?"

The Carriers had been locked in the library all night after the two dangling spies had been found. Clearly there had been resistance bubbling under the surface of all that apparent obedience. He had no doubt who would be behind it: their blind king, the one they called Primo.

"Burn the library down at the first sign of attack. And let them know their fate beforehand so they will have some time to regret their treachery. It will fuel their screams."

"And Santiago, Master?" asked the Siguri chief.

Kaparis looked at the cowering wretch. It was a life hardly worth the kill – and yet… No, he had an idea. They were fond of him, the Carriers.

"Take him up to the library and kill him. Make the Primo pull the trigger."

Santiago wailed and Heywood gasped – "Bravo!" His Master was back to his best.

"To the Polaris!" Kaparis ordered.

In the anterior tympanic artery in Kaparis's brain, Finn sashayed like a snowboarder down the twisting blood vessel on the scoot. The further he went, the more the walls closed in, the louder the whale song became.

Nico's idea was that, if Finn could reach the bony labyrinth of the inner ear, he could make direct contact with it with his helmet, and it would act as a sound box, so the whale song vibrations would make sense. If so, he should be able to shout back and be heard too.

The artery suddenly split into several smaller tributaries and Finn had to take his pick and crawl up towards what he hoped would be bone.

"It's tight now. I'm crawling along," he reported.

"Keep going until you reach a white membrane. It should be covering the bone," replied Nico.

And just as she said it, Finn saw the membrane up ahead, shining like ice.

"Got it."

His body was almost plugging the narrow vessel now, the blood cells having to wriggle past.

"OK, I'm there. I can feel something, slight vibrations…"

He dragged himself forward a few last inches and touched his helmet to the bone, and sound instantly exploded through his head, clear as day.

But it wasn't from the outside. It was over the comms:

"ARRRRGGH! HE'S BACK!"

Screams in his helmet. Nothing but screams and struggle.

"Carla! Carla, what's happening?"

Finn heard one last blow, then… a familiar manic cackle…

Kaparis twitched, stopped. He could hear something… something deep in the itch of his innermost ear. Screaming?

"Pan?" said Kaparis, as if recognising a long-lost son.

There was a last strangled yelp and the itch was gone.

Finn scrambled madly backwards, back down the blood vessel, back towards the craft.

Not Pan... not with Carla and Nico in the *Vitalis*... surely not...

TCH-KASH! An electronic whiplash smacked up the comms line and exploded in his ears, followed by sharp pain as the line attached to his belt suddenly tightened and yanked him immediately down – down at tremendous speed – down, crashing fast against the tight tide of blood, Finn on the spinning, twisting, powering end of the line.

He *SLAM-SLAMMED* off the arterial walls, trying to stop, wanting to scream as he cut through the blood flow, the jellyfish red cells pummelling his torso – *dhu-dhu, dhu-dhu, dhu-dhu, dhu-dhu* – *dhu-dhu, dhu-dhu, dhu-dhu, dhu-dhu* – blood blood blood – thumping and roaring as he *SLAMMED* round another arterial junction.

The new vessel he entered was wider, the pressure intense but not as violent.

Finn took a moment to draw breath, nailing the obvious – Pan was back.

He must have hidden. Must have attacked Carla and Nico. Must have taken the *Vitalis*, dragging Finn along now like a distant water-skier...

Then there was a change...

Dhu-dhu, dhu-dhu, dhu-dhu, dhu-dhu...

The blood still thumped and roared, but he was no longer being dragged along. He seemed to be stable in the flow. The *Vitalis* must have stopped. Anchored?

Get back to the ship, Finn thought. *Get back now.*

The scoot was dragging at his left ankle, useless in such a strong flow. He reached down and flipped the clasp and it went spinning off into the darkness. He grabbed the guide line in front of him instead and began to pull himself up it, hand over hand, over and over, faster and faster.

He had to do it. He had to reach the *Vitalis*.

Kaparis staggered forward on his own two feet and reached the Polaris escape vehicle.

Heywood was waiting, and had thoughtfully mixed him his favourite cocktail.

"Heywood, you are the truest servant any man could find." Kaparis angled the straw round to take a sip and suddenly felt soaringly relieved and pleased with himself. He was moving again, and he had cracked Boldklub, and he always so loved a daring escape.

And what a future to escape to! He had solved Ethan Drake's Time = Place *conundrum.*

There was so much to be done in the seven cities, the seven wells.[22]

He was helped into the payload bay of the Polaris and a harness was

[22] [INFORMATION REDACTED] G&T order no. 22378/b

brought down over his head. Heywood would take the seat opposite. Then Hudson was dragged into the escape vehicle by two Siguri and crammed into the small space on the payload-bay floor.

"Ow! Is that really necessary?" he asked.

FEBRUARY 22 07:21 (GMT+3).
Romanian-Ukrainian airspace, 5,000ft

A blistering white-gold sun crested the horizon, mighty engines roared, and a fleet of aircraft banked left as they approached the target area.

A fleet capable of unleashing half an army.

Within the C-130 Hercules command aircraft, Al and Commander King watched screens that showed the magnificent and forbidding Monastery of Mount St Demetrius of Thessaloniki, as seen from a dozen different angles by the forces on the ground.

All that those forces ranged against it were waiting for now was the final order.

Journey time to target was seven minutes.

"Well? What are you waiting for?" demanded General Jackman on screen.

Commander King looked across at Al as he buckled himself into a parachute harness.

"A sign," answered Al. And King knew what he meant. The troops, the technology and the weaponry at their disposal were of the highest calibre. And yet they were about to make a desperate gamble. They needed something more. They needed to believe in their own luck.

"Sir! The dome!" a technician called, and there it was.

The great dome was beginning to split in two.

THIRTY-ONE

FEBRUARY 22 07:22 (GMT+3). Great Cavern,
Monastery of Mount St Demetrius of Thessaloniki

*The Polaris was eased up the launch ramp until it was almost vertical,
pointing up the shaft towards heaven. Around the Great Cavern an alarm
was sounding, and technicians and others were taking cover. Although
the first stage of the rocket launch was powered by compressed air, the
force would be enough to rip any fool standing close enough to pieces.
The main rocket engine would not ignite till they had cleared the dome.*

Computers ran ten thousand automatic checks.

*Santiago watched alongside the two Siguri deputised to take him to his
death, sheltered behind a bank of computers. He cried. He had let down
Hut-sun. He had let down the angels. He had let down the Primo.*

Inside the payload bay of the missile, trapped between the devil and his ridiculous butler, the boy prisoner Hudson issued a chilling warning.

"Um, I don't know how long this is going to take, but I should warn you – I suffer from travel sickness."

"Oh, for goodness' sake," said Kaparis.

"It's just, if I haven't got a bag, things could get messy..."

"Have we got a bag we could put over his head?" Kaparis asked Heywood. But Heywood wasn't listening. Heywood was concentrating manically on the sound being emitted from the Geiger counter behind his Master's head.

"That's code, sir! Morse."

.-. .-. / .-. . .-. .-. .- .. -. .. / -.- --- -. -.- --- .-. / -.. .-. .-. -.- . / -.. .
.- -..

"'Pan here... regained control... Drake dead.' He's done it, sir! He's done it!"

"HAAAAHHAAA! PAN!" cried Kaparis, just when he thought the day couldn't get any better. "Throw the idiot out! We don't need him any more! Be gone, imbecile!" he roared, as Heywood opened the payload door and shoved Hudson rudely out.

Thump – thump – THUMP – "Ow!" said Hudson as he tumbled out of the missile, bounced off the launch ramp and finally hit the cavern floor.

"Take him with the other idiot and have the Primo shoot them both!" ordered Kaparis to the Siguri who ran forward to grab him.

The payload door of the Polaris shut again and a single piercing BAAAAAAARRRRRRRRRP signalled the start of the countdown.

Hudson rubbed his eyes. Well, at least I won't throw up, he thought, as he was dragged off by his Siguri guards. He stumbled, hardly able to see a thing. Somewhere in the Polaris he'd gone and lost his glasses...

"Ten... nine... eight..."

Kaparis was so, so pleased. The adapted Polaris engines would propel them to Mach 6 and allow them to splash down in one of six pre-programmed, lakeside locations...

"Seven... six... five..."

They would be three hundred miles away by the time the G&T realised they had lost them on radar, the stealth-coating making the missile entirely undetectable once it had slowed and begun to fall.

Where would they go? Which base next?

"Four... three... two..."

The Ethiopian Highlands? Atlantis? Babylon?

"One..."

How he loved a countdown...

"Zero!"

PSCHHHHHHHHHHRRRRRRRRORORORORORRORORORRRR – compressed air exploded from jets at the base of the missile and shot the Polaris up the launch ramp – *RORRORRRORR* – along four embedded rails – *RORRORRRORR* – one for each of the stubby fins on the rocket's tail – *RORRORRRORR...*

In one of which had fallen Hudson's pebble-thick prescription glasses.

The tiny, momentary drag that the glasses caused as they were vaporised, in such a tiny, tiny fraction of time, was just enough. Just enough for the guidance computers to have to react and adjust the angle of thrust – once, twice, three times – as the Polaris picked up speed and began to ascend the shaft; oscillations that were exaggerated in tiny increments as it rose in the compressed airflow, confusing the guidance programs further, so that by the time the missile reached the end of the shaft it had wobbled fatally off course.

And so, instead of clearing the open dome dead centre, the rising Polaris, already at 200mph, ignited its main rocket on a tilt that drove it straight through the golden skin of the false dome – CRAAAAASSSKSKSKSHSSKLSLSSH – the entire craft suffering a massive spiral fracture from nose to tail, its constituent parts separating and exploding open like one of those bake-your-own tubes of croissant dough, but in a fraction of a second; and instead of cookie dough, fuel and metal...

FEBRUARY 22 07:26 (GMT+3).
Romanian-Ukrainian airspace, 3,000ft

Seen from the air, a column of fire and disintegrating rocket engine streaked sideways from the shattered dome of the monastery like a cosmic snort.

PCARARSHSHSHHRTSFRSHSHAHAHHHHH!

"OK," said Al, stunned in the C-130 command aircraft, "that's definitely a sign."

Commander King gave the order – "GO!"

"GO!" said the jump masters, and parachutes began to bloom from a dozen aircraft.

"GO!" said the commanders of special forces in the valley, and a hundred grapple guns fired claws up cliffs and over parapets.

"*Allez!*" ordered Henri Clément as he and five other members of the équipe bleu poised on the cliff face around the wheelhouse sprang from the rock, pulled hard on their ropes and swung up through the trapdoor in the wheelhouse floor in a move worthy of a *parfum de Paris* advert.

FEBRUARY 22 07:27 (GMT+3). Great Cavern, Monastery of Mount St Demetrius of Thessaloniki

In the Great Cavern, fire and fine debris rained down the shaft from the shattered dome like hell's tickertape.

Technicians, Tyros, the medics and Siguri staggered forward to stare up the shaft.

Santiago stared too. *The Master? Dead?* He moaned in fear. What awful consequences might follow?

Hudson, lying in the dirt, hands still bound, broke from his daze. "Santiago! We must get away!"

Santiago looked at the backs of their Siguri captors as they walked, stunned, towards the shaft. Voices yelled for fire hoses. Sirens began to sound the invasion.

Chaos was their cover. Santiago hauled Hudson up and they ran for the monorail carts.

FEBRUARY 22 07:29 (GMT+3). MONASTERY OF
MOUNT ST DEMETRIUS OF THESSALONIKI

In the dome, Kaparis woke.

There were flames and smoke all around, twisted girders. The Polaris payload bay had been ripped apart, its contents cast into the web of structural metalwork. He and Heywood were caught like flies, still strapped in their seats, Heywood's face horribly burnt.

Kaparis saw a sky full of smoke and parachutes...

He must get out. He hit the release on his harness, then on Heywood's.

FEBRUARY 22 07:30 (GMT+3).
Romanian-Ukrainian airspace, 3,000ft

WHOOOFUMP! – WHOOOFUMP! – WHOOOFUMP!

Al looked up as the chute deployed and prayed they weren't too late. He had no idea who or what was on that rocket, but if it was

Kaparis making an exit, there wasn't going to be much left of him...

He blanked out the fear, gritted his teeth and thought only of Finn, trapped inside that body. *I've scoured the face of the earth for you, you glorious boy – last link to my sister, last of the Allenby line. And even if you're getting smaller and smaller all the time, God help me, I'm going to find you...*

Beside him, Delta looked down through the smoke trails obscuring their descent and made out the patchwork of monastery roofs. She saw bright muzzle flashes. At last... action. The snap, crackle and pop of a firefight as the first paratroopers landed. She braced her M27 against her shoulder, and fired a few rounds, just to say hello – *DRTRTRTRT!* Oh, she was ready!

Kelly guided his chute ahead of them both and picked out a suitable landing spot, wielding his own M27 one-handed. But there was little left to hit. What little opposition there had been on the rooftops had been quickly extinguished.

"On me!" called Kelly, and he hauled his chute to the right to bring them to a gentle halt on a slope of icy terracotta tiles – *crunch – crunch – crunch.*

FEBRUARY 22 07:32 (GMT+3). Monastery of Mount St Demetrius of Thessaloniki

In the High Chapel, the Abbot howled. The one true Master... obliterated?

𐀏

Where did that leave them?

Who was in charge now?

A sudden toxic flash of greed shot through him, greed for power, as for the merest moment he thought he might assume supreme control… And then – *DRTRTRTRTRTRT* – his inner coward quickly returned as gunfire shot out the windows.

He scurried off as the Siguri covered his retreat – *DRTRRTRTRT!*

What to do? The Master's orders were to resist till the last drop of blood was shed, but those orders were now orphans. Perhaps it would be better to preserve as much of his Master's legacy as could be saved? Yes. That would be much more respectful.

"BACK! FALL BACK!" commanded the Abbot.

Down in the library, the Primo heard every bullet, scream and stun grenade.

He could also sense Tyro confusion and Siguri fear in their two dozen jailers.

As the first stray bullets began to whistle and crack through the ancient glass of the library windows, biting chunks from the walls, the Primo made his call.

"Now!" he cried, and seized a handbell.

Ding-a-ling-a-ling-a-ling-a-ling!

As one, the Carrier children rose screaming from their shacks. They threw anything they could at their oppressors, a hail of crockery, cutlery and improvised wooden spears, followed by a thousand little fists.

Many of their captors fell immediately under the assault. Some guns discharged – *DRTRTRRTT!* – but they were quickly silenced, or even taken and fired on their Siguri owners, who quickly turned and fled.

A great cheering broke out.

"Barricade the doors and windows!" ordered the Primo. "Take cover!"

When Santiago and Hudson reached the top of the monorail, the Siguri guarding the entrance were nowhere to be seen, likely having thrown themselves into defending the monastery. They found tools and cut the plastic ties that bound their wrists, then ran up the stone steps towards the sound of battle.

In the catacombs, they ran straight into a party of retreating Tyros.

"Back!" Santiago cried, and he pulled Hudson down a narrow skull-studded gangway leading to the base of the disused south tower – *DRTRRTTTT!* – bullets echoing in their wake.

When they reached a spiral staircase, in terrible repair, Santiago screamed "UP!" and pushed Hudson ahead of him. "Go, Hut-sun! Out!" he urged, as he pulled and kicked at loose masonry to block the path of their pursuers.

Hudson climbed, but without his glasses he was half blind. He saw light coming through what he thought was a doorway and ran straight through it...

... and found himself in cold air, falling...

SMASH! Hudson hit snow and stone and light and dark as he

tumbled over and over and over – THUMP! – ending up in a deep, deeply layered, winter-long snowdrift.

His senses blended into one tremendous pain – "AAAOOOOOOWWWWWWWW!" *Well*, he thought, *that's it. This is what dying must feel like.*

Then everything went black.

"HUUUUUUUT-SSSSSSUN!" Santiago called, uselessly, over the din of battle from the ruined tower.

He could see the gash in the snow-clad scree slope below. Hudson must have hit it and carried on down into the endless forest. He must save him!

But first he must find him. *How?*

Inspiration struck in the form of a scurrying rat...

To the kitchens!

FEBRUARY 22 07:38 (GMT+3).
Romanian-Ukrainian airspace, 3,000ft

Seen from the screens of the circling C-130 command aircraft, troops were swarming up the cliffs and across the rooftops like ants over a wedding cake.

The success of the initial assault seemed total. They had complete control of the roof and ramparts, and some units were already pushing deep into the complex.

Commander King had every right to feel relieved. But he felt nothing of the sort. For he already knew what Allenby would be thinking. And Allenby was probably right. In his mind, he replayed a clip of the Polaris blasting through the dome to oblivion, and hoped against hope that their worst fears would not be realised…

FEBRUARY 22 07:38 (GMT+3). Monastery of
Mount St Demetrius of Thessaloniki

Al scrambled up to the base of the ruined dome. Fuel was still burning in a streak across the roofs opposite.

He looked into a tangle of metal and smoke… into a hell. Surely no one could have survived… Except the devil himself.

There!

Through a curtain of flame, Al caught a glimpse of a figure, like a great ape, swinging and grabbing its way down through the twisted girders…

Good heavens, it moves… thought Al, appalled.

THIRTY-TWO

Dhu-dhu, dhu-dhu, dhu-dhu, dhu-dhu.

Pull... Pull... Finn hauled on the tether, into the everlasting red, hauled without a hope of finding its end, dragging himself on up the line.

Then suddenly he could sense light, something glowing beyond the first few feet of rushing cells. Pull... Pull...

Yes! Just inside an opening in the artery wall ahead, in a branch off the main blood vessel. He pulled harder and reached the opening. The lights were there. The lights were near.

He turned off his helmet light and let the blood flow carry him straight down the new arterial branch towards the *Vitalis*. Precisely as he did so – as he careered towards the anchored submarine – he saw him.

There, plain as day in the open hold, was Pan, dagger in hand, having just cut through the guide line where it was caught in the hinge of the hold doors. He must have cut it from the reel and not realised for a few minutes – vital minutes to Finn – that it had snagged on the hinge.

A second later and Finn would have been a goner. Now he was merely hurtling out of control and untethered towards the *Vitalis*...

He could see Carla and Nico lashed together on the bridge. The open hold was his only chance. His adrenalin spiked and, using all his strength, Finn swam hard and mad for it. Pan looked up from the hold just in time to – *SLAM* – get a whole load of Finn slamming into him and knocking him clean out of the hold. With a jolt, the short tether connecting Pan to the *Vitalis* left them both dangling, spinning and fighting in the torrential flow.

Finn clung to Pan as he clung to life, locking his arms around his waist and digging his fingers into his wetsuit. *Don't let go, don't let go*, he told himself, while Pan, furious, tried to rip, kick and punch himself free. They heard each other's desperate rasping breath, their grunts and curses.

Dhu-dhu, dhu-dhu, dhu-dhu, dhu-dhu.

"DIE!" croaked Pan, and he began to batter away at Finn's helmet. Finn was unable to let go and beat him back. Pan was too strong. Finn was losing his grip...

Caught in an eddy of the flow, they spun like ballerinas for a few seconds. Then Finn saw his only, lousy, option – let go and try and race Pan back up the short tether to the hold, with arms that were already exhausted by his recent epic haul. But he had no choice.

With a primal cry and a thrash of hands, Finn monkeyed his way up Pan's body and managed to grab the tether.

Pull! Pull! He felt Pan claw at his legs, but he wouldn't let go. Not now.

Pull! Pull! The muscles in his arms burnt as Pan clung to him and he hauled them both up the tether. "COME ON!" he yelled to himself, and kicked back. His foot struck something hard and he felt Pan drop back.

Pull! Pull...! When at last Finn reached the hull of the *Vitalis*, he dared to look back...

There was Pan, right behind him, but choking on blood and plasma, which was filling up the inside of his helmet. Finn's kick must somehow have broken it, shifted the seal...

Finn showed him all the mercy at his disposal, all the mercy Pan or Kaparis or the whole damn lot of them had ever shown.

He kicked out again.

Pan's helmet flew off and there was a shell-burst of air from his tanks as he screamed uselessly after it into the naked flow, clawing desperately at the air line fixed at his neck, letting go of the tether as he fought to divert the bubbles, to cram them into his lungs – dangling and spinning and drowning and dying...

Finn pulled himself into the hold and out of the force of the flow, pulled until he reached the tether's end. Then he unclipped it and let it whip out, releasing Pan's body into the deep blackness of Kaparis's brain.

"He's there!" Al had yelled over the radio, as soon as he'd laid eyes on Kaparis. "Send in Stubbs! I'm going in with the assault group!"

"Oh glory," said Stubbs.

"Oh glory," parroted Li Jun who was especially fond of him.

Stubbs and his escort would drop with a trio of super-nano detection devices he and Li Jun had knocked together in the previous two hours – a blood filter made from an old hoover, an ultrasound fitted to a nano-radar rig, and an electron microscope they had butchered and reassembled for portability.

Commander King radioed the landing master.

"Eagle to Storm One, do we have control of the drop zone? Can you accept Crown Jewels? Over."

Stubbs rolled his eyes at his code name.

"Storm One to Eagle..." crackled the reply. "Bring him in."

The noise level went through the roof as the drop hatch in the tail of the aircraft opened. A burly paratrooper grabbed Stubbs and hitched himself to him as a jump buddy.

Li Jun wailed.

Grandma didn't even look up from the screens at the opposite end of the aircraft where, together with a technician who could speak Portuguese, she was poring over old medical records wired over from Brazil...

Stubbs and his paratrooper escort stepped out of the back of the aircraft and disappeared into thin air.

WHOOOFUMP!

Stubbs gasped as the chute opened – at the physical shock, but also at the sight of the snow-clad carpet of the Carpathians, and at the burning jewel they were falling towards.

FEBRUARY 22 07:47 (GMT+3). Monastery of Mount St Demetrius of Thessaloniki

DRTRTTRTT! DRTRTRTRRTRTTT! BANG!

The main force was pressing into the heart of the monastery, the defenders having fallen back to the Forum.

KATHUMP! The kitchen doors blew open on a charge and Henri and the équipe bleu burst in.

DRTRTTRTT! DRTRTRTRRTRTTT!

Pots and pans pinged and crockery shattered as they were met with a hail of fire that would have cut down a regiment. But the members of Commando Hubert had trained with the acrobats of an avant-garde circus, and each was perfectly at home in a kitchen.

The defenders didn't stand a chance.

Yvette performed bullet-evading somersaults while firing twin Uzi machine pistols. Jacques shot out a shelf of cast-iron pots, dumping the lot on three Siguri; Marie and Helga rolled a huge cauldron as cover down the right flank to take out another three. Toni sent oil and other ingredients raining down on the fleeing remainder by shooting out the store jars above them.

Henri tasted a sauce, added a little salt.

In the Forum, the Abbot only tasted defeat. He watched the Siguri scramble out of the kitchen and fall back, the enemy closing in. While the Tyros would follow orders and fight to the death, the Siguri were all too human – they needed to be led, forced. *I am no master of that*, he thought.

He made a decision. He yelled, "CEASE FIRE! DEMAND TALKS!"

The Siguri were eager to oblige.

The Tyros looked at him as if he was mad. They were armed.

For a moment, the Abbot thought that maybe he'd been a little hasty. Then he knew he had.

From on high came a thunderous voice: "WHAT TREACHERY IS THIS?"

There, at the top of the Forum, ignoring every bullet, a magnificent figure staggered into view, a half-dead butler in his arms. Burnt black and blue, hair slicked back with blood, wearing a Siguri breastplate and a shredded silk dressing gown, like some steampunk warrior – Kaparis, a god among men.

"The Master! He is risen!"

A great animal roar went up.

The Abbot fell to his knees.

"HOLD EVERY POSITION! CONCEDE NOTHING!" Kaparis yelled down.

Dozens of Tyros and Siguri ran back to the posts they'd recently abandoned, the Tyros in a state of honourable rage. A gang ran to aid Kaparis in his descent, relieving him of Heywood.

"Get him to the Cavern. The medics – tell Leopold to save him or die."

As the sounds of battle increased, Kaparis descended, his eyes never leaving the Abbot. He took an AK47 from a Siguri fighter on the way.

"A miracle..." murmured the Abbot as he staggered towards him.

Kaparis towered over him.

"Master! We fell back to this strong point! I offered to talk in order to set a tra—"

BANG.

Kaparis put a bullet neatly through the Abbot's forehead.

It was always important to set an example. The day was not lost. It had only just begun. He could still get away. He would leave a surprise. A booby prize for a prize booby. It would require effort and sacrifice, but what was the point of having an army if they were not prepared to die?

He just needed a hostage or two, or a hundred...

302

The Forum was eminently defendable and their concentrated force could easily be directed against any point of attack.

"Thirty of you – with me. The rest of you – start diversionary attacks while we take the library, then fall back here and hold the core. FIGHT TO THE LAST!"

THIRTY-THREE

Kelly and Delta were creeping through the Tyro dorms when half a dozen figures burst in from the Forum, running and firing – *DRTRTTRTT! DRTRTRTRRTRTTT!*

"INCOMING!" Kelly and Delta let rip with their M27s – *DRTRTTRTT! DRRRTRTTT!*

Only three of the attackers, all Tyros, managed to survive and find cover – *DRTRTTRTT!*

Over the comms link, to the circling C-130, came the explanation: "They're counter-attacking in a dozen places at once…"

"Got one right here!" Kelly reported. "They'll be diversions! Only one attack will be real! Find it!"

DRTRTRTRRTRT!

Commander King assessed the battle in real-time via dozens of flickering live feeds from tactical headgear. Each counter-attack had been short and aggressive, but easily repelled – all but one: the main passageway down to the library.

DRTRTTRTT! DRTRTRTRRTRTTT!

"Library! They're breaking for the library!" shouted King as he saw the last of his paratroopers driven back.

Kaparis, firing awkwardly from the hip, personally obliterated the last of the defending troops in the main passage – DRTRTTRTT!

Oh, it was nice to be back on your feet.

He had two-thirds of his force left, heavily armed and with their blood up.

DRTRTRTRRTRT! DRTRTTRTT!

As they approached the ancient library doors, Kaparis insisted on stumping forward to take the lead. A charge was laid.

BANG!

Carriers screamed as the doors flew off their hinges. Ancient pages scattered like confetti.

Kaparis, blasted, appeared in the doorway. An icon made flesh.

The Primo turned to face the attack. He had ordered the Carrier children to take cover in the shacks, but fear and pure excitement had brought many of the younger ones out to huddle around him.

"WHO DARES DEFY THEIR MASTER?"

The Primo's blood ran cold.

Kaparis braced his gun against his hip and fired – DRTRTRTRRTRT!

Bullets ripped over the Carriers' heads and they screamed and scattered. The Primo remained bolt upright on the dais. This was their sanctuary. He had failed them. Now he must take responsibility.

"OUT, RATS! EVERY LAST ONE OF YOU!"

How Santiago finally made it through the chaos and back to the kitchens was a mystery, but somehow he did. Narrowly avoiding being cut to pieces by a stream of fire from Yvette's Uzis, he held up his hands to protest his innocence and galumphed across the stone floor and through the door to the ratters' yard.

YAP!

Yo-yo met him with a wet kiss while the rest of the pack ran round ineffectually in yapping circles. Santiago reached into the folds of his rags and brought out a paper bag full of unsightly aged sick. Hudson sick...

All the dogs took a good long sniff.

Yo-yo knew the owner well – *YAP!*

"Hut-sun! *Aduc! Rechercher!* Go!"

As they returned in triumph to the Forum, members of Kaparis's library raiding party grabbed an injured paratrooper in the gangways and stripped him of his hi-tech tactical helmet. It was taken to Kaparis.

"Open a line to your Commander!" shouted Kaparis into the lens of the camera embedded in the shell of the helmet. He turned it round and gave it a good view of his adoring Tyros, his brutal Siguri, his Carrier hostages, and the Primo on his knees.

The transmitted image was crisp and clear on Commander King's screen in the C-130 Hercules above.

Then Kaparis turned the helmet camera on himself.

There he was on screen, able-bodied, his hair slicked back with blood, armed and armoured, towering over the Primo and the cowering children.

"Commander King!" Kaparis demanded.

"Dr Kaparis, we meet again," said Commander King through the speaker in the helmet. "I see you are returned to health. And yet you are surrounded and your forces are defeated."

"My forces will fight to the last drop of blood. I demand you withdraw or I will engage in a slaughter of innocents that would make even King Herod blush."

He turned the helmet to let it take in the terrified Carrier children. King had no choice. "All units: hold your fire."

In moments, guns across the complex fell silent.

Kaparis almost laughed. The great weakness of Western civilisation was assigning value to lives so obviously worth nothing.

"What do you want, Kaparis?" asked King.

"A holiday. Time to recuperate," he smirked.

"If you give yourself up now, you won't be mistreated in any way. Your achievements are of significance. Rooms are being prepared for you in the Tower of London."

"Haaaaaa! Flattery! Do you really think me so shallow? Play games and their blood will be on your hands."

He took a killing knife from a Siguri and held its razor edge to the soft throat of the Primo, drawing a bead of blood from the surface. "And this one will be the first."

The Primo felt the blood trickle down his neck.

"I want those two Chinook helicopters you have flying around outside to land on the roof of the High Chapel and be left there with their rotors running. My own people will pilot them. I want a radio and radar blackout, and if we are followed at any appreciable distance, I will start throwing Carriers from the aircraft. Do you understand? Would you like a moment to digest? You may also like to consider that I have captured Infinity Drake and Carla Salazar, and I have taken the work of Ethan Drake so far forward that, if you kill me, you will be killing the future in ways you cannot possibly understand. No one will thank you. Your pathetic organisation may attempt to persecute a genius, but humankind knows when it's on to a good thing."

"Humankind enslaved by you?" said Commander King.

"Humankind in thrall of me," said Kaparis, beaming. "After all, I have

the Boldklub sequencing equations now, as you must be well aware. And believe me, my resurrection is only the start of it!"

Commander King digested this. World leaders digested it. Al, who had just been patched in, and who was at that moment creeping down the gangways to hook up with Delta and Kelly, also digested it.

Meanwhile, Grandma, up at the front of the plane, popped on her reading glasses and read a communication from the Director of the Brazilian National Crime Agency, one she had urgently requested…

"Now," said Kaparis, "I'm going to count down slowly from ten, and if I haven't had a positive answer by the time I get to zero, I will kill the first hostage. Then we will move on to the second, et cetera. Do you understand, Commander? Can you count, Dr Allenby? Then let us begin. Ten…"

King put Kaparis on hold and opened a separate channel to Al.

"What do you say, Allenby? Is what he's saying credible?"

"He's just shrunk a bunch of people to a hundred thousandth of their size. So it must be."

"Nine…"

"We've got to keep him alive," said Al. "He's got Finn, he's got the kids, and he's made some kind of breakthrough. We need to get a handle on it."

"Eight…"

"As I read it," said General Mount, "we've got him in the bag anyway. He can get on that aircraft, but there's no way in the world he's going to get far."

"Seven…"

"He's right. Two Chinooks can't just disappear," said General Jackman.

"What about the radio and radar blackout?" asked the Russian president.

"Six..."

The NATO leaders all knew top-secret "invisible" quantum radar stations had been established across Europe. "We have ways," said King.

"Five..."

"He flies them to the middle of nowhere – we pounce," said General Mount.

"Four..."

"But we'll be straight into another hostage situation," said the French president.

"Three..."

"We've all been here before; we have specialists. It may get messy, but there's only one way this is going to end," said the British prime minister.

"Two..."

"It's a no-brainer. Give him the choppers," agreed the US president. "There's any number of ways we could play this out. In any of them, we win back those choppers."

"One..."

Kaparis tensed the muscles of his forearm, ready to slit the Primo's throat.

"Zer—"

"STOP!" said Commander King "OK. You've got your chop—"

"WAIT!"

A shout came from the front of the C-130 command aircraft. It was Grandma, who was making her way down the plane towards them. "I've got something!"

Commander King hit hold. "Got what?"

"Ondine! When she got away from Kaparis – she wasn't mad, she was *pregnant*."

"What?" said King.

"What?" said Al on the ground.

"*What?*" said the various leaders of the free world.

Grandma hurried down the cabin, brandishing a printout of the message she'd just read.

"Pica! That's what gave it away," Grandma said. "An absolutely classic case."

"What do you mean, 'pica'?"

"Ondine wasn't mad when she tried to escape him. She was suffering from pica. It's a condition of pregnancy – a craving to eat the strangest things. In mild cases, coal and chalk and so on. In extreme cases, women suffer wild mood swings and even try to eat the walls."

"Walls?"

"Yes! It's something to do with the taste of plaster," Grandma said, demanding the microphone from King, who, to his eternal credit, went with his instinct and handed it straight to her.

"Hello? Is that you, dear?" asked Grandma.

Kaparis shivered as he suddenly realised Violet Allenby was speaking through the helmet. Their time together in the South China Sea had not been a pleasant one, nor had it ended well.

"Mrs Allenby, get off the li—"

"I've been looking for your wife and child," she interrupted, "and thought perhaps you could help me clear a few things up."

"What?" hissed Kaparis.

"We've discovered medical records that confirm that a patient was treated at the Convent of the Little Sisters in Rio de Janeiro, Brazil, in 2002. There, a certain 'Maria Santos' was treated for three months for post-natal depression and injuries sustained during childbirth."

"What nonsense is this? King! I demand—"

"She disappeared from the convent on New Year's Day 2003 under suspicious circumstances. The Brazilian authorities investigated, and it was found she'd registered under a false name. Because of a rare blood condition – to do with a panther parasite – they were able to identify her. It turns out her real name was Dr Ondine St Emmanuel de Morales."

Kaparis could barely speak for fury. Who would dare think him weak enough to believe such a thing... Violet Allenby was goading him.

"The authorities believe she was murdered. But not before she gave birth to a child. Your child."

"I have no child!"

"You do, even if you didn't know about it. Your wife, I strongly suspect, was suffering from pica at the time of your accident. These hospital records show that, at some point after she escaped from you, she had your child. Then she fled to Brazil."

Far beneath, Al was listening in. *Wow, what a mum...,* he thought – and not for the first time.

"No doubt she tried to hide it from you, so this will have come as a bit of a shock... *emotionally*," suggested Grandma.

"*EMOTIONALLY?*" *Kaparis finally managed to roar.*

"But then, there's never a perfect time to reveal these things, I suppose. The important thing to bear in mind here is that there is a child out there somewhere – *your* child, David. Ondine didn't hate you, or want to hurt you. She was sick. You don't need to *hate*, David – you have loved and been loved, and a child was born of that love. And once you have love, well, you don't really need to rule the world."

There was a long pause. Al, Commander King, Grandma, the waiting world – all held their breath. Had she somehow managed to get through to him? Had she somehow managed to touch his heart?

They could hear something... Sobbing? *Was he actually sobbing?*

"*Love!*" *laughed Kaparis in contempt, as the bubble burst and he laughed and laughed and laughed. Love? What lies! Violet Allenby had gone and overplayed her hand. If children were born of love – well then, there could be no child, as that woman – his wife – had never loved him. Any fraction of doubt he'd experienced was just Ondine reaching from beyond the grave to torment him.*

"*My dear, deluded lady! I've never felt love in my life,*" *said Kaparis.* "*Never given it, never taken it. Power – oh yes, Ondine had power. Power to lie and wound and weave spells. Oh, she was good, was Ondine – and you are undoubtedly cut from the same cloth! Now, set the two Chinooks down on the roof, withdraw your forces to the periphery and clear the gangways. You have three minutes or I will begin the cull. That is all.*"

And with that he tossed the helmet away with a newly acquired flick of the wrist.

King watched the spinning camera feed and it felt as if all his efforts were being tossed away.

"Well," he said to Grandma, "I suppose it was worth a try."

"Have faith, Commander," said Grandma. "It's not over yet."

"Great effort, Mum," said Al over the comms. "But surely we're not going to take him at his word, King?"

"Of course not," said Commander King. "Most likely he won't be on those choppers. This is Kaparis we're talking about. A man who loves games, bluff and double bluff."

"What games?" asked the British prime minister.

"Well, there's the rub," said Commander King. "There must be another way out of that place. And we've got three minutes to find it."

"To the chapel roof!" cried Kaparis, and there was a burst of cheering, a primitive, wicked shaking of fists and a brandishing of guns – DRRRT!

Poor fools, thought Kaparis, even as he milked their adulation.

THIRTY-FOUR

The first Tyros, with the first of the hostage Carrier children, emerged at the door of the bell tower that led out on to the High Chapel roof. They weren't afraid, weren't scanning for snipers or looking for cover. They were arrogant. They were proud.

The Chinooks clattered in to touch down before them. The air crews quickly got out. Then the Tyros and hostages poured out of the tower towards them.

And in the middle of them was Kaparis... Hidden, covered, smuggled, just enough of a view to identify him – his head covered in blood, his Siguri breastplate, his...

Wait a minute. Al, unable to resist, had run back up to the parapets to see for himself. As Kaparis was rushed into the back of the Chinook, he saw his head flop forward.

There was a hole in the back of it.

This was not Kaparis, this was some corpse.

"Delta! Kelly!" he shouted over the comms. "It's not him! He must be escaping! The moment those choppers are out of the way, get as far down the complex as you can. He has to be heading for the caverns."

At the entrance to the catacombs, Kaparis pulled on the dead Abbot's robes and laughed as he got ready to make his escape.

Long ago, Ondine had managed to escape from her prison in these caverns and now it was time for him to follow her lead. She could be horribly clever, and cleverly horrible. A combination he had found irresistible.

Everything was ready. He had ordered the Tyros to escape with the hostages in the Chinooks, directing them to fly into the centre of Bucharest and to disperse as best they could.

The Siguri were to hold out in the Forum for as long as possible.

Drake was dead. The G&T defeated.

There was just one last act to perform.

He tightened his hold round the blind boy's throat and continued dragging him down into the caverns with him.

"Can you see where you're going, boy?" he taunted, throwing the proud wretch onto the floor. "You betrayed me, you led the vipers to my den, and you shall die here, alone, in the dark, unfollowed and unmourned. Let me

leave you with this one final, purest truth. Many pathetic souls inhabit this earth, and for what? To suffer and to die for their masters," said Kaparis, drawing the knife.

"You are not my master," the Primo dared to gasp in the face of death. "I am my master."

Kaparis roared at this final insult, and drew back to strike the mortal blow...

"I WOULDN'T DO THAT, IF I WERE YOU!"

Kaparis froze. The voice came from inside his head...

"HE'S YOUR SON!"

There it was again, loud and clear. It couldn't be... and yet it was. It was the voice of...

Infinity Drake.

In the Forum, the Siguri steeled themselves and checked their weapons. There were forty or so of them left. Their strategy was simple. They would turn their fire, as one, to whichever one of the dozen doorways presented an attack. Like a deadly game of Whac-A-Mole.

They would fight to the last drop of blood, as they had been ordered.

From the Tyro dorms, via a probe, Kelly observed the defensive set-up.

"Whac-A-Mole," he said. Delta nodded.

"Henri! All units! Masks on," Kelly ordered over the comms. "Gas attack. Stun grenades and suppressing fire. Imperative we hit them all at once."

"*Absolument*," confirmed Henri from the kitchens.

"Control, count us down from thirty seconds," said Kelly.

Kaparis twitched back from the blind boy.

It's working, thought Finn, wedged tight against the bones of Kaparis's inner ear. He had crawled back along the narrow blood vessels, still determined to mess with his head as originally planned, only to arrive in time to overhear everything, including Grandma's voice. He felt like he was almost home.

But this was no moment to celebrate. He had to save the Primo.

"He's your own flesh and blood..." he continued, taunting Kaparis.

"NO!" Kaparis threw down the Primo, then smashed his hand against the side of his own head.

The shockwave boomed through Finn.

The Primo lay, winded, on the cold stone. Who was the Master shouting at? Was he possessed?

Kaparis stared at the Primo's face. Was there something familiar about it? The angle of the cheekbones? The resolute jaw? No no no...

"He's yours!" shouted Finn. He had no idea whether this was *actually* true, but as the Primo was from a local orphanage, he knew it *could* be. And that was enough to stall Kaparis until he could come up with something better.

"Impossible!" barked Kaparis. The knife twitched in his hand. Do it now, he told himself. Stop this nonsense. From the Forum he could hear fighting:

DRTRRTRTRTR! DTDRTRT! BANG BANG BANG!

Kaparis sheathed the knife and grabbed the Primo – that sack of skin and bones that he was suddenly freaked by, frightened by – and drove him through the catacombs towards the caverns. He must talk to Heywood immediately.

"Ask him!" Finn yelled as they fled. "He was brought here from a local orphanage – no doubt where your wife abandoned him."

"They are all orphans!" said Kaparis as they reached the stone steps and he tossed him down.

"He is fourteen years of age, he is dark like his mother…"

"NONSENSE!" said Kaparis, kicking the Primo down ahead of him as he descended. The Primo tumbled madly, trying to cling to whatever he could.

At the bottom, Kaparis hauled him up and held the dagger to his throat again.

"Where were you born, Carrier boy?"

"I do not know."

"Born to a mother – or just found on the streets and handed in?"

"I do not know."

Kaparis drove the Primo against the wall, as if trying to bash the answer out of his body. From above, he could hear automatic fire and the sound of heavy feet approaching.

DRTRRTRTRTR! DTDRTRTRTRT!

The enemy were closing in.

He pulled the Primo along the stone passage and forced him into a monorail cart.

DRTRRTRT! – DRTRRTRT!

Not far behind, coming fast down the stone steps, the lead elements of the assault force – Kelly and Delta among them – gave chase...

FEBRUARY 22 08:31 (GMT+3). Great Cavern, Monastery of Mount St Demetrius of Thessaloniki

The cart hurtled down the crystal flume into the belly of the earth, sucking Kaparis towards a moment of truth.

"He's yours, he must be yours..." Finn pressed on, trying to appeal to Kaparis's monstrous ego. "Look at him and look at what he's done..."

In the bottom of the cart, the Primo struggled to understand the white-knuckle ride, tried to figure out the forces at play.

"He's fourteen years old, he runs *everything* in this place – *blind.* His natural intelligence must be staggering."

Kaparis stared at the Primo's scarred eyes.

320

"What a brain! What determination! You think that just happens?" Finn asked.

Kaparis computed the probability of such an outrageous claim, just as the cart turned the final curve and dropped to level out.

"You have to be *born* with that kind of leadership. He's *yours*," Finn insisted as they pulled into the Great Cavern.

It was a mess. Fuel still burnt in the shaft and more debris had fallen from the dome. Technicians and Siguri were rigging explosives around the rings of particle accelerators and banks of computers, ready to destroy it all and take out as many invaders as possible. In the remains of the operating theatre, the medics fought to save Heywood.

They were shocked to see their Master swing his semi-animated body out of the cart, dragging the Primo after him.

"He is *you*, and you made him blind by sticking those spikes in his eyes. Butcher!"

"He is nothing!" cried Kaparis, dragging along the blind Carrier boy. "He cared for the wretched Carriers! No Kaparis would ever do that. The primacy of the few is ingrained within us – the few who survive and prosper because they are the embodiment of self-interest, creatively selfish to the core of their being. This boy is a communist, a ragged revolutionary. This boy is the antithesis of everything I believe in!"

"Only because you *made* him that way though. You blinded him and made him a slave. And he became king of the slaves. Like father, like son!"

"Like father, like son – HA! And like your father, you shall die!"

"My father is not dead! You can't kill him and you can't kill me! You've met my grandma, you've heard her. You can't kill love, no matter what you do. It's just a matter of time and place. 'Time equals place', you said it yourself."

Kaparis shoved the Primo up against one of the explosive-laden particle accelerators, and, like it was an ancient stone in an ancient place of sacrifice, he drew his dagger for the third and final time. He must do it, now. He must end this.

"Look into your heart!" cried Finn, growing desperate.

Kaparis drew the dagger back and...

THUD. Arrrrgggggh! Somehow, he had missed. His half-recovered nervous system must have misdirected the blow, or -- it made him sick to think it -- could his subconscious have intervened and somehow willed the blade to miss?

Finn did not know the Primo was still alive until he spoke.

"Let me live, and I swear I will kill you," he told Kaparis with all the bitter authority he had left.

The words chilled Kaparis to the bone. What arrogance, what sang-froid...

"Ha! A chip off the old block," said Finn.

With a grunt of rage and emotional confusion, Kaparis threw the blind boy to the ground.

"Don't let him move!" *Kaparis ordered a technician, who was watching in awe, and he staggered off towards the operating theatre, where Leopold and the other medics were still fighting to save Heywood's life. The boy's words kept spinning round his overheated mind. "No, no, no, no..." He must kill him, destroy the runt. His line on earth could not continue through a slave. But first he must know.*

"Heywood! HEYWOOD!" he cried.

From the mangled wreck of a body came a weak groan. "Master..."

He was still alive.

"They say Ondine bore me a child. This is not true!"

"It is not true..."

"HA! I knew it!"

Relief exploded through him, blooming out from his heart, a heart which had grown tight with dread, with guilt, with emotion he could not begin to understand, so disturbed had he allowed himself to become. Oh, what a fool! What a—

"She bore you a jackal..."

"... WHAT?" demanded Kaparis, the euphoria popped.

"I wanted to spare you, Master... When we found out how she'd escaped from the cavern, I retraced her steps... She'd been found by a woodcutter, who realised she was pregnant. His wife nursed her and she stayed with them until she had the child. Then she ran from it. It was a runt - deformed by the panther cells she'd injected... I killed the woodcutter and his wife, but not the child. It was part of you, Master, a holy wretch - I could not... so I left it in the snow for the wolves..." finished Heywood, his eyes slowly closing.

Kaparis felt a sense of horror overwhelm him as he realised who that child might be.

"Never! Not that thing... NEVER! Wake up, man! WAKE!"

But Heywood would never wake again.

From the far end of the Great Cavern came a flash and the noise – BANG! – BANG! – BANG! – of stun grenades. The enemy was at the gates.

In Kaparis's inner ear, Finn's head was thrown back by the ear-splitting force of it.

Kaparis barely cared any more. He was scrambling out, running away, from the truth, from his past, from the word echoing through his mind. "Santiago...!" Running away from his son.

NO! IMPOSSIBLE. A plot. Torment. He knew nothing, he told himself, nothing.

Yet he knew everything.

He knew what to do.

THIRTY-FIVE

FEBRUARY 22 08:46 (GMT+3). Body of D.A.P.
Kaparis

DRTRRTRTRTR! DRTRRTRTRTR!

"I can hear gunfire!" Finn reported back to the *Vitalis*. "They're closing in!"

"We can't risk letting him escape, Finn. We've got to do this and get out before it's too late!" said Carla from the bridge.

"Hit it!" cried Finn. "Reel me in!" Immediately, the tether line tightened at his belt and – this time more gently – he was dragged back down the narrow blood vessel and away from the bone cluster of the inner ear, back towards the *Vitalis*.

Heart thumping, Al slid after the troops down the monorail tunnel
on his backside, the flashes and bangs of the battle ahead echoing
up, turning the descent into a ride down hell's own helter-skelter.

DRTRRTRTRTR! DRTRRTRTRTR!

The Great Cavern was a sound-and-light show too, the crack of
gunfire echoing off the walls, muzzle flash shimmering through the
stalactites as the invaders fought their way along the end of the tunnel.

It was time for the final showdown. It was time to get Finn back.
And Al was ready.

"Do it now, buddy," he prayed to Finn. "Whatever it is, do it
now…"

---

*In the centre of the henge, Kaparis was bent over the Primo, dribbling with
furious anger.*

*The Primo had been lashed to one of the great stones. By killing the
Primo, he would take revenge. He would kill the very idea that he might
have ever had a child.*

"Pretender! Vilest scourge! SLAVE!" he ranted. "You will die!"

DRTRRTRTRTR! DRTRRTRTRTR!

The barbarians were at the gates. It was time to blow the house down.

"Set the final charge!" he ordered the last of the Siguri, as he staggered out of the henge.

The Siguri switched on laser sensors. The accelerators would remain intact until the moment anyone stepped into the circle, then the sensors would trip and the whole thing would blow, Primo and all.

The voice in Kaparis's head seemed to have stopped. He should never have listened. If Infinity Drake had not already drowned in his blood, he would soon meet some grimly fitting end. He would eventually run out of air, or they would retrieve the craft first. One way or another, Infinity Drake was finished.

Kaparis stumbled towards the last remaining exit. To the river.

Ondine had escaped all those years ago by leaping into the underground torrent. She was carried along through the mountain until she emerged a few minutes later in a spring in the valley below. She had relied on her supernatural lung capacity, on a knowledge of flow dynamics, and on stupendous luck. After Kaparis had finally worked out what she'd done, he'd taken the precaution of having a grenade-sized scuba device planted just below the waterline. Much more civilised.

Now it was his turn to take the same leap. He reached the precipice and looked down into the thrashing waters – DRTRTRT! – then he looked back. An enemy soldier had almost managed to reach the henge before being cut down. The Siguri were about to execute him. Then Kaparis realised who it was.

"STOP!" Kaparis boomed over the sound of battle. "Bring him to me."

The Siguri dutifully grabbed a limb each, and carried Kelly, groaning, to Kaparis at the river.

FEBRUARY 22 08:48 (GMT+3). Body of D.A.P. Kaparis

Deep inside Kaparis's head, in the network of blood vessels that fed the ear, Infinity Drake had re-entered the *Vitalis*.

The great submarine was already powering down the external carotid artery, impeller arms thrust forward, drawing itself up the flow of blood towards the neck.

Finn tore off his tanks and helmet and ran up to the bridge. Nico was calling the shots at the arterial map while Carla drove.

"Get ready to hit the brakes and twist hard right when we reach the junction!" ordered Nico.

Carla sent the craft surging forward, ready to curl back into the flow of the internal carotid artery back up into the brain.

"How far down are we?" said Finn.

"We should get there any moment now," said Nico.

WOOOOSHH – the *Vitalis* hit the wide-open, red blizzard of the carotid artery and took the internal branch back into the deep brain. Carla swivelled the impellers to break their ride.

"Keep her steady in the flow and drift right across! Find the opposite wall!" called Nico over the noise of the engines.

"Find the wall, Carla!" Finn added helpfully as – *THUMP* – they hit the other side of the artery and bounced back.

"That's it! Now keep her steady… keep her steady…" called Nico as she traced their progress up to the back of the eye.

"There!" shouted Nico, at a fast-approaching tributary. "Hit it!"

Carla fired the anchor lines – *Tzoot!–Tzoot!–Tzoot!–Tzoot!*

The *Vitalis* had taken them as far as she could go.

If Nico's reading of the anatomy was correct, they had wedged the submarine into the internal carotid artery at the back of the eye, just off the ophthalmic artery. A big enough explosion here would, with any luck, cause a frontal lobotomy[23], but more importantly it offered them their quickest way out of the bone cage of the skull.

"The eyes have it," Finn had concluded earlier. "If they find him with a brain injury, and assume we've caused it, the first place they're going to look in is the eyes."

Carla turned the power sliders to the max and the impeller arms went crazy trying to drag the anchors from the flesh, but the anchors held and the blood and plasma were whisked into a frothy goo. The heat indicators from the nuclear reactor began to rise.

"GO!" shouted Finn above the screaming of the engines, and they descended to the open airlocks where Nico was waiting with their subaqua gear.

---

[23] A now-discredited psychiatric surgical procedure whereby most connections to the prefrontal cortex of the brain were severed.

They had full tanks, they had a laser scalpel, they had their scoots – and who knew how much or how little time. Clinging to each other, they swam out of the open hold and scooted clear of the chaos the mighty *Vitalis* was leaving in its wake.

Nico led them shooting down the ophthalmic artery, then they turned to surf into the retinal supply. Before they joined the new flow, she touched them to explain: "This is the main artery to the retina. It will take us straight along the optic nerve. If we just stick to the main branch and follow it all the way to the end, we'll hit the back of the eye."

"Great, let's do it!" said Carla.

"Go!" said Finn.

All three powered forward on the scoots.

Dhu-dhu, dhu-dhu, dhu-dhu, dhu-dhu, dhu.

The flow caught them and they surfed its turbulence, staying as close to the centre of the current as they could as they were carried upwards in a twist to join the darker mass of the optic nerve just beyond the artery wall – then arrow straight along it.

If they could reach the retina and cut their way through the back of the eyeball, they'd arrive at the conjunctiva, which would be lubricated by the saltwater sea of Kaparis's tears. And from there they could swim all the way round to the front of his eye, where surely Al would want to look…

All they could do was swim, and hope.

"Well, well, well... Captain Kelly, you can be my messenger. Wake him!"

A bucket was dipped into the rushing water and the ice-cold contents emptied over Kelly's head. His eyes briefly snapped open. Instantly he wished they hadn't. His body was shot up along one side and bleeding hard. Before he could pass out again, Kaparis grabbed his jaw to insist he hear him out.

On the empty bridge of the *Vitalis*, the engines screamed and the reactor alarm sounded – *NEEW-eu- NEEW-eu- NEEW-eu- NEEW-eu- NEEW-eu.*

The yellow radiation hazard symbol flashed and flashed – WARNING MELTDOWN! CORE HEAT CRITICAL! WARNING MELTDOWN!

In the retina at the back of Kaparis's eye, forward momentum had been lost, but for Finn at least, the spectacle was dazzling.

The main artery had split into dozens of smaller blood vessels at the retina, and Finn, Carla and Nico found themselves having to squeeze their way along a narrow arterial tube.

Lights – reds, yellows, blues – were rippling through the layers of light-receptor cells all around them, like the aurora borealis.

"How far?" Finn demanded of Nico.

Nico knew they couldn't go much further and that anywhere at the back of the eye would do.

"Go for it!" said Nico.

Finn took the laser scalpel off his back and pulled the trigger. A lightsaber shaft of perfect blue light burst from its end and immediately divided the artery wall and the flesh of the retina above it. The gap cleaved open and they were able to push through a thick duvet of nerve cells and on into the light, into the infinite pool of clear gel beyond...

And there, to Finn's utter astonishment, the light resolved itself to became a coherent image, a face...

He gasped and his own eyes filled with tears. "KELLY!"

"Listen to me," said Kaparis, eyeballing Kelly. "I want you to take a message back to the G&T. Tell Allenby he's finished, that he'll never catch me. But be sure to thank him: I've learned so much. It is a great pity we never got to work together, but then the strong must always defeat the weak. Tell the world I am ready to parlay, ready to receive their offers and trade my forgiveness in return. But there's only one Master now, and there always only will be while I have breath left in my body."

Back in the *Vitalis*, the siren stopped.

ASSSTSTSTSTSTSTSTSSSSSSSSSSSSSSSSSSSSSSSSSSSS...

The reactor did not explode in the first vital moment as planned. Instead, its fuel began to burn and it dropped like a white-hot diamond, through its housing in the craft, then through the hull, then on and down, as hot as the core of the sun, through blood and brain tissue, as it built towards critical mass...

The first thing Kaparis noticed was an irresistible urge to twitch his left eye.

The first thing Kelly noticed was that Kaparis had suddenly stopped talking.

The first thing Finn, Carla and Nico noticed, at the back of the eye, was the sudden orange glow behind them. Instinctively they clung to each other.

The second thing Kaparis noticed was the worst pain any human had ever felt.

At nano-scale, the explosion was huge. At normal scale, it was just enough. Enough of the nuclear fuel in the reactor had reached critical mass and detonated – not as planned beneath the frontal lobes, but directly behind the left eye, gravity having taken it burning through the optic canal and out of the skull because Kaparis was leaning over

Kelly. So although the eye socket protected the brain, nothing, sadly, could be done for the eye.

The energy released naturally took the path of least resistance out. *SSSSSSKAAAAAABAAABBABAAAALOOOOOOSH!*

Kaparis's eye literally exploded.

"ARRRRRRRRRRRRRRRRRRRRRHGGGHHHH!"

Finn sensed a moment of perfect noise and blinding light as they became instant nothingness.

"ARRRRHGGGHHHH!" *Kaparis screamed as his eye spattered across Kelly's face.*

Kelly had seen many horrors, had caused a few. But he'd never experienced anything as revolting as this. He passed out.

"ARRRRHGGGHHHH!" *Kaparis clutched his burning empty eye socket.* "INFAMY!" *The pain. The frustration. The shattered remnants of his eye all over Kelly.* "ARRRRHGGGHHHH!"

BOOM! BOOM! DRTRTRTRT!

The enemy closing in.

The indignity!

Kaparis did not linger – SPLASH!

Into the blackness and the maelstrom, into the gaping yaw of hell he dived, the freezing, rushing water possessing him, spinning and sending him down, down into the ice-cold deep...

"ARRRRHGGGHHHH!"

THIRTY-SIX

Finn was in a dream. It was a dream he often had, of walking along
a perfect white beach on a beautiful day with a load of people he
knew, and ahead of him was his mum – she was always ahead – and,
as he ran along the perfect white sand, he reached out for her and
she reached back to catch his hand, and always at the moment their
hands were about to touch... he would wake, or she would disappear,
or the dream would change. And every time, even though he knew
he was in a dream, he thought, *One day, it's going to happen; we're
going to touch...*

He woke up with a gasp.

He was still in the mask. He was breathing. He was floating in a perfect whiteness, a perfect white ocean. Was this the end of life? Was this heaven?

Someone was swimming towards him. *Mum?* He looked closer. It was Carla.

"Are we alive?" he asked, incredulous.

"I think so," said Carla, unsure herself. "Look!"

There was another body coming towards them, from below, deep in the water, riding a scoot at speed through the whiteness – Nico. Shouting, insisting, already sure.

"His eye! We're on the surface of his eye!"

"Kaparis's?"

"I don't think so..."

The implication was clear, but so incredible that it took a moment to sink in.

The face. Kelly. The blast.

They couldn't be...? Could they?

Finn still had the laser scalpel across his back.

"DIVE!" he shouted.

DRTRT!

The last shots were fired by the units of the relieving force that Kelly and Delta had led down the monorail tunnel. The last of the Siguri raised their arms and signalled their surrender. Technicians, cowering among the stalagmites in the crystal fringe of the Great Cavern, did the same. Troops spread out, ordering them out.

Yvette Dupuis spotted it first – the technicians being herded out of the stalagmites were avoiding crossing the henge.

"*ARRÊTEZ!*"

Instantly, the troops in the Great Cavern came to a halt.

Nobody moved. The injured groaned. In a wisp of fine dust, she spotted it. A perfect line of laser light leading from the bottom of one of the particle accelerators to the next. A trap.

"*ICI!*"

In the minutes that followed, while the booby-trap explosives rigged around the henge were being dismantled, it was established that Kaparis had got away. A search was initiated for a secret escape tunnel and specialist divers were summoned to take a look in the river.

Kelly was located, badly injured and unconscious on its bank. Al, Delta and even Stubbs were all there when he was brought round.

337

Kelly saw their faces... and knew the mission must have ended in some kind of disaster.

"Kaparis got away," said Al. "Did you see him?"

"I..." said Kelly, wringing out his traumatised brain, trying to remember as the medics worked on his wounds. "I can't think, I..."

Stubbs, distracted, picked up what he thought was a pickled egg. It turned out to be half a fried eyeball.

"That's his! I remember!" yelled Kelly, recalling the moment it was propelled directly down at him. But his mind was shot by battle shock and he couldn't remember the message Kaparis had growled down at him before his head exploded, or which way he had gone.

For once, Delta didn't hold back. She abandoned emotional control and cried. She let herself sob for Carla. After they had come so far...!

Al put an arm round her. He felt her sorrow and knew her despair. Any words of comfort or reassurance stopped dead in his mouth. They had lost him, and perhaps their last best chance. He'd tried everything. He knew Finn would have tried everything too. In the heart of the mountain, the pit of the earth, he thought he'd never been at a lower point in his life... Would Finn exist for him now – like his mother and father existed – as a dream more than a reality, a memory more than a hope?

Then his own mother arrived. Al would have to tell her the bad news, and the thought of this broke him, the thought of letting her down and breaking her heart all over again...

Violet Allenby was helped out of a monorail cart. She took a good look at the Great Cavern and thought it the womb of hell.

Stubbs watched in silence as Kelly was moved onto a stretcher. Stubbs was no good at times like this. He didn't get on with emotion or upset. He would just take his bag of engineering tricks and hide himself away. Try and find a cup of tea. Polish up his screwdrivers and micrometers...

Kelly saw him turn away as they lifted the stretcher, saw Delta wailing, saw Al saying something to Grandma, saw her shoulders trying not to sag, saw the whole mad cavern...

Flash, Flash, Flash went his eye, bluish flashes pricking his vision, like a twitch. But it wasn't a twitch. Again, *FlashFlashFlash*, then immediately slower – *Flash, Flash, Flash* – repeating in a pattern, over and over. *FlashFlashFlash* – *Flash, Flash, Flash* – *FlashFlashFlash*...

"Stop!" he cried to the medic attending him. "Something's happening to my eye!"

In the ocean of Kelly's eye, Finn fired the laser scalpel down through what he prayed was the pupil. Bubbles ballooned in the tears along the line of the flashing blade, and he prayed as hard as Carla and Nico prayed.

Suddenly white light bloomed around them.

FlashFlashFlash – *Flash, Flash, Flash* – *FlashFlashFlash*...

"Can't you see it?" Kelly asked the medic who was staring into his eyeball through an ophthalmoscope.

"Describe it again?"

"It flashes blue like in a rhythm: *FlashFlashFlash* – *Flash, Flash, Flash*

– *FlashFlashFlash*. Three fast, then three slow, then three fast again, like in a pulse. Maybe it's my pulse or..."

He stopped dead.

FlashFlashFlash – Flash, Flash, Flash – FlashFlashFlash.

... / --- / ...

SOS.

Save our souls...

Kelly shot up and off the stretcher and screamed.

"STUBBBBBBS!"

Ow, thought Hudson. *Owwwwww*.

He had passed in and out of consciousness several times, and always the pain was too much, or the cold was too much. He was encased in snow and he would soon be entombed. And though the snow immediately around him was beginning to melt, he knew he'd never be spotted, even from the air.

Owwwwww.

He felt like he'd broken every bone in his body. And now he would die here...

Snow death, slow death, he thought. *I could have used that in one of my poems*. Then he saw the snow melt away from the very tip of a very tiny bright green shoot, right in front of his face. *New*, he thought. *Spring*, he thought.

Owwwwww... and he closed his eyes to pass out again.

Wowwoowww... Owww... Wowwow wow wow wow bow wow wow!

His eyes snapped open.

Not far off, zeroing in on six different trajectories, kicking up snow and bashing into one another and hitting trees with idiot force, ran the ratters at full speed, the scent of the kill – or at least of Hudson – in their nostrils, Yo-yo pulling ahead of the others, sensing him near, sensing him strong – *YAP YAP YAP!*

THIRTY-SEVEN

Kaparis had emerged freezing from the rock, bubbling up from one of the black springs that ran from the tree line to the pasture. He had staggered out, the Abbot's robes he was wearing soaked, his eye socket a pit of agony.

He had walked for hours by the time he reached a dilapidated wood-cutter's hut.

He shivered in the ruins of it. A dead place in a frozen valley. Pathetic signs remained of the simple life once lived there: rotting furniture, pages of magazines...

And suddenly, there at his feet, he saw it. A tiny, delicately carved rattle, an extraordinary and complex little thing made from a single piece of wood.

What craftsmanship, what hours and dedication it must have taken to create. What... love.

And for whom?

He dropped it back in the snow. He knew the answer. He could feel it.

It was the end of the story that Heywood had told him. It was the story of his son.

An hour later, he started his long walk. He would head west towards the Alps. He was now dressed in rags he'd found in the woodcutter's hut and he made use of a staff. His wounded eye was covered by a hat pulled low over his forehead. He would stay off the beaten track until he was well clear of the mountains, then he would summon his forces. He would recover in the Alps, in his vaults, in the impenetrable heart of his empire and of Europe itself.

And then.

When he was ready.

He would begin.

FEBRUARY 25 09:09 (GMT+3). Great Cavern, Monastery of Mount St Demetrius of Thessaloniki

WOOOOOOMMMMMMMMMMMM!

The accelerator had whipped up a whirlwind of pure energy. The sound was deafening.

WOOOOOOMMMMMMMMMMMM!

The crucial moment had arrived. The tipping point. All it needed was the final order.

The chief technician announced: "Ready to commence Boldklub sequence."

Al nodded. They had spent thirty-six hours reconnecting and testing the henge in the Grand Cavern. They had not seen daylight. They had not slept.

A switch was thrown. Power surged.

WOOOOOOMMMMMMMMMMMM!

In a flash, the hot area became its magnificent self, a dynamic orb of perfect white light. It was impossible to look at directly, but everyone positioned round the Great Cavern was focused on it, praying for a miracle.

Commander King was, certainly.

Stubbs, who had successfully filtered Infinity Drake and his companions out from the fluid in Kelly's eye, definitely.

Grandma and Al, for sure.

There had been talk of rebuilding and recalibrating the henge back at Hook Hall in line with the "Time = Place" breakthrough Kaparis had made, but Al had quickly established that it would be faster and wiser to revive the system where it was. Besides, if he'd had to wait, he would have lost his mind, either to anxiety or to overexcitement. And besides, it was great getting to play around with someone else's toys, especially after Li Jun had retrieved all the blitzed operational data from the control computers, a task that should have taken more than a billion hours to complete – and would have done, if Li Jun herself had not written the crucial line of code in the self-destruct program.

Tests had been run. Results had been analysed. Finn and Carla and Nico had waited, under the lens of a microscope, communicating via a crude system of flashing lights.

Now there was only one light, throbbing away at the centre of the henge.

Grandma closed her eyes. Delta held her hand, nearly wringing it off.

A notification alarm sounded on the control panel.

REANIMATION 100% COMPLETE flashed across the screen.

Al gulped. With a shaking hand, he hit the keyboard. Cut the power. Heart thumping clear out of his chest.

At once the orb evaporated into a million pinpricks of sparkle, and faded like a wish. All that was left was the shape of the orb still present on the retina. Eyes blinked it away.

And at the centre of the henge, three figures stood, posed as if in a statue from antiquity...

Quite still. Holding each other...

Then the first one moved.

Gasped.

And Delta Salazar let out a cry and ran into the henge to embrace her sister.

And Nico too staggered out towards her bemused husband.

And Finn...

Infinity Drake blinked, blinked at the world anew, a world of lights and faces and shapes at the edge of things, a world he opened his mouth and lungs to scream his approval of, to swallow whole – or at least he would have done had his grandmother not met and enveloped him at ramming speed, almost bowling him over and drowning him in happy, happy tears...

And Al ran too, ran in on the ecstatic scene – ran in, saw something, and stopped...

He felt his heart seize in horror... No, please no. Something had gone wrong... He had changed. Something had happened in the reanimation. Finn seemed to have been warped or distorted or... Had they gone too far?

Grandma stood back and, to the delight of the waiting world, hovering respectfully outside the henge, introduced her grandson in the manner of grandmothers throughout history by saying...

"Hasn't he grown?"

Which was a fair estimation, and perhaps not unsurprising, given he had been trapped first at 9mm tall then at just 9 microns tall for over a year.

And Al's heart burst as he embraced him, as he realised Finn had not become some freak. He'd become a teenager, a young man.

"Hasn't he grown!"

And Infinity Drake could not speak for the joy that stopped his throat and filled his eyes and the relief, oh! the extraordinary relief, as he smelt it – smelt it and sensed it and felt it – on them both, on them all.

"Hasn't he grown!"

"Shut up, Mother! Of course he's bloody grown!"

Home.

PART
FIVE

PART
FIVE

THIRTY-EIGHT

JULY 6 14:58 (GMT). Langmere Secondary
School, Buckinghamshire, UK

The day had been long. Too long.

Sun had baked the desks and the smell of ink and plastic and overheated teens gave substance to the stale air. Everyone had that end-of-term feeling, with nothing to do but mark time before the start of the summer holidays. Some teachers set up amusing tests, some stuck on a DVD and disappeared, and some unrepentant dullards pressed on, "tackling the curriculum".

Finn had biology with Mr Penna and an irritating hour had been spent writing up an experiment. They worked in silence as Penna had totally lost it about three times. It was mundane to the point of madness.

349

And Finn loved it. Absolutely loved it.

He loved normal. He loved sitting in this room full of big and splendid full-sized human beings, loved being able to pick up a pen, loved seeing and being seen, loved fitting into the world so perfectly, loved living a life he'd so nearly lost. The miracle of just *being* made him want to cry with luck. It made him old. Weird, maybe. He didn't fit in as well with everyone as he'd used to. But he didn't care. There were just enough others like himself.

He looked at the pen in his hand, at its point trailing ink across the page, and for a moment his imagination saw the massive rolling ball-point thundering towards him, a thing the size of a house, careering forward with massive force, spilling and spewing a slick blue sea which engulf—

He jolted awake as the bell went and the class broke up. Released.

July 6 18:27 (GMT). Hook Hall, Surrey, UK

Hook Hall never looked more glorious than in late June and early July. The flower borders sang with colour and the cream stone of the manor was perfect against the sky blue – and there was no more glorious occasion at Hook Hall than the annual 'Frocs and Docs' Summer Ball. The one time of the year when the assembled brainiacs, soldiery and support staff could really let their hair down.

All day, vitally important projects had been abandoned in favour of attention to dress and dance routines as each department prepared for the climactic 'dance off', a prospect that brought Stubbs out in hives. Never before had he made such a spectacle of himself, but he had solemnly promised Li Jun he would at least try and pretend to be trapped in a glass box as the centrepiece of the Ad Hoc Engineering entry.

In the sick bay, Captain Kelly, trying to remember how to tie his bow tie, planned an acrobatic showpiece on crutches on behalf of the SAS.

In the master bedroom, Commander King tied his bow tie as if he had been born to it, which of course he had. He would make the annual address and take absolutely no part in any dancing, thank you very much. *Unless Violet Allenby forces me to*, he thought fearfully, as he saw her car pull up the drive.

Grandma parked up. She had the boys with her. Finn got out in a grump. She had made him wear a very old suit of Al's that was clearly too big for him. Hudson got out in a purple velvet tuxedo *he had made himself*, and the pair of them walked towards the hall like a pair of freak-show rejects.

Santiago laughed at them from the fountain.

"Ha ha! Monkeys!"

He had found it difficult to cope when he'd first arrived at Hook Hall, but the formal fountain in the drive had caught his sense of wonder – the simple beauty, the play of water and light. Now, when he wasn't being rehabilitated from a lifetime's abuse and slavery, he was always to be found there.

DNA analysis had proved beyond doubt that Santiago, not the Primo, was the son of Kaparis. No one had told him yet. Maybe they never would.

The Primo, who had effortlessly embraced modernity, now shared a cottage in the grounds with him. The other Carrier children, back in their countries of origin, were all on a rehabilitation programme supervised by the G&T. Those Tyros who had been captured alive were under the care of Grandma in a secure institution a few miles north of Hook Hall. Progress was slow, but her work with Li Jun had proved that, once some kind of emotional contact had been made, she could rescue their humanity. "Normal teenagers feel everything and know nothing," Grandma would say. "With Tyros, it's the reverse." Given time, no one doubted that she would achieve success.

Grandma hurried off to meet the "admin girls" (none under the age of fifty) so they could work on their Motown medley. Hudson went to exchange punches with Santiago at the fountain, while Finn went on into the hall. The caterers were setting up and the final decorations were being put in place.

Finn went in search of Al, but found his office empty. In the mess on his desk, Finn could see that Al had been studying his father's notes – the same infamous papers that Kaparis had had copies of. Since their adventures in the mountains, the notes had become an obsession for many of the Hook Hall scientists. The "Time = Place" paradox had changed their understanding of everything—

How? Finn would ask, but Al would refuse to answer. "Not until *I* really get it."

Wacawacawacawaca...

A helicopter was coming in to land on the airfield at the back of Hook Hall.

Finn ran round and, of course, there was Al waiting in the rotor wash as Delta and Carla Salazar arrived from the US. Delta stepped out first and wrapped herself round him. *Yuk.* Finn turned away. He'd never be able to cope with old people in love.

Carla clearly felt the same, getting away from them as fast as she could and greeting Finn with a high-five, a hug and an "Aren't they disgusting?"

Carla looked well – amazing – but she was clearly still miserable. She'd found it more difficult than Finn to adjust, especially at high school. She was struggling to unlearn some of the things she'd experienced, and spent more time on Skype with Finn than she did with her old friends. Her stepmother was concerned, and there was talk of her spending a term at school in the UK.

"Hi, how's it going? Or shouldn't I ask?"

"I'm fine. Just grouchy from the flight... You look like a clown."

"Thanks. Bring a prom dress?"

Carla indicated the bag over her shoulder, as if she was carrying something vile.

"No way are we dancing."

"No way," agreed Finn, as Delta and Al rocked up and Delta headlocked him hello. Then she and Carla left to find their rooms and get "fixed up" for the ball.

"No pressure," said Al, "but if you don't look absolutely perfect, we're having you deported."

As the day faded to evening, Al and Finn retreated to his office to find him a tie.

"Where the hell is it? I know there's one here somewhere…" Al said and switched on the desk lights. Again, Finn saw his dad's last words spread out in hieroglyphs of advanced physics.

"Over the summer, will you try and teach me what some of this means?" asked Finn.

"If I ever manage to understand it myself," said Al.

"Don't lie, because Stubbs virtually told me – you've started rebuilding the henge," said Finn, skewering him.

"You know, Grandma wants you to have at least a year off from all this stuff," was all Al could say in his defence.

"And you too! Does she know about the new henge?" said Finn.

"You'd better not breathe a word, you little…"

"Just as long as you tell me how far you've got," said Finn.

Al looked across the papers, the accumulated mystery of it.

"Well, I can give it my best shot, but don't expect firm answers as there's a long way to go."

"Fine," shrugged Finn.

"Well, the 'time equals place' stuff throws open a whole load of questions. Basically, it means that all time is space – in the same way that all matter is energy."

"Huh?"

Al smiled and tried to put it as simply as he could.

"Some people think the only way of explaining all the contradictions of physics and quantum physics is to assume that there are an infinite number of parallel universes, parallel realities, where all possibilities can exist. It's a convenient idea and it gives us a way to explain away things like where all your mass went to when we shrunk you, say. In theory, you should have been nine millimetres tall and eight stones heavy, but your weight – your mass – disappeared proportionately. We think your dark mass, the mysterious stuff that makes up ninety per cent of everything in the universe, disappeared as you shrank; we think it went somewhere else. Where? Our best guess is that it slipped into one of these parallel dimensions."

"Yeah, you said that before. I remember," said Finn.

"Right. Now I think it went somewhere else *in time*," said Al.

"In time?"

"Yes. If you assume time equals place, it changes everything. You start to think, not of an infinite number of parallel universes, but in terms of an infinite number of moments of future time (future because you can never go back in time), with every point in that future time relating to a place. We can then say your dark energy was pushed to a place and time in the future, and when you needed it back, you got it back again."

"But hold on – you just said you *can't* go back in time, so how could it come back?" said Finn.

"Exactly. You can't go back in time, but maybe you *can* go back in time that *hasn't happened yet*," said Al, beaming.

Finn's brain was hurting, but also hoping. He could tell when Al was excited about something big. "You think that's where my dad might be?" Finn dared to ask. "Some place... in the future?"

Al laughed. "I do and I don't. As yet, I can find no way to test all this. For now, let's say it's just a matter of faith."

"Grandma will be happy," said Finn.

"I think your father was only just beginning to understand this too. The notes aren't at all clear. There seem to be seven places, or seven ancient cities, that somehow have a link to this, and a link to water, but how they tie in I have absolutely no idea."

"Venice..." said Finn. "You used to go to Venice after he disappeared."

"That's right. He mentions this church in Venice – I went back time and time again, but I could find nothing. Frankly, most of this seven cities stuff doesn't make any sense."

"But you do think," said Finn, trying to put it all together, "that there may be an infinity of possible moments – in which he may exist?"

"Or not," warned Al.

"And each moment relates to a place. A place in the real world?" said Finn.

"Yeah, all maybe just a fraction of a moment ahead of us, so we can never quite get there, or far in the distant future."

"Wow," said Finn.

"I know," said Al, delighted as he always was by his nephew's sense of scientific wonder.

Finn reached out into the space just ahead of him.

"So he could be just there... just in front of me..."

"He could. Or he could not. I have to admit we've got a hell of a way to go."

"But in time..."

"In time – lie all the answers," said Al, just as he found his tie – "Aha!" – and he held it up as proof of his assertion.

As night fell, the guests began to arrive, the music started to play, and Finn and the other teenagers gathered in their finery at the fountain. The Primo, courtesy of Commander King's tailor, looked a million dollars and extremely distinguished in his dinner jacket. Tragically, he could not see Li Jun swathed in sleek blue silk beside him. Hudson was quite disturbed by it, and stood the other side of Finn and Santiago, who had been forced into a white shirt. Finally, Carla came out in a little black dress, scowling and glorious.

They all hung out together for a few more minutes before going in.

"So, I've spoken to my stepmom and she says she'll look at us moving over for a year," announced Carla.

"Yay!" said Hudson. "You are going to hate our school!"

"Well, nothing's definite, and she's bound to want to send me to some private place, but in the meantime, I can definitely stay here with Delta for the summer."

"That's great!" said Finn.

357

"What do you think we should do? We should all do something together," said Carla.

"I have an idea," said Finn innocently. "Let's go travelling. I don't know why, or even when exactly, but I do know where to start..."

In Venice, in the dead of night, just off the Grand Canal, a gondola pushed its way down the Rio de l'Alboro towards a tiny and quite ancient church.

Its passenger, incongruously alone, one eye concealed beneath a decorative eye-patch, typed a final instruction on his phone to his Scots architect, and pressed Send. Then he sat back, satisfied, justified.

From a nearby palazzo, Beethoven's late string quartet in C sharp minor drifted out across the canal. He did not hear it, was not prompted to reflect on eternity as any normal mortal would have been, so full was he of his own thoughts.

Thoughts of himself. Only ever of himself. And of himself going on and on, for ever.